chosen
book one

Copyright © 2018
Rebecca Thomas

All rights reserved. This book or any portion thereof may not be reproduced or used in any manner whatsoever without the express written permission of the publisher except for the use of brief quotations in a book review.

This is a work of fiction. Names, characters, businesses, places, events and incidents are either the products of the author's imagination or used in a fictitious manner. Any resemblance to actual persons, living or dead, or actual events is purely coincidental.

Printed by Createspace.com

Title Font: Blackout by Zulfan Iskandar
Used under commercial license.

Cover Image by luisclaz on Pexels
Back Cover Image by Sindre Strom on Pexels

ISBN-13: 978-1721017560
ISBN-10: 1721017569

Prologue

"I warned you that you were too sensitive for this work, Caleb."

Caleb brought his dark eyes to meet Master Mahmid's, "And sympathy was never your strong suit."

As someone who had lost his parents at a young age, Caleb knew that people expected him to be used to death. In fact, it was quite the opposite. He didn't see any problem with mourning a life, particularly when you had spent almost every day of the last four years with them. Madeline had been a good friend. It was unfortunate that one so kind of heart had been given this destiny. She could have done so much more with her life if only she had been left to her own devices, but fate always had other ideas.

"Madeline fought valiantly for someone so gentle, no one can deny that," Master Mahmid said as he moved a step closer, his feet barely making a sound against the stone floor. "What I am saying is that you can't afford to be devastated by every death. You will see many lives come and go, each one as special as the last. You can't guide them properly if you let the fear of their inevitable demise drive you."

Caleb disagreed, but he knew that arguing with Master Mahmid was like beating your head against a brick wall. The Elders had the experience, they knew what was best. So many people had tried to convince him as much. Their method was to treat a person like a weapon. When the weapon broke, they put it away and found another one. He couldn't do that to people, not when they were giving their lives for this.

"How about I worry about my emotions," Caleb suggested, "And you tell me where I'm going next."

Master Mahmid sighed and looked up into the rafters. Caleb could tell he was feeling uneasy because of their location. Usually Guardians would never step foot in a church, but Caleb had needed to say goodbye to Madeline, who had loved this church, and Master Mahmid had happened to find him there. They didn't believe in the way institutions used religion, but they never paid disrespect to anyone who believed.

"Our Oracles believe that the next viable candidate can be found in London," Master Mahmid said.

"How long?"

"They are not sure. This Chosen seems to be shrouded in a haze."

Caleb had always had very direct orders about where to go next and who to find. He'd never heard of an Oracle not being able to see a Chosen.

"How can that be?"

"It happens sometimes. Usually it's to do with distance, Oracles tend to have limited vision," Master Mahmid said.

This was news to Caleb. He'd never thought to ask.

"What's my cover?"

"We're sending you to teach history at King's College London for now. When the Oracles have more information, we'll forward it onto you."

"Integration level?"

"Ultimately, it's up to your discretion, but I wouldn't get close to anyone outside of those who already know about our order. Remember, when we track down the Chosen, you will have to put aside any relationships you may form to focus on your new trainee," Master Mahmid reminded him.

Caleb nodded. *Ultimately*, it would depend on time. How long he stayed would dictate whether he tried to make friends or not, probably for the sake of his own sanity.

"When do I head out?"

Master Mahmid looked around the building again first before responding, his eyes glancing at each name engraved on the churches' walls. "You can have until Monday, then you should get on the first flight to Heathrow."

Master Mahmid rarely showed such generosity. Maybe he understood the gravity of this loss after all.

"I'll contact you when I get there," Caleb assured him.

"As always," Master Mahmid agreed as he turned to leave, his long robes unsettling the dust between the cold slabs.

Caleb sat for a few minutes longer, staring at the bright day outside. Hopefully Madeline was enjoying it too, wherever she was now.

"Until we meet again," he smiled softly, then pushed up onto his feet and disappeared through the doors into the light. He had a new life to start.

One Year Later
Chapter One

It was a blisteringly hot day in the center of London. Kiara was lying flat on her back on a bench outside Somerset House, eyes closed, soaking in the sun's rays. Anyone who wasn't a tourist or who had somewhere to be was hiding away inside the nearest air-conditioned building or huddling over a fan trying to dry the sweat off their brow. Not Kiara, though. Her Mum always said it was because she was a summer baby, born on the first day of August. A hilarious excuse considering she was a redhead and her pale skin could freckle at the mere sight of sunlight.

Kiara reckoned it was something simpler. England was such a cold and rainy place that whenever the sun came out, she made the most of it, however hot. The sunlight also made her happy and relaxed, something she didn't feel as much now both her parents were gone.

It was only a week until Easter. A week until a nice, four-week break spent skating, filming and occasionally studying with her girlfriend, Hallie…

"Wait."

Kiara opened her eyes and lifted her wrist to check her watch. She was going to be late to meet Hallie after her history class.

Her fingers just about closed around her backpack as she hoisted it from the ground beneath her seat and set off at a run, going around the end of the building towards the university. White stone rushed by on either side as she steered away from the river, across the path and up to the door of the main building. Three flights of stairs later and she made it with only seconds to spare.

"Why are you panting?" Hallie asked in her loud, American accent from the middle of the lecture hall after most everyone else had filed out of the room.

"I was running laps around the building while I was waiting for you," Kiara managed a grin between deep breaths.

"Liar."

Kiara loved it when Hallie smiled. It spread out across her whole face, framed by her curly, crazy brown hair on each side. Hallie got those curls from her Dad, which Kiara had always thought was ironic considering he was sun-kissed at most, whereas her 'Momma's' family was originally from Nairobi.

"I've just gotta ask teach over here about something from class today, then I'm all yours, babe. Come in and wait."

Even though Hallie was a film major, she adored her extra history modules. This was no doubt helped along by the teacher, who definitely knew his stuff for someone relatively young. And, as Hallie liked to remind her, he was easy on the eyes.

"Oh, hey Kiara," he smiled softly as he looked up from tidying his notes.

"Hey Caleb."

Hallie and Kiara hung around talking to Caleb so much in and out of class that they were on a first name basis.

"What about me?" Hallie protested.

"I talked to you a minute ago when you almost didn't let the class leave because you had so many questions about the Armenians."

"But it's so fascinating. No one ever talks about happened to them during World War I," Hallie enthused.

"What did happen to them?" Kiara asked, leaning on the edge of Caleb's desk.

"Genocide!"

"Oh wow, yeah." Kiara tried not to snort at Hallie's declaration of such a terrible word. "How come I've never heard about that?"

"Because the Turkish government won't recognise it as one," Caleb chipped in as he placed his work in his backpack.

"God forbid they acknowledge killing hundreds of thousands of people for what it really is," Hallie said scathingly.

Kiara nodded her head in agreement.

"Actually, you've just reminded me…"

"What did mass murder remind you of?" Hallie smirked.

"I've got this project due for my sociology class based on how insurgency affects migration levels and I need help."

Hallie pointed at Caleb. "He's your best bet, there doesn't seem to be anything he doesn't know about when it comes to the history of the world. Believe me, I test him every lesson."

"She does," Caleb chuckled, "And I can. How does tomorrow sound? 2 o'clock in my office?"

"Yes, that gives her the morning to burn off the hangover we're totally going to be suffering with after the partayyyy this evening," Hallie answered for her, beaming.

"I can feel my brain cells dying already," Kiara said mournfully.

"Have fun, but be safe," Caleb told them.

"So long as we have each other, nothing can go wrong," Hallie asserted, slinging her arm around Kiara's shoulder.

"I don't doubt it."

~

Caleb had begun to doubt that the Elders had sent him to the right place. Almost a full year of teaching at King's College under his hat and he'd heard barely any news about the possible new Chosen. Every time he asked, the Oracles were still unclear on when they would appear. Being a Guardian was supposed to be his life's purpose, so it was frustrating that he couldn't fulfill his duties, that his life was out of his control. Students like Hallie made it easier. She was so eager to learn about history that it almost made up for it.

While he was in London, he had been keeping in touch with a source from MI6. There was a lot going on in the city and around the world that he could be helping to solve, but he was forbidden to do so by the Elders without a Chosen at his side. Without the Chosen's powers, he could very well get himself killed.

As he dropped his bag down behind the door to his flat, he scooped up his mail with the other and had a quick flick through. Couple of bills and a flyer for a rave that was going on in Lambeth that evening, nothing interesting.

His flat was small, which was fair enough for someone with his salary. He hadn't bothered trying to do anything with it either, just bought some simple furniture from IKEA and set up the keepsakes he carried with him everywhere. An old lotus lantern, some pictures, and a bear that wore a bracelet with a Chinese symbol. If it wasn't for those, anyone who walked in would have no clue who lived there.

Caleb tossed his mail down on the coffee table and, as he looked back up, caught a quick glance of himself in the mirror. He looked tired. The circles under his eyes were getting to be as dark as his hair and his olive skin looked pale. It didn't help that the country's weather liked to swing between seasons like there was no tomorrow. It felt like winter only last week. Part of him wished he could have been back in California instead, relaxing in his Aunt Mee's house while he waited.

His eyes flickered over to the picture of her on the windowsill, standing with her arm around his Dad. He had been four when his Dad died on a flight from Seoul to LAX. Caleb had gone first with his aunt, something about his Dad needing to tie up loose ends. He had also been nursing a head wound at the time from the car crash that killed his Mom. It was now a scar hidden along his hairline. Aunt Mee always said that it was because of the bump to the head that he didn't remember his Mom very well or what happened that made them move so suddenly. She wouldn't tell him anything about her, other than she used to help people. It was never enough for Caleb, but no one else was around to give him the answers he needed.

Caleb's phone ringing cut through his nostalgia, bringing him back to the room.

"Hello?"

"Caleb," Master Mahmid's voice sounded hopeful for once.

"What is it?"

"One of the Oracles has had another vision. It will happen tonight."

Caleb let out a sigh of relief.

"There are several Oracles in the city, do we know which one will give them their prophecy?"

"No, I'm afraid not. You will have to visit them all in the morning and see which one found the Chosen."

More waiting.

"Don't worry, Caleb. All the time you've spent in the city will be worth it."

"I hope so," he said.

There was a small chance that this was all a cosmic joke. He would have to wait until tomorrow to find out if his faith was warranted.

Chapter Two

Jen's parties were always wild. Hallie and Kiara had been part of the same friendship group for two years now, ever since Freshers Week, so the gaggle of five girls knew each other well. Jen would be the richest if it wasn't for Hallie's Dad's mobile app business. She was certainly the richest based in London. Her parents rented a whole townhouse for her in Kensington and she generally wanted for nothing. However, she was only a little bit of a spoilt brat, which was better than most twenty-year-old's in her position.

They started out at Jen's house for pre-drinks before heading into the center for that rave everyone was talking about after Hallie's morning editing session. It was ridiculous. The music was so loud Hallie could barely think, let alone talk. She kept one hand on her girl at all times to stop other pretty dudes or ladies from getting any funny ideas. It wasn't unusual for her to lay someone out for trying to hit on Kiara, particularly if they got pushy.

Kiara always reciprocated the hands. It had taken her a while to get used to all the touching at first, Hallie was her first anything, but once she had, they barely kept their hands off each other. It wasn't like there was anyone around to police them.

The rave was intoxicating. Everyone was pressed together, moving in synchronous bounds in time to the thumping beat. Hallie could feel the beads of sweat dripping down her neck, Kiara breathing strawberry, peach and rum on her face as they danced so close they could almost taste each other.

'I love you,' Kiara mouthed, grazing her lips against Hallie's.

Hallie kissed her in reply, smiling through it.

She counted herself lucky that she had Kiara in her life and that she had met her when she did. It was the first day of university and Kiara hadn't been sure that she even wanted to sign in. Her Mom had died two weeks earlier after losing her fight with cancer. Kiara had promised her she would still go to school when it started, but on the day, she found herself dithering in the entrance to the library, struggling to go up to the welcome desk. That was when Hallie had found her. If she hadn't encouraged Kiara to be brave then, they wouldn't be here now. She would have missed out on one of the best things to ever happen to her.

They danced for hours, completely losing track of time. It was after midnight when they found themselves back out on the street, looking for something else to do. None of them could sleep right now, they were too buzzed. They stumbled from streetlight to streetlight, following their feet more than anything else, chatting all the way. Eventually, Theresa piped up from the back.

"We should totally do truth or dare."

Hallie giggled as she pushed up the strap of Kiara's dress back onto her shoulder.

"No one is sober enough to say no," Jen slurred.

There was laughter in agreement.

"Who goes first?" Hannah asked.

"ME!" Hallie stuck both her hands up in the air and grinned. She was always the first one to dive head first into a fun situation.

"Truth or dare?" Kiara asked her.

"Mmmmmm, truth," she decided.

"Other than me, who out of the group would you snog right now?" Kiara smirked wickedly, making Hallie snort.

"Are you trying to give me ideas?" she asked as she eyed up the other three girls. They started posing for her, but they were so drunk it looked hilarious rather than sexy.

"Theresa, because she has such pretty pink highlights. They're so bold, I love it."

"Awww, thank you," Theresa crooned, running her hands through her hair.

"You're welcome, sweets."

"Who's next?" Jen asked as no one immediately volunteered.

"I think it should be Kiara," Hallie said.

"Does it have to be?" Kiara pouted. None of the group were shy, exactly, but Kiara wasn't a big fan of making a fool out of herself.

"It's only fair as you got to ask me the truth."

"And you can't pick truth," Hannah chirped up.

"Yeah, otherwise it would be boring," Jen agreed.

Kiara let out a deep sigh. "Okay, dare."

The girls knew they had to make it a good one because the chances of Kiara doing another after this one was slim.

After searching around for a moment, Theresa pointed at a building across the street and said, "I dare you to get your palm read."

All the girls followed her finger to the old shop with the wooden board above its door which read, 'Mystic Mindy's Magic Shop'.

"Ohhh, that's priceless! You have to do it!" Hallie bounced up and down.

She seized Kiara by the shoulders and pushed her over the cobblestones before she could protest.

They couldn't see much through the front window as every inch of the display was covered in trinkets, scarves and items which could possibly be 'magical'. Inside was much the same. It was cluttered, but not in a way that looked like a mess. The colour theme was pinks, purples, and reds, with smatterings of glitter and sequins. A bell tinkled over the door when they opened it and a woman's voice came from the cashier's desk.

"You ladies are out late."

Based on the sign outside, Hallie was not expecting a cute, petite woman with big hazel eyes and mousey brown hair down to her shoulders to be looking at them from behind the wooden bench. She was wearing a simple black summer dress with flowers on it and was smiling warmly.

"Uhhh, yeah, we've been at the rave down near the waterfront," Hallie explained.

Clearly the other girls were baffled as well because none of them spoke.

"Are you Mindy?" Kiara asked, eventually.

"Oh, no, I'm Lily. I just run the shop. Mindy should be out shortly," she informed them. "Are you all looking to have your palms read?"

"No, just my girlfriend," Hallie nudged Kiara over towards the desk.

It could have been because she was drunk, but she could have sworn that Lily was looking at Kiara like she already knew her.

"Which one of you is Kiara?" an elderly voice asked from behind them.

They all turned on their heel, a little freaked that Mindy already knew her name. The elderly woman was a lot more like what they were expecting. Full length everything, scarf around her head, rings on each of her fingers.

Kiara hesitantly lifted her hand.

"Come over here, dear. Sit. The rest of you can make yourselves comfortable."

Still feeling creeped out, the ladies positioned themselves on various chairs and stools around the small, round table in the center of the room. Kiara sat nervously in the seat opposite Mindy, her chest rising and falling a little quicker now that the lady appeared to be more legit than the fortune peddlers at Blackpool that Hallie had tried last summer.

"Place your hand out flat on the table for me, dear, palm facing upwards."

Kiara did as she was told. Hallie looked back at Lily who was watching intently, her focus on Kiara more than Mindy.

Mindy gently traced the lines on Kiara's palm with her wrinkled forefinger, muttering to herself. Hallie couldn't really hear what she was saying, she wasn't sure they were real words.

"You will have a great deal of love in your life," Mindy said eventually, looking Kiara in the eye. "It will come from a handful of close people, some you know already and some you don't know yet."

Kiara glanced back at Hallie who offered her a reassuring smile. One of those people had to be her. She loved Kiara so much and she didn't see that ending any time soon.

"You will soon uncover old secrets, kept from you for a long time. It will change your life."

That sounded more like the sort of thing that psychics would say to catch the person's attention, make them hopeful for the future.

"And you will do great things with this change, however..."

Mindy drifted off and closed her eyes, looking pained. Hallie couldn't tell at this point whether it was an act or not, the upset looked so real.

"Your life will be shorter than most."

Hallie felt a lump lodge itself in her throat.

"How short?" Kiara asked quietly, sounding unsure as to whether she believed this woman.

Mindy took Kiara's hand in both of hers and clutched it tightly, squeezing her eyes more tightly shut, like she was concentrating harder than she ever had in her life.

"Five."

The ladies looked at each other, confused.

"Five what?" Hallie asked.

"Five years. To the day."

Her eyes flew open and she stared right at Kiara, like her eyes were piercing Kiara's soul.

"Five years until Kiara Shaw is no more."

~

The silence was deafening. Of all the things Kiara thought some psychic shop lady might say, predicting her death, to the day, was not one of them. She sat there with her mouth slightly open, unable to comprehend whether this was real. Why would someone who peddled dreams and fantasies say something like that to someone? That was definitely not the way to get new customers.

Kiara was still deep in thought when Jen loudly blurted out, "Pffft, yeah right!"

"Shut up," Hallie slapped her hard in the arm, eliciting a quiet whimper.

Mindy let go of Kiara's hand and said, "It is up to you whether you believe it or not, but I suggest you use your time wisely."

As Mindy rose from her chair, Kiara found herself faltering.

"No, wait, I have questions."

"I'm afraid that's all I can tell you. You will have to get your answers elsewhere."

As Mindy disappeared into the back, Hallie stepped forward and wrapped her arms around Kiara's shoulders.

"Don't worry, babe, it's not real," she murmured, pressing her lips to Kiara's cheek, trying to comfort her.

Kiara looked at Lily, who gently shrugged her shoulders. Hallie was right, it couldn't be real. Mindy was just playing with them, trying to make it more dramatic. Or she was trying to make it seem like everything was more urgent so that Kiara would go out and make those changes herself, be the prophecy.

"Not real," she agreed, finally.

"Let's get the hell out of here," Theresa said, hopping to her feet.

"Yeah, let's," Kiara said, wrapping one of her hands around Hallie's.

They were halfway down the street, heading towards the tube station when Hannah asked, "Wait, did we pay back there?"

All of them were so drunk, no one noticed.

"No, damn," Kiara said, feeling a little guilty.

"They didn't ask and don't deserve it for being so freaky," Jen said.

No one disagreed with her. The mood was decidedly sour now, which didn't suit any of them.

"We need to get some of the fun back, how about we play a different game?" Hallie suggested, obviously not wanting to end such a good night on a low.

"How about I Spy?" Theresa said.

It was innocent enough, there didn't seem like any danger there.

"All right, I Spy with my little eye, something beginning with… P," Hallie said.

Hallie's P for 'potted plant' and Hannah's S for 'street light' kept them guessing all the way back to the station. They were making their way onto the empty platform when Hallie finally guessed it.

"How is it your turn again?" Jen whined, leaning up against the tiled wall.

"I'm just that good," Hallie grinned.

Kiara wasn't even really playing. She was still distracted by what Mindy had said. Five years didn't seem like a long time at all. And what had she said about secrets? Something about her finding out stuff that had been kept for her for a long time? She wanted it to sound like a load of junk, but there was something about the way that Mindy had looked when she was speaking--

A shriek cut through her thoughts. Kiara looked up just in time to see Hallie, who was standing right on the edge of the platform, slip and fall out of sight with a crash.

"No!" she gasped, running forwards to the edge and looking over.

Hallie was lying across the dirty tracks, her face contorted in pain, tears streaming down her face.

"Hallie! Are you okay?"

"Oh GOD, that hurts!" Hallie cried, pulling her arm across her face so the others couldn't see her quietly sobbing.

"Stay there, I'll go get someone," Hannah said, running off back up the stairs. Theresa and Jen were both stood beside Kiara, the three of them trying to figure out if they could do anything before Hannah got back. Then they heard it. The quiet whoosh of an approaching train. Kiara's head whipped around to look at the sign. It was due in one minute.

"Hallie, Hallie, I need you to get up," her voice was frantic now, the three of them beckoning Hallie to them.

Hallie could hear the train too, the panic stopping her tears for now. She tried to lift herself up, but when she tried to put weight on her leg, she buckled and screamed.

"I think I've sprained my ankle," she said through gritted teeth, trying again but to no avail.

Before she really knew what she was doing, Kiara was kicking off her heels and lowering herself down onto the tracks. The other two yelled for her not to at first, but it was the only way to stop Hallie from becoming a tragedy.

"Come on, I got you," Kiara said, hoisting Hallie up onto her feet.

Out of the corner of her vision she could see the train's headlights, they needed to get moving.

"Move it, move it."

Kiara supported Hallie over to the edge, pushing her towards the other two's outstretched hands. "Go, go, please!" she pleaded, trying to hurry them up.

The rush of air before the train was blasting her now, blowing her hair across her face. With one final push, she felt Hallie's waist leave her hands and she overbalanced, falling back. There was a blinding light and tremendous, ear-breaking screeching, then everything went black.

~

"NOOOOOOO!" Hallie banged her fists against the stopped train's windows, her eyes so blurry with tears she could barely see.

Theresa and Jen were holding her, but she couldn't feel them. She couldn't feel anything but the anguish. The train doors opened, and the driver stepped out, shocked, wobbly on his feet. Hallie shook the two girls off and hobbled over to him, intending to take out her agony on him, but she was so unsteady that he had to catch her when she swung at him.

"I saw her at the last second," he murmured, shaking.

Hallie pushed him away, wiping her eyes so she could see him this time and sock him properly, then she noticed something.

"Shouldn't there be… person all over the front of the train?"

It sounded so stupid when it came out of her mouth, but it was true. There should have been splatter or something, something of Kiara to show that she was dead. She didn't know whether it was the horror speaking, or the denial, but when the driver looked over too, he was equally confused.

"Move the train," she ordered, thrusting him back towards the driver's seat as she went to peer around the front.

There was no sign that anyone had been hit by anything. Not on the lower part of the carriage, not on the wheels.

"Move, move, MOVE!"

As the tube driver edged the train forwards slowly, Hallie hurried as quickly as she could back down the platform to the other two girls and waited. Inch by inch, the train rolled away from the spot where Hallie had fallen to reveal a hole between the tracks. Kiara was there, hanging onto a broken pipe for dear life, choking from the dust.

It was that moment that Hannah and two station workers burst back onto the platform, looking around at the scene.

"Get down there and help her!" Hallie said shrilly, desperate for them to save Kiara before she fell and really did die.

They scampered down onto the track and pulled Kiara up in the nick of time, making sure she and the ground beneath them were stable before breathing a sigh of relief. It was a miracle. Kiara was alive.

"I was so scared," Hallie said, pulling Kiara into her arms as soon as she was back on the platform, "I thought you were dead."

"Me too," Kiara breathed, both of them unable to comprehend her terrible and brilliant luck. What were the odds of that happening to anyone, let alone someone who had just been told they had five years left to live?

"Never do that again," Hallie ordered, squeezing her even tighter.

Kiara let out a soft laugh, "I'll try."

"Girls?"

They held onto each other a little longer before turning to face the man in the high-vis jacket who had just helped save Kiara.

"You'll need to stay a little while to talk to the police and get checked out by paramedics, but then we'll make sure you get safely home, okay?"

"Okay," Kiara nodded, still overwhelmed with relief.

"You're one lucky girl," he added, squeezing her shoulder, "Don't take what comes next for granted."

Hallie and Kiara looked at each other and smiled a little.

"Don't worry, I won't."

Chapter Three

Caleb wasn't sure how this was possible. Five Oracles in the city and not one of them had a visit from a new Chosen last night. He had double checked with all of them before calling Master Mahmid to see whether anything had changed. Nothing had. So, it was entirely possible that there was someone out there in the city right now, none the wiser to the fact that they had abilities which could help change the world. It was his job to find them, but it had got so late in the morning that he had to go back to the university to give two classes and sit his office hours, so students could come see him for guidance with their dissertations and other essays.

On any other day, he might have broken his flawless record and taken a sick day, but he remembered he had said he would help Kiara with her project. Hallie and Kiara were important to him, so he wouldn't let them down if he could help it.

It turned out that Kiara was the one who almost missed the meeting.

"I'm sorry, so, so, sorry," she said as she ran through the open door.

"No worries, sit down, breathe. All the important things," he said.

Kiara offered him a grateful smile before nudging the door closed and seating herself in the chair by his desk.

His office had more stuff in it than his whole apartment, because of the nature of his work. There was a lot of stuff that you could research online these days, but there were a lot of books that he used for his lectures that he had to keep on hand, should he need them for classes or to lend to students. Between the bookshelves, there was a direct line between the door and his desk, the spare chair, and that was about it.

"You're the last person I'm seeing today anyway, so don't sweat it."

"Thank you for doing this, I really appreciate it," she said, pulling her work out her bag. There was something about the way she was still struggling to catch her breath that suggested she was more tired than normal.

"Did you not get much sleep last night with all the partying?" he asked.

Kiara looked up at him confused for a moment, then remembered.

"Oh yeah, the rave. Yeah, we were out until the early hours, I barely got any sleep," she admitted.

"We can do this some other time if you want, if you need to go back home and catch up on some sleep."

"No, no, I want to do it now," she assured him, but then fumbled her papers, spilling them all over the desk and floor.

"Shit," she cursed, then slapped her hand over her mouth.

Caleb laughed. "Don't worry, it's not like I don't swear."

"My Mum would be so ashamed," Kiara said as she crouched down to start scooping up the mess she'd made.

That was when Caleb noticed her hands.

"Kiara."

It took a moment for her to look up at him. "Hmm?"

"What happened to your hands?"

They were covered in cuts and bruises.

"Did someone hurt you while you were out last night?" Had someone hurt Hallie? He felt his blood begin to boil pre-emptively.

"What? Oh, no," she shook her head quickly before the anger could build any further. "I had an accident."

"An accident?"

Kiara got back up and sat down, placing the papers down carefully this time.

"It was so freaky. I don't even know how to explain it."

"Try," Caleb said, concerned now. Anything that busted up her hands that bad couldn't have been a simple accident.

"The five of us were heading home after the rave. We went to get the night tube home, like normal, but Hallie fell onto the tracks."

Caleb's head shifted back, alarmed.

"She's fine, just a sprained ankle. It's fine."

Caleb didn't feel relieved, but he gestured for her to carry on anyway.

"Hannah went to get help, but there was a train coming. I got down onto the tracks myself to help Hallie back up. I got her up safely, but I stumbled just as the train was coming. I thought for sure I was dead, but the next thing I knew, I was falling. I grabbed out for anything, clasped my hand around this pipe that was there and held on until they figured out I wasn't dead and came to get me. That's why my hands are so bad."

That was one hell of an accident, Caleb would give her that much.

"I'm so lucky and so happy that I'm alive and safe, and that Hallie is safe. I wasn't going to bring it up, I didn't want you to get that look on your face, like the one you're doing right now."

Caleb loosened his expression and looked at her properly. "Sorry, I just... You're right, you're very lucky."

The odds in that moment had to be stacked against her, a million to one. Ten million to one... He'd encountered flukes before, they happened all the time when Chosen were first starting out, but he'd never heard of anything quite like that before.

"Fingers crossed nothing like that ever happens again, hey?" he said, making her smile and nod.

"Absolutely. Being scared shi- uh- less once is enough for me," she caught herself this time, even though he'd said it was fine.

There was a moment of silence between them, then Kiara looked back at the papers on the desk.

"Maybe we should...?" she suggested.

"Yeah, yes, of course."

Caleb started sifting them back into a proper order for her, then she seemed to remember something.

"Oh! Hallie asked me to ask you if you want to get coffee with us this weekend? Her exact words were, 'When you almost get mowed down by a freakin' train, you realise you should probably spend more time with the awesome people in your life.' Lucky you," she smiled.

Caleb chuckled. "Nice impression. And yeah. I'm going to pretty busy, but message me when you head out and I'll meet you."

"Ace."

~

"There you are! I was starting to get worried!" Hallie declared when Kiara rounded the corner, heading for her student flat.

Kiara and Caleb had spent at least an hour together going over all of her notes for her project to check that they were up to scratch, then she'd found herself taking several detours on her way back, just so she'd have more time to think. She hadn't mentioned the whole 'a fortune teller told me I'm going to die in five years thing' to Caleb because he was so clearly upset about the accident that she didn't want to worry him any more than she already had. He probably would have thought it was a whole load of bollocks anyway. He was a smart man, there was no way he would be sucked in by something so ridiculous as palm reading.

She, however, was letting it play on her mind a little too much. The whole thing had seemed dubious until the train incident. Now she *wanted* to continue to poo-poo the idea but couldn't shake the feeling that the two things were connected. Also, the secrets thing, that was bugging her big time. How did the woman know that there was stuff in her life that was a mystery to her? Surely it wasn't something she could read off her or her friends in the room? Her Dad was the biggest thing in her life that she was missing. She only knew things that her Mum let slip by accident, and even then, that happened so infrequently that she couldn't paint a real picture of the man. She didn't know how he'd died either; it wasn't reported in any newspapers, not even an obituary.

Kiara never understood why her Mum never remarried, or why she never saw any of either parent's families, or where half of the things she was talented at came from. Most of her life was a mystery, she guessed, except for what she had now. Hallie being the key thing.

"I'm sorry, I needed to clear my head," she said, wrapping her arms around Hallie in a tight hug.

"I get it, just shoot me a text next time, okay? Otherwise I'm going to think that fate has caught up with you because you cheated death," Hallie squeezed her, stealing a kiss before Kiara could pull away.

"Oh God, no. Please don't put that idea in my head," Kiara snorted.

Hallie zipped her mouth shut, then quickly stole Kiara's keys so she could let them both into the flat. It was tiny because it was all Kiara could afford with her student loan. Her Mum hadn't really left her anything in terms of inheritance and she kept passing on Hallie's offers to let her use her trust fund to help. That money was for when Hallie wanted to make her first big movie or start her first charity, Kiara asserted. She could get by on very little, she'd been practicing it for most of her life.

There was a small kitchenette with a microwave, fridge and sink, and an even smaller bathroom where you could pretty much pee and wash your hair at the same time, then there was the main room which was mostly taken up by her desk and her bed. The bed doubled as a sofa, which was great, because it meant she and Hallie could chill there while they were watching TV or playing games on Kiara's old console.

"What did you need to clear from your head?" Hallie asked as she dumped her backpack and shoes at the foot of the bed and flopped down on top of the duvet.

Kiara shook her head, "Nothing really, just everything from last night is still floating around in there."

"Me too, babe. But don't worry, it's all over now. We're safe."

Kiara wasn't as sure as Hallie, about most things really, but there wasn't much point worrying about it when they were together.

Hallie patted the bed next to her and Kiara settled in. She wrapped an arm around Hallie's waist as she pressed her forehead against her shoulder. Hallie was quite tall for a girl, whereas Kiara was average height, which meant that they fit together really well.

"Caleb was up for coffee, by the way," she said quietly, just in case she forgot to mention it later.

"Sweet. I think we need a little more sensible and cute in our lives after that madness."

Kiara nudged her with her head. "You're all the cute I need."

"I love you too," Hallie smiled, curling up closer to Kiara.

Kiara was sure that she could lie with Hallie like this forever if she had the choice, if they didn't have to get on with their lives at some point. But for now, she was content to snuggle. And, apparently, to sleep.

Chapter Four

Hallie was so glad it was the weekend. Usually she would spend her Saturday and Sunday balancing doing work for class and spending time with Kiara, but after they both almost died, she wanted to spend every moment she could with her girlfriend and her friends. It was better to embrace life while they had the time and energy. This thought was regardless of whether or not that palm reading was real. She knew she wouldn't feel this empowered forever, that it would fade, and she would get back into the grind that was life. But for these two days, at least they could enjoy themselves.

After a three-hour call with her Mom and Dad, of course.

Usually her parents didn't speak to each other, but something as dramatic as this had to bring them together in joint concern. Her Dad's company was based out of Brisbane, which was where he lived and worked now, but for a few years while her parents were together, they were all situated in New Jersey, which was where her Mom still lived. Their divorce wasn't exactly amicable, but they still both cared for her deeply. And Will, of course, her older half-brother. Will saw her Mom as his second 'Mum', which was great. He used to come out and visit all the time, when their parents were together and when they weren't any more. Hallie and Will used to be thick as thieves until he disappeared without a trace a couple of years before she went to university. Not even their Dad knew what he was up to, it was like he had vanished off the face of the Earth. Hallie hoped he turned up some day. She might even go searching for him once she graduated, he wouldn't want her to jeopardise her degree for him.

Once her parents were both suitably reassured, she hobbled out to the coffee shop she had agreed to meet Kiara at around lunch and shot Caleb a message like he asked. It was a small place near Waterloo Station which she and Kiara liked to hang out in sometimes after their classes were done. It was cosy inside, warm colours highlighting an otherwise bland colour theme. They had jammed as many sofas and armchairs in there as possible. Oh, and a ton of cushions. It was warm enough to sit on the wooden furniture outside, so she grabbed herself an iced mocha and nabbed one of the tables, so she could wait for her friends in peace.

To her surprise, it was Caleb who showed up first. Kiara must have still been on the underground otherwise she would have texted.

"Hey, I'm glad you could make it," Hallie grinned up at him. His black hair was more tousled than usual, and it didn't look like he had got a lot of sleep.

"Funnily enough, I was in the area when I got your message. Lucky happenstance," he smiled in return. "Let me get a drink and I'll join you," he added, not giving her a chance to ask about the bags under his eyes.

"Black coffee, bold choice on a day like this," she said when he returned, gesturing around at the sun and the people in as little clothing as possible.

"I can't stand it any other way. Never been able to figure out why," Caleb admitted.

"Family thing?" she suggested, sitting back in her chair a little.

"I, uh, wouldn't know. I don't really know much about either of my parents, let alone how they took their coffee."

Hallie hadn't meant to step into territory like that, but then she shouldn't have assumed he had a normal family. It wasn't like any of her friends did.

"I'm sorry, I get these bouts of foot in mouth disease..."

Caleb chuckled. "Don't worry about it. We've never talked about anything like this before. Besides, I lost them both a long time ago, my aunt raised me, so I wasn't alone."

He was right. Hallie prided herself on being his star student, and she and Kiara talked to him more than some of ladies in their friendship group sometimes, but he had never mentioned anything so personal. He was definitely a private guy. Until now.

"I'm glad you had someone. Everyone needs someone."

"They do," he replied with a small smile, suggesting there was a lot more to that story.

Maybe she would ask someday, when it was more appropriate.

"Hey, how's your ankle?" he asked, looking at her bandaged foot in a flip flop.

"Oh, it sucked so hard for a couple of days, but it's already starting to feel better. I'm more worried about Kiara, she's still freaked about the whole thing."

"Well, that's understandable. I think anyone would be if they almost got run over by a train."

"Duh," Hallie snorted. "It's not just that, though. Didn't she tell you what happened before we went to the station?"

Caleb looked confused. "No?"

"We dared her to get her palm read by this old lady, Psychic Mindy… Mystic Mind? I don't remember. It was weird from the start. She knew Kiara's name somehow, then when she sat her down, she started telling her stuff that wasn't generic at all."

She glanced at Caleb as she was speaking, sort of registering that the expression on his face was changing from one of curiosity to one of concern.

"Then she topped it all off by telling Kiara that she only had five years to live. To the day, she said. It was so freaky, seriously. I can't believe anyone would say that, it's so terrible, right?"

When Caleb didn't say anything, she looked at him properly.

"Hey, Earth to Caleb?"

"Hmm?"

"I said it's so terrible, right?"

This time, Caleb didn't get a chance to reply. They were both distracted by the sound of a car horn beeping on the street. Hallie looked around to see Kiara, headphones on, attempting to cross the street, oblivious to everything. She walked into the path of a passing bike, who veered in front of a car which was about to collide with her. The car then stopped in front of her, preventing her from stepping on top of a water main which suddenly burst through the tarmac, spraying everyone with water. Any one of those things could have hurt or killed her, but she narrowly missed all three?

The now startled and wet Kiara pulled her headphones off and stared at Hallie and Caleb, who were both completely flabbergasted.

"What was that?" Hallie choked, unable to move from the shock.

Caleb, however, managed to get onto his feet to check on the driver and the cyclist. When he found they were fine, he pulled Kiara out of the chaos, both of them now soaked through.

"What the...? How did the...?" Kiara spluttered, unable to finish a sentence.

"Are you okay?" Caleb asked instead, checking her for any injuries when he knew very well she couldn't possibly have any. They saw everything with their own eyes.

"I don't know. I think so?" she looked over herself as well, still baffled.

Hallie wasn't saying anything. How could so many life-threatening instances happen in the space of a few days? Three within a minute?

"Good," Caleb said, although it didn't sound like he was glad. If anything, he sounded... upset.

"Hallie?" Kiara sounded worried now.

Hallie got up and pulled her into a hug. "How is this possible?" she whispered.

"I don't know," Kiara murmured back.

They held onto each other for a few moments, then turned back to Caleb who looked agitated.

"Are *you* okay?" Kiara asked him.

"What? Yeah, just... shocked, of course. I think we should get out of here."

Kiara didn't look so sure.

"He's right, I'd rather not have to talk to the police again for the second time in a week." Not when Hallie couldn't explain any of the things that had just happened. No one was hurt, it wasn't going to count against them morally.

"Okay," Kiara said, taking Hallie's hand. "Let's go."

~

Once Caleb had made sure that both of the girls were safely back at Hallie's place, he had departed pretty quickly. If this had been any other situation, of course he would have stayed. Whether that was because he was being a good friend or because it was his duty as a Guardian, it would have been the right thing to do. But Caleb wasn't thinking straight.

When he hadn't found the Chosen that morning after trying his other sources, he was sure he would never find them. He had gone to get coffee with the ladies thinking that he would go back to his place after and tell Master Mahmid that they should give up, there was no point wasting time. Something had clearly gone wrong. At least he got that last part right. Kiara had slipped through the cracks somehow, something he was sure hadn't happened in the entire history of their order. It was something he was going to have to look into, but for now, he had to decide what to do about this dilemma.

With every Chosen he had guided, it was straightforward. Even if he didn't meet them the moment they were given their prophecy, he never accidentally befriended them first. In this situation, Master Mahmid would tell him to put his feelings aside. What mattered most was that the Chosen fulfilled their destiny, whoever they turned out to be. The world was more important than one person. But in this instance, Caleb wasn't sure.

For one, Kiara had been through a lot in her life. Never having a Dad and barely scraping by with her Mom, before she too had to leave, it was a lot for one young woman to handle. Her timeline now was a given, there was no changing it. But the least he could give her was five good years filled with normal things, possible happiness.

And for two, Caleb wasn't sure he was fit to train her. His emotions could get the better of him with people he didn't know before he trained them. With a friend? How was he supposed to knowingly put her in danger? Even if she couldn't die, she could still get seriously hurt. Also, how would it affect her relationship with Hallie? It was tough maintaining relationships with anyone while you were going through training, then when you were out in the field… He didn't want this to be the reason for their demise. They were too good together to let something like this come between them.

Caleb was trying to decide what to do when his phone buzzed in his pocket. He was surprised it wasn't broken or dead after being drowned in all that water.

It was Master Mahmid calling.

Clutching the sopping piece of technology in his hands, he briefly considered not answering. That would only make Master Mahmid suspicious.

"Caleb," Master Mahmid said right away when Caleb put the phone to his ear.

"Yeah?"

"Have you had any luck tracking down the Chosen?"

Of course, the truth was that she'd fallen straight into his lap, like some strange and horrible twist of fate. But, based on the reasons he'd given himself for not involving Kiara in this life, he didn't think he could be honest with Master Mahmid. For the first time ever, he was going to lie to his mentor.

"What? Oh, uh, no," Caleb said, pretending to sound distracted.

"How can this be?" Master Mahmid was as perplexed as Caleb was, just for a different reason.

"I really don't know. I've tried everything, no one has heard anything or knows who it could be," he said, feeling bad.

They didn't always get along, but there was a trust between him and Master Mahmid. He didn't enjoy breaking it.

Master Mahmid let out a sigh, clearly trying to think of a solution rather than admit defeat.

"Stay where you are for now and leave it with me," he said eventually. "If I can't turn up anything, we'll reassign you."

Caleb really hoped he didn't find something, for Kiara's sake.

"Yeah, okay," he said, not letting his feelings seep into his words.

He was about to say goodbye and hang up when Master Mahmid added, "It's been a long time since we've spoken face to face. If nothing turns up, at least it'll be good to see you."

Caleb could feel his guts twisting inside. Why did the man have to go and break out the sentiment right now? A part of him wanted to come clean there and then, but he knew that if

Master Mahmid found out then he could salvage that relationship, whereas he couldn't take back ruining Kiara's life.

"Yeah, it'll be good. Look, I've got to go prepare my classes for next week. Let me know if you find anything."

Master Mahmid confirmed he would and rang off, leaving Caleb standing there, feeling like a jerk. It wasn't a feeling he was accustomed to and he hoped it didn't linger long. He was making the right choice for Kiara, that was enough.

It had to be enough.

Chapter Five

Kiara hadn't seen Hallie for two whole days. She honestly couldn't remember the last time they had been apart for that long. It was partly her fault. After Hallie had hurried off home following the accident, Kiara had spent most of that time in her apartment doing nothing. Her worries were gnawing at her from the inside. The fluky accidents had scared her into thinking that maybe the prophecy was true. In less than five years, her time could be up, meaning that all the plans she had for her life were pointless. There would be no real future for her and Hallie either, which was why she hadn't bothered trying to contact her. Hallie would try to reassure her, tell her that she was being silly, and she didn't want that right now. Her paranoia was real.

As the hours ticked on, Kiara realised that Hallie wasn't trying to contact her either. Maybe she had realised just how dangerous Kiara was to be around at the moment and was staying away out of self-preservation. It seemed unlikely, but her mind wasn't in a reasonable place.

It was the middle of Monday afternoon. Kiara should have been in a lecture on Modern Christianity, but she didn't feel like listening to a two-hour spiel about how the religion functioned in today's society. It was a good thing that she didn't go because she would have missed the knock on the door. It was loud and quick, like whoever it was outside was in a hurry.

"Oh good, you're here," Hallie said when Kiara crawled out of bed to answer.

Her nose wrinkled, and she pulled a face.

"Babe, when did you last take a shower? And what the heck is going on in here?"

There were a few takeaway boxes littered about the small space and her bedsheets were a tangled mess because she had spent most of her weekend there.

"I was wallowing," Kiara admitted as Hallie walked by her and started picking stuff up, so she could throw it in the bin. She was wearing a massive backpack, which was unusual for her. Shoulder bags were her thing, or just carrying what she needed in her pockets.

"What's in there?" she asked, pointing at the backpack.

"Research," Hallie replied.

"About what exactly?"

Hallie rinsed her hands in the sink to get the sweet and sour sauce and pizza crumbs off them, then sat on the edge of Kiara's bed.

"About everything that's going on with you, of course. What do you think I was doing all weekend?"

"I don't know really."

Hallie looked concerned now. Despite everything that Kiara had been through, she was usually more put together than this.

"Come, sit," she ordered, tipping the contents of her backpack onto the bed and fanning them out.

There were a couple of big books with sticky notes marking pages throughout, a bunch of print outs, and her own notes. When had Hallie had time to sleep?

"How did you find all this?" Kiara asked, picking up one of the printouts.

"It turns out that googling freak accidents brings up a lot of crap. Put that together with palm readings, future, and/or prophecy, however, and you start to get some stuff with a little more substance. Obviously, there was still a lot of stuff about wackos who believe that they were blessed by whatever deity to roam the earth immune to death, but when I delved deeper into history, I found that there's myths and legends about people who couldn't die -- until they did."

The piece of paper Kiara had chosen was an article from an old newspaper, back in 1921. It was the life story of a Jameson Holt. He was supposed to have miraculously saved the lives of several men, women and children around New York city, a sort of vigilante, until his untimely death by heart attack. Jameson was only 25 when he died and was a picture of health.

"There's stories like that one dating back to the first and second century, and those are just the ones I found in two days. Who knows how long this sort of thing has been going on," Hallie said, showing her another couple of stories, then a few pages from one of the books.

"How do we know they're not all fake or blown way out of proportion?" Kiara asked, unsure what she believed about all this.

"We don't, but how else are we supposed to explain what happened to you in the days following Mindy's palm reading? It is like the universe is yelling at us that something weird is going on here."

Kiara had been so wrapped in her mortality that she hadn't thought about it that way. Maybe she shouldn't have let it get her so down, but what else would most people do if they were told they were going to die? There had to be some time to process. Hallie had decided to process everything for her.

"How are we supposed to figure out if this is real?"

"Well, I thought maybe we could take all of this stuff to Caleb, see what he thinks," Hallie suggested.

"Maybe he'll have heard other stuff too, he knows so much about history after all," Kiara added.

"That's more like it," Hallie said, glad to see that Kiara was willing to see if any of this made sense. "But first, you definitely have to have a shower. No one needs to see you with two-day old bed head."

"No one else, you mean," Kiara snorted, slapping Hallie with one of the articles.

"I speak for everyone in this case, you look much purdier without cheese stuck to your vintage tee."

Kiara looked down and laughed when she found out that Hallie wasn't joking.

"Okay, jeez, I'm going, I'm going."

~

Caleb was finishing his last class of the day when two faces appearing in the doorway caught his attention. He hadn't heard from either of the girls after Saturday's events. If all went to plan, everyone would let it go and get on with their usual business. Eventually, the death-defying events would slow down, and Kiara would be able to live life like any other person. Hopefully, to the fullest.

Things rarely ever went to plan, though, not with so many unknown variables.

It seemed Kiara managed to keep Hallie from barging straight in before everyone had left, the pair of them only coming in once they were alone.

"How are you feeling?" Caleb asked Kiara first, showing genuine concern.

"I had a bit of a lazy weekend--"

"Understatement," Hallie interrupted, earning herself a poke.

"But I'm doing better now. How about you?"

"Yeah, fine," he nodded, not about to go into his own festering guilt spiral of a Sunday. It had been difficult to plan classes when he was so torn over his decision.

"I, on the other hand, am sleep deprived because of all this," Hallie announced, opening her rucksack to show him a tree's worth of books and papers.

"Getting a head start on that assignment on gender roles during wartime, huh?"

"No, something much more important."

Caleb and Kiara followed Hallie over to one of the benches where she proceeded to take everything out of her bag and spread it out for him. He wasn't comforted by the headlines he saw. They were exactly the same sort of thing that had come up when he started looking up the stuff from his Mom's journals back in the day.

"What's all this?" he asked, feigning ignorance. He had already lied to Master Mahmid, he wasn't about to come clean now.

"You see, I started thinking that maybe the fluke accidents weren't flukes at all. Especially after what that psychic,

Mystic Mindy, said to Kiara. I started looking into it and it turns out that there are other people in the past who have defied death on more than one occasion. I've never seen the word miracle mentioned more than I have in the last 48 hours."

This was bad. It appeared both of the girls had begun to buy into this theory. Of course, it seemed plausible after what they had seen and experienced. But they couldn't be allowed to believe it if he wanted to keep this under wraps.

"Do you think it's possible that this is a real thing?" Kiara asked.

"People being told that they have so long to live and the universe, sort of, preventing them from going before that time," Hallie clarified for her.

Caleb took another few moments to look over the stuff before shaking his head, uncertain. At least, to them he appeared uncertain. In his mind he was going straight to the bad place for telling so many lies.

"I don't think so. Things like this usually get over exaggerated, hyped up by the media to make them seem sensational in order to sell more papers. As for the books, they're probably talking about instances people couldn't explain back then. Like when adrenaline kicks in and people can do the sorts of things they couldn't usually do without that fight or flight reflex."

"What about what happened to Kiara though?"

"A spell of equally horrifying but ridiculously good luck? It can happen."

Both the girls looked disheartened about him shooting down their idea. It had been one thing lying over the phone, but doing it to their faces...

"I'm sorry, but based on other things I've read, it doesn't seem possible," he said, trying to console them.

"It's okay," Hallie said, stuffing all the papers back in her bag. It didn't sound like it was okay, not in the slightest.

"Do you think there's any truth to what the psychic said?" Kiara asked, looking directly at him.

"No, probably not. But I think the sentiment behind what these psychics usually say is true, you should live every day like it's your last. Cherish what you have, because the next moment it could be gone."

Kiara nodded your head. "Yeah, makes sense."

Caleb had to give her something. Hopefully she would take it to heart.

"I'll see you in class on Wednesday," Hallie said, taking Kiara's hand so that she could steer her out of the room.

"Bye!" Kiara called back as they rounded the door and disappeared.

Once he was sure they were gone, Caleb slumped against the bench and buried his head in his hands. With any luck, that would be the end of it so far as Kiara and Hallie were concerned. He wanted to put it behind him as well. It would be simple enough to see out the rest of the year and then say he was transferring to another college, probably one stateside. There was one thing he wanted to know before he left though, to satisfy his curiosity if nothing else; who the hell was Mystic Mindy?

Chapter Six

Despite the way it looked when they left Caleb's office, Hallie wasn't ready to give up on her theory. She had spent too much time trying to make this craziness make sense, it had to be something other than dumb luck.

"I don't think he's right," Hallie said as they walked out the main doors.

"How are we supposed to know?" Kiara asked.

Hallie scratched the top of her head in thought, slowly coming to a stop in the middle of the path.

"We've got to find some way to test it out. If you survive for a third time, then it must be true."

They went back to Kiara's place to throw ideas around while they tidied up and ordered a fresh set of takeaway food. One large Hawaiian pizza and a lot of internet searching later, they had a plan.

A period of hot weather like the one they had just had was always followed by a crazy thunderstorm. They checked the weather forecasts and started working out exactly how they were going to test out their theory without getting Hallie killed in the process. Once they were settled, they went to bed, but neither of them got much sleep. The nervous anticipation was too much for them.

It took two tubes, a train, and a long walk to get them far enough out of the city to find fields. All the while, dark storm clouds were bubbling up overhead, threatening to release all their fury on what lay below.

"I think it's going to start soon," Kiara told Hallie as they both made their way out into the middle of one of the fields.

There were no trees around for the lightning to catch, just some small hedgerows all the way down the other end of the field, and Kiara was a couple of feet taller than them anyway. This should work, so long as she could get the lightning to strike where she was standing. They weren't sure what was going to happen exactly, but they were both willing to try it in order to prove that Kiara couldn't die.

They both heard their first rumble of thunder as they neared the center of the field. Another quickly followed.

"All right, I think it's nearly here," Hallie said.

She got down on the ground, so she could flatten herself against the earth and take herself out of the running as a target for the weather.

"Here goes nothing," Kiara nodded, making sure to get some distance between her and Hallie.

"You're going to be fine, babe, you'll see," Hallie called out to her, confident in herself and her assumption.

A bright flash of lightning nearby made them both start. Hallie counted how long until the rumble of thunder; only two Mississippi's. It was almost upon them.

Another thirty seconds passed before they saw a spectacular fork of lightning hit a tree in a field across the road from theirs. If it didn't happen in the next minute or so, then it probably wouldn't happen at all.

Hallie was close to giving up hope when all of a sudden, she saw it. With the loudest bang that she had ever heard in her life, the sky around them erupted with light. The bolt of lightning crackled through the air, splitting into four bits before it hit the ground, each one narrowly missing Kiara as she stood there, frozen to the spot.

As it faded away, both of them remained absolutely still just in case another struck right away.

"That. Was. AMAZING!!" Hallie yelled at the top of her lungs, scrambling to her feet so she could go over and hug the crap out of Kiara.

It took Kiara a few seconds to hold her back, still stunned that she hadn't just been fried to a crisp.

"I was right! I was totally right! Caleb can suck it!" Hallie cheered, feeling like dancing around.

It was a good thing she didn't.

Out of nowhere, the air exploded again. Hallie couldn't see a thing as Kiara pulled her tightly against her body and put an arm over her head, the light from the bolt temporarily blinding them both. It was only because of Kiara that they both got out unscathed.

Once it was over, they both quickly crumpled to the floor and lay on their backs, staring up at the dark, angry sky.

"Oh my God," Hallie choked.

"That was so close," Kiara said, her voice barely there because of the shock.

"Oh my God, oh my God, oh my God."

Hallie was freaking out. Adrenaline was pumping so hard through her veins that she felt like she was buzzing from the inside out.

"That was incredible."

"Yeah, it sort of was," Kiara looked at her and grinned, clearly feeling the rush.

Now they both understood why people risked life and limb to do this sort of stuff, the feeling that followed was out of this world.

Another rumble of thunder went off further away just as the skies above them opened and a torrential shower poured out of the clouds, making them laugh.

"I love you, you know that, right?" Hallie shouted at Kiara over the noise.

"You bet your sweet arse I do," Kiara said, rolling over to kiss Hallie.

Hallie caught her before she could pull away and deepened the kiss, revelling in the moment while she could. She didn't care if they got covered from head to toe in mud, it was totally worth it. This was a moment that they would keep with them for the rest of their lives, however long or short they ended up being.

~

"Uh, Mystic Mindy?"

Caleb honestly wasn't sure what to expect. When the girls told him what had happened the night that Kiara received her prophecy, he couldn't figure out how it was possible. The birth of an Oracle was always predicted by another of their kind. They were registered when they were born, usually visited by Guardians and other Oracles while they were growing up in order to hone their ability to find Chosen, and then they notified the Elders whenever a new Chosen was about to appear. He'd never heard of any living outside the system. Possibly, until now.

"No, but I can get her for you if you..."

The brunette behind the counter trailed off when she looked up. It was like she recognised him. Maybe she did, it might explain a lot. This didn't look like a place that an Oracle would usually keep. It was so tacky, but that could be so that they could hide in plain sight.

"You must have a lot of questions," she said.

"A lot, yeah. You're the Oracle?" he asked, starting with the simplest question that came to mind.

"Sort of," she said, moving to change the sign on the door to closed. This was a conversation they would both rather remained private.

"Sort of?"

"Follow me, please."

Through the back of the shop, things started to look a lot more normal. Walls painted in cream, standard brown coloured carpet. There was a flight of stairs which led to an apartment, hers he assumed. It was bigger than his and better kept. She definitely liked to keep things neat and organised.

"I clean to distract myself from my thoughts," she explained without him asking anything. It could have been an observation that people had made before or--

"Yes, I can hear your thoughts."

Caleb stopped where he was standing, his mind going blank with panic, which made her laugh softly.

"I don't usually listen in if I can help it, I just wanted to see what you were thinking about all of this," she reassured him. "Please, sit."

"I'm starting to wonder whether I'll be able to get a word in edgewise," he tried humour, unsure whether she was still listening.

"I'll let you ask the questions," she smiled.

They both sat down on her very comfortable two-seater, the brunette smoothing out her dress, so it covered her knees. Where should he start?

"What's your name?"

"Lily," she said, looking a little embarrassed that she had forgot to introduce herself. He imagined it happened a lot when you could simply read the other person's mind to find out who they were.

"How is it that no one knew about you?"

"I wasn't born an Oracle like everyone else, it's just an extra part of what I can do," she explained.

"It doesn't run in your family?"

"Both of my parents were orphaned as children, they had no idea if my grandparents had powers. If they did, they didn't inherit them."

If they all died young, then it was possible that something else was going on.

"How about Chosen, do they run in the family?"

Lily pressed her lips together, leaving him hanging for a minute before nodding. "My brother was one."

"Who was your brother?" Maybe Caleb had heard of him.

"Peter Shaw."

Wait...

"Shaw? Like, Kiara Shaw?"

"Yes, she's my niece."

Caleb was lost. Obviously, his expression conveyed this because she continued without him having to ask another question.

"I was the one who gave Peter his prophecy. It was only eighteen months. Another Oracle must have seen it too because the next day a Guardian turned up at our door to explain everything. Ezra Mahmid was the one who trained him. They spent pretty much every waking moment together for a year and a half. But Peter never told Ezra that he was married. Or that his wife fell pregnant a couple of months before he died. They had been told that this sort of thing could run in families. If their baby ended up being a Chosen, they didn't want anyone to know. While Peter knew that he was doing good, didn't want his kid to suffer the same fate if it could be helped, he wanted his child to live her life to the full, however long it ended up being."

Lily paused there, partly to let him process, but also because it looked like her emotions were starting to get the better of her.

"How did you manage to obscure Kiara from us?"

"I've become friends with all the other Oracles in the city over the years, I asked them not to tell the Guardians if they had any visions about Kiara. Other Oracles would have been too far away to see her specifically."

"And you orchestrated it so that you, or more Mindy, got to tell her the prophecy, so that we wouldn't find her?"

"A plan I was sure was going to work."

"You didn't see that I would find her?"

"I have control over my psychic powers, but I'm at the mercy of my visions. I only saw it right before it happened, there was nothing I could do to stop you from finding out."

Caleb sighed. It was a shame that someone like Kiara had to be involved in something like this, it wasn't fair. It wasn't fair for any of the Chosen, really.

"I appreciate that you are trying to keep it from the other Guardians, that you're trying to protect her," she said with a small smile.

"Of course," he smiled in return, his eyes lingering on her face. It was funny, now he knew that she and Kiara were related, he could see the family resemblance. They both had the same eyes, pale skin, big smiles.

"Is that why you haven't reached out to her, because you're also still trying to protect her?" Caleb asked.

Lily nodded.

"It must have been hard for you to tell two of your family that they're going to die," he said quietly.

"The hardest thing," she agreed.

Caleb was sorry for her and sorry that he couldn't do anything to change this situation, not without giving everything away.

As silence fell between them, Caleb could hear that there were so many thoughts still buzzing through his head. Her answers had brought up even more questions, there was plenty that he still wanted to know. But he didn't get a chance to ask another because her face screwed up with pain and she let out an anguished yell, crumpling back against the sofa.

"Lily, what's wrong?" he asked, leaning forward and reaching out to steady her with his hands. She was so cold all of a sudden.

"Vision," she choked out, so that he wouldn't distract her.

Caleb remained quiet until she relaxed, her eyes fluttering open.

"What did you see, is it another Chosen?" he asked, still holding her.

"No, it's Kiara and Hallie, they're going to get hurt."

Caleb looked startled, gripping her arms a little tighter out of worry.

"When? Where?"

"Tower Bridge. A little while after the rain clears."

They both looked over at the window behind them and saw that the skies were already growing lighter, the rain a faint drizzle.

"Go," she said, pushing him up onto his feet. "Quickly!"

Caleb didn't need to be told twice, he ran as fast as his legs could carry him.

~

Kiara and Hallie could still feel the rush of what they had just experienced as they made the long journey back into the city. For lightning to curve around Kiara like that… It meant that what they believed had to be true. They were three for three; Kiara couldn't die.

"Hey," Hallie said, pointing at the sign with all the tube stations on it. "Do you want to do something even more reckless?"

"Is anything more reckless than what we just did?" Kiara asked with a laugh.

"Want to go to the top of Tower Bridge?" Hallie said, wiggling her eyebrows.

An intrigued smile slowly spread out across Kiara's face. "You can get us up there? Isn't it closed?"

"Is there anything that money can't buy?"

Hallie didn't usually flash around her cash, but she was feeling invincible and she wanted to expel her energy while she was feeling brave enough to be adventurous.

"Let's go, then."

They both hopped off the tube when it stopped, running even though there was no need. They had so much excitement to burn, they couldn't help themselves. Hand in hand, they jogged up to the bridge's entrance and bribed their way in. They had to swear they wouldn't do anything that would get the security guy in trouble, which they obviously did, crossing their hearts and everything.

There were so many stairs to the top, Hallie wasn't sure it was ever going to end. But when they did reach the last step, the view outside was worth it. On the walkway, there were glass panels in the floor, showing the road and river below. It was a bit vertigo inducing, but seriously cool! While Kiara was taking it all in, Hallie wandered up and down the walkway, having a poke around. Looking up, she noticed a wooden hatch in the ceiling, the latch unlocked.

"I bet the view is even better from up there," she called to Kiara, beckoning for her to come look.

It took some effort and some teamwork, but with Hallie standing on Kiara's shoulders, they were able to get the hatch open and Hallie climbed through. Turning around, she stuck her hands back down so Kiara could jump, and Hallie could pull her up. It was a bit slippy but they both managed to situate themselves close to the edge without falling off.

Looking out across the Thames from there was absolutely amazing. The sun was setting, turning the lingering clouds a gorgeous shade of pink. It was the perfect way to end one of the craziest days of their life.

"I didn't even notice the rain had stopped," Kiara remarked, looking across at Hallie with a grin.

"No, me either."

They had been too busy having fun.

"Thank you for today. If it wasn't for you, I wouldn't have figured out how epic this could be. Caleb was right, I should live every moment I have left to the fullest," Kiara took one of Hallie's hands and pressed a kiss to her palm, then hugged her hand to her chest. "You're the best girlfriend ever."

"Why thank *you*," Hallie beamed, pleased that she managed to change Kiara's mind. If they couldn't be together forever, then they were going to have to make whatever time they had left the most spectacular years of anyone's life ever.

They sat there for a little while, just soaking it all in. Then Kiara began to shiver.

"Apparently you're not immune to the cold," Hallie joked, tugging Kiara towards her so that she could embrace her.

Unfortunately, the motion was too harsh and with the ground underneath them still slick with water, they both lost their grip.

"Crap!" Hallie cried out, slipping out of control. "No, no, no!"

Kiara tried to grab onto something, anything, but there was nothing. The roof disappeared completely as they soared over the edge. There was a brief rush of air as they both fell, a high-pitched scream, then what Hallie could only assume was her end. By God, did it hurt.

Chapter Seven

It was the screams that Kiara heard first, cutting through everything else. Next, she registered the sound of the rushing water, then the throbbing helicopter rotors approaching through the city. It sounded like utter chaos.

For a brief moment, she couldn't remember what happened or where she was, then it all came flooding back; the bridge, falling, Hallie…

"HALLIE!" she spluttered, flailing around in the water as she tried to look for her.

Out of the corner of her vision, Kiara saw someone dive into the water, causing even more screams from the crowd that was gathering along the river bank. She didn't look to see who it was, instead she focused on trying to find Hallie. The river was so murky it was almost impossible to see anything. It didn't help that they were also starting to flow downstream. Kiara wasn't sure how long it had been since they fell, Hallie could be anywhere.

"Kiara!" A familiar voice cried out to her from nearby and she whipped her head round to see Caleb swimming towards her, his arms slicing through the current to bring him closer to her.

"Are you okay?" he was barely able to finish asking his question before she interrupted him.

"Where's Hallie? Can you see Hallie?"

Caleb knew that she wouldn't let her help him until they found her. He searched, looking for any sign of her, then dove under the water. The wait on the surface was painful. Every second ticked by slower than the last. Her heart leaped into her throat when he came back up with nothing, but all he did was take another huge breath and then go straight back down again.

"Please," she begged, praying that their stupid stunt hadn't got the love of her life killed. She would never forgive herself if that was case.

After another agonizingly long wait, Caleb resurfaced, bringing Hallie with him. She wasn't conscious. Kiara couldn't tell if she was even breathing.

"Can you swim?" he yelled to her.

Kiara nodded. In theory she could, but right now she couldn't tell how injured she was because of the cold water. Caleb was already paddling away as quickly as he could, tugging Hallie along as he went. It took her a couple of movements to get it right, but slowly she also started to make her way to the bank. It was difficult when she couldn't take her eyes off Hallie and Caleb.

Once he reached a ladder, he hoisted Hallie over his shoulder and started the climb. It was a strange thing to think in that moment, but Kiara had never realised he was that strong. He always looked so skinny under those jeans and baggy t-shirts.

By the time Kiara managed to make it over to the ladder, someone was already climbing down to help her up. It was only when she was pulled out of the water that she realised she was bleeding. Her arm was so badly broken that there was bone sticking out of it. If she wasn't so traumatised and scared, she probably would have thrown up.

Up on the river bank, the crowd was being held back as best they could by a few police officers. Hallie was lying on the floor, a paramedic performing CPR on her, while a breathless Caleb crouched by her side, his brow furrowed deeply with worry.

"I need to--" she pointed at her girlfriend, wanting to see if she was going to be okay. The emergency services guy could stop for long enough for her to see that, it was the least he could do.

Kiara didn't know how long it took, but when Hallie choked back into the land of the living, her knees gave out from under her. The emergency services guy caught her before she could hit the ground, carrying her over to one of the ambulances that had just arrived.

"I need to check you over and get you to the hospital," he said.

"Is she going to be okay?" Kiara asked, tears in her eyes.

"It's too early to say," he told her honestly. "From that sort of fall, it could go either way." Even that was too generous. It had to be at least a hundred feet. The only reason Kiara was alive and talking right now was because of that stupid prophecy.

"Caleb," she tried to shout for him, but the exhaustion and pain was catching up with her.

"It's alright, I'm here," he said, appearing from behind the guy placing her down on a gurney.

"It was so stupid. We were so stupid," she started to cry.

Caleb ran a hand over her wet hair, his expression a mixture of sadness and guilt. "You're both alive, that's what matters. I'm going to ride with Hallie to the hospital and make sure that she gets the best care possible, okay? The moment you're out of surgery, I'll come find you and keep you updated."

"Okay," she sniffed, shivering like crazy.

"Look after her," Caleb told the emergency services guy as he pulled away, running over to the air ambulance so he could join Hallie.

Kiara hoped with every ounce of her being that Hallie would be fine. It was the last thing she would remember thinking before she blacked out.

~

Indescribable wasn't an accurate enough word for the well of emotion twisting Caleb's gut. It was beyond that; a searing flame that wouldn't let him settle on any one horrible feeling. Guilt was definitely a huge part of it. Keeping everything from the girls had only made things worse. If Kiara had known what she was getting herself into, if she'd had it confirmed rather than shot down, the two of them never would have been on top of that bridge in the first place.

Sadness was another part. It was his job to look after both of the girls and they were both broken. Thankfully, Kiara was more hurt emotionally than physically. A broken arm and a couple of broken ribs, the doctors were calling it a miracle. Hallie, however, was going to be bandaged pretty much head to toe if she made it out of surgery. If he hadn't gone to see Lily and she hadn't had the vision, Hallie probably would have drowned in the Thames.

It had only been a couple of hours since they had all been rushed to the hospital. Kiara was out of surgery, but still sedated. She looked so pale from the cold, it was taking her a while to warm back up. Hallie had a long way to go before anyone would confirm whether or not she was going to survive, and even then, who knew what permanent damage would be done.

Caleb knew that he owed them both an explanation. He planned to give them one the moment they were both together again and conscious. If Hallie died and he could have prevented it, then the conversation was going to be even harder.

It was morning before Kiara came around. Caleb refused to go home and spent the whole night in her room, staring off into nothing, the same thoughts going round and round in his head. Mostly he was swearing to himself that he was never going to do anything so misguided and idiotic ever again. Master Mahmid and the Elders set rules for a reason, from now on he was going to follow them, if they let him stay a Guardian.

"How is she?" were the first words out of Kiara's mouth. She was groggy, but she was still worried about Hallie.

"The doctors came in an hour ago to update me. She's out of surgery and in the ICU. She's still in a precarious state, but they're saying she could survive, so long as nothing else goes catastrophically wrong."

Tears rolled down Kiara's cheeks. Caleb wasn't sure whether they were out of relief or guilt, it could be both.

"It's all my fault."

"No, it's not, it's mine," Caleb said, pulling his chair closer to the bed. "Believe me, if I had been honest with you from the start then none of this would have happened."

Kiara looked confused. "What do you mean?"

"You and Hallie were right. There are people out there who can't die and there's a reason behind it. I want to explain everything, but it should wait until you've recovered."

Kiara looked like she wanted to protest, but then her gaze moved over to the door. "Are you a doctor?"

Caleb followed her line of sight and went pale. No, it wasn't a doctor. Although Master Mahmid sure looked like one in his shirt and tie. It was unusual to see him in civilian clothes. What wasn't unusual was the look of disappointment on his face.

"How did you know?" Caleb asked him, although he suspected he knew the answer.

"The Oracles," Master Mahmid said.

Caleb could hear the anger in his voice. There was no way any of Lily's friends were going to keep being quiet after what had happened yesterday.

"I'll be back," Caleb told a very puzzled Kiara, rising from his chair.

He followed Master Mahmid down the hospital corridor and into one of the private family rooms, where he locked the door behind them.

"What were you thinking?"

Caleb had experienced Master Mahmid's anger before, but not quite like this. His Israeli accent was so much more pronounced when he was furious, Caleb noticed.

"I was trying to protect her."

"By keeping her in the dark? By letting her run around by herself with no idea what she can do? Have I taught you nothing?" The last rhetorical question was particularly thunderous.

"I'm sorry."

"And so you should be! You put the lives of two innocent young women in danger because of your misguided ideas. I warned you against making friends with people outside of our line of work, that becoming close to people is a weakness."

Caleb understood why Master Mahmid thought as much, especially in this situation, but he still didn't fully agree. It was a coincidence that he was friends with the person who ended up being the Chosen. However, it was his choice that had led them here and he was beyond apologetic.

"Will the other one live?"

"They're saying it could go either way depending on how the next twenty-four hours play out."

"You better hope she survives, otherwise there will be no coming back from this for you," Master Mahmid told him.

Caleb was surprised that there was a chance of him coming back at all. He'd managed to convince himself overnight that this was it, his time as a Guardian was over. It appeared that might not be the case.

"You're not kicking me out?"

"Believe me when I say that I should, and I would if…"

Master Mahmid cut himself off, shaking his head. Caleb knew not to push for an explanation, it would only get his head bitten off.

"The moment they are both well enough to understand, you explain everything. You don't leave out a single detail. Am I understood?"

Caleb nodded.

"I'm going to go back to the Citadel and do damage control. I want you to report back there in one week to explain yourself. After that, you will return here, and train Kiara as originally planned." This was, of course, so long as Hallie lived. If she didn't then he was most likely going to be forced into obscurity to live out his days guilt ridden and alone.

"I understand."

"Good, because one more toe out of line and even I won't be able to save you."

Master Mahmid was completely serious. Caleb was shaken enough by this to fall back into line. If they were looking for a model Guardian, that was all they were getting from now on.

Chapter Eight

The next several hours were some of the hardest that Caleb and Kiara had both suffered through in their lives. Caleb was able to wheel Kiara up to see Hallie once, but she had been heavily sedated, and they couldn't enter the room. It was imperative that she didn't get any infections. He had been right to assume about the number of bandages. The only part of Hallie that wasn't covered by bandage or blanket was her face, and even then, her skin was pale and the dark circles under her eyes made her look like she was dead or almost there.

After that, they had to return to Kiara's room where they waited. One of the male nurses offered Caleb a spare pair of the clothes and the opportunity to shower in the staff changing rooms, which he accepted. It would be good to wash the lingering Thames from his hair and his body. He appreciated that they didn't make him go home, even though he wasn't family. Hallie's parents were both on their respective flights from Australia and the US and Kiara didn't have anyone.

Well, that wasn't technically true.

Following his shower, Caleb went to get some fresh air. It was 5am and there was very little going on. The city around them was quiet except for a few cars here and there. He leaned his forehead and elbows against the wall, taking a minute to let his emotions wash over him away from the prying eyes of others.

Caleb stood like that for a few moments, his breaths short and fast as he tried to not lose too much control. He felt someone gently touch his shoulder and peered round to find a blurry Lily standing there.

"Hey," she said softly, pulling on his shoulder a little so he would let go of the wall.

Usually he didn't accept hugs from strangers, but Lily didn't feel like a stranger. Obviously, she was upset too. Her niece had just fallen off Tower Bridge, that was terrifying even if you knew that she couldn't die.

Lily wrapped her arms around his waist and placed her head against his chest, holding him firmly but comfortably. He wasn't exactly tall, which made her tiny by comparison. It didn't take him long to place his own arms around her shoulders and press his cheek to the top of her head. She smelled faintly of lavender, which was soothing. They needed soothing right now.

Caleb lost track of how long they stood there like that, it was only when the tears finally dried up that he pulled away.

"Thank you," he said.

"It looked like you really needed it."

She was right, there hadn't been anyone else around to comfort him. Master Mahmid rightfully yelled at him and the girls were both in pieces.

"I'm sorry I didn't see it sooner, if I had known what they were going to do…"

"No, there's absolutely no blame here, I was the one who was supposed to be responsible for them. It's me who has to shoulder this."

"So long as you don't take too much of it," she said. "Remember, the girls also chose to do this, so it's not all on you."

That was the sort of sensible thing that he needed to hear. He didn't know whether she was reading his mind right now, but it was appreciated either way.

"Do you want to come upstairs and meet her?" he asked. Family could be the thing that Kiara really needed right now.

"Won't it be too much?"

"I don't know. But I think that honesty is the best policy from now on."

"Of course," Lily said.

This was a big moment for her. She'd had to keep herself a secret for so long, from everyone including her only remaining family member, everything was about to change.

"Take a breath," he said.

Lily did. A couple, actually, just to be sure.

"Ready?" he asked.

"Yes," she nodded. "Lead the way."

~

Kiara was drifting. The pain medication they had her on made her head fuzzy, which made it difficult for her to think through everything that had happened. She kept considering asking Caleb what he had meant before that man showed up at the door, then the thought would slip away again. The same happened when she thought to ask who it was and why they were so angry. One thing remained whenever the other questions passed by and that was her heartache over Hallie. They were coming up on 18 hours into their 24 hours with no real news. Caleb had said that no news was good news, but she couldn't help the fear that Hallie was going to slip away up there, and they wouldn't know about it until it was too late.

Caleb had been gone for quite a while when he finally returned. He lingered in by the door until her attention fell on him.

"Clean?" she asked, her drowsiness coming through with her words.

"Very," he said, his hair still damp from the shower.

Kiara couldn't muster a smile, so silence fell instead.

"Do you feel up to meeting someone right now?"

"Is it that guy from yesterday?"

"No, not yet. It's someone who I think could make things better."

Kiara wasn't sure what he meant but nodded her head. She would take anything right now to make this easier.

From behind him, a woman appeared. She had short brown hair and a dress on under her long coat. Wasn't she…

"Lily?" Kiara murmured, unsure. She had only met the woman once after all.

"Yes, hi. Can I sit? I've got something to tell you."

"If it's that I'm going to die, we covered that already."

Lily looked pained. "No, it's about the secrets that have been kept from you. I think you finally deserve the truth."

Kiara was so confused.

"Caleb?"

"Please, hear her out. I'm going to be right outside if you need me."

After a moment, Kiara agreed to both things, watching Lily as she came and sat down beside her in Caleb's chair. She couldn't tell whether it was the drugs or the lighting, but now that Lily was so close, she looked like someone.

"What secrets are you going to tell me?" she asked, looking into Lily's hazel eyes.

"The ones your parents kept from you. There's a lot that needs to be explained and I know that Caleb will do a lot of that, but it's important for you to know about your family in order to understand what comes next."

"You knew my parents?" she asked, having never come across anyone who had before.

"Very well, I spent a lot of time with them when I was growing up. Because, you see, I'm your Dad's sister."

Kiara stared at her, hard. "What?"

"Your Mum never told you because she didn't want you to know about your family's history, about the tragedy that lay there. She was hoping to spare you from it, that all of this would never happen."

"The dying?"

"And the stuff that goes with it. You see, Kiara, you're something called a Chosen. Your Dad was one too."

"A Chosen?"

"Centuries ago, a woman called Sitara discovered that there were people out there in the world that could see the future. A man called Kyros told her that there was this guy in a local village who was destined to die in a matter of months, but before then, he would save them all. It turned out that Kyros was the first known Oracle. Sitara watched over the man who was supposed to be their saviour and saw things that she could barely believe. In a fight, weapons would bend around him like he had an invisible force field. When he saved a family from drowning, he almost lost his own life, but a freak wind blew him and the water back to shore. Until finally, one day, raiders came to sack the village. It was his bravery that saved them all, but he was killed in the process, a few months after Sitara first heard the prophecy. She decided to try and find more like him and she became the first Guardian, starting up an order of people who were supposed to train and guide those chosen by the Oracle. Hence the name Chosen."

The story was a lot to take in. It sounded like some of the stories which Hallie found, except neither of them had suspected that there was something huge going on behind it all.

"So, I'm like that man, the one who saved the village?"

"Yes. Caleb and the man you saw before are Guardians, and I'm an Oracle."

"It was your prophecy?"

"Yes, I let Mindy do her own thing with everyone else. I sometimes help her get inside their heads. But with you, it was important that she told you the truth, just in case. I didn't want you to waste the time you had left, even if your Mum wanted you to stay away from the dangerous part of it all."

Kiara's head was spinning. Her Mum had lied her whole life? About her family. About her Dad. About everything. How was she supposed to take all this? What else didn't she know?

"How... How did my Dad die?"

"It was on a mission in Ethiopia. Him and his Guardian, Ezra Mahmid, were there to help save some aid workers who had got caught in the fighting. They were able to get everyone else out alive, but only if your Dad stayed behind to hold the soldiers off. He didn't make it back."

Kiara pressed her lips together and closed her eyes, refusing to let the tears start again. She was so over crying at this point.

"Why couldn't my Mum just tell me the truth? Why didn't you?"

"If there was a chance that you could live a happy life without being tainted by all of this, then we both would have done anything to protect it. I saw what it did to your Dad, what he had to give up in order to be a hero. Your Mum didn't want that for you."

Kiara choked up a little. "Why did Caleb lie?"

"He was trying to protect you too. Guardians don't usually get to know their Chosen beforehand and that's down to me. Me hiding you from them messed everything up and I'm sorry."

Kiara didn't say anything, she just clenched her fists in an effort to stop herself from falling apart.

"This is so… so…" she tried to say.

"I know," Lily replied, placing her hand over one of Kiara's closed fists briefly. She chose not to linger just in case Kiara didn't want her touching her.

"What am I supposed to do with all this?" Kiara asked, managing to open her eyes again without anything spilling out.

"Don't make any decisions right away. Caleb is going to explain everything else once Hallie is awake. Give yourself some time to think it over and make your own choice. We're all so sorry we took that away from you."

Kiara didn't say anything else, she just looked off at the wall. Lily was thankfully smart enough to know that she was done with the conversation.

"I'm going to leave my number with Caleb. If you want to know anything else, just ask him for it."

Kiara glanced at Lily and then away again, slowly tilting her head in acknowledgement. She was grateful when Caleb didn't come in right away after Lily left as she wasn't sure she wanted to talk to him either right now. It was going to take her a while to sift through all the lies and figure out what she was supposed to do. She needed to do that by herself for once.

~

Caleb and Kiara didn't talk much after Lily's visit. Instead they both mustered through the waiting period quietly, Caleb grading papers and Kiara flicking through the TV channels whenever she needed something new to watch. Hallie survived the rest of 24-hour period without any hiccups, but they waited another full day before trying to wake her up, just to be safe. Kiara and Caleb nervously waited around outside the room as they took the tube out of Hallie's throat and performed all the necessary checks to make sure there wasn't any brain damage or loss of motor function. Her parents were both delayed by bad weather, otherwise they would have been there too.

"Well, it's still early days, but everything seems to be okay," the doctor said when he exited the room. "So long as there aren't any unforeseen circumstances, she stands to make a full recovery."

The two of them breathed a massive sigh of relief, looking at each other properly for the first time all day. While Kiara didn't hug him or anything, it looked like maybe her feelings of betrayal were beginning to fade now that she didn't have to worry as much about whether Hallie was going to live.

"Can we go in and see her?" Kiara asked.

"Yes, but take it gently. We don't want to stress her out too much while she's still fragile," the doctor told them.

"We will," Caleb promised, then gestured for Kiara to go in first.

"Hey," Kiara said to Hallie as she approached the bed, leaning forward to kiss her ever so carefully on the lips. "I was so scared I was going to lose you."

"Me? Never," Hallie croaked, managing a small smile.

Kiara took the seat by the bed, leaving Caleb leaning against the doorframe.

"The doctors told me that you were the one who pulled me out of the water," Hallie said to Caleb, her expression telling him how much she appreciated it.

"I wouldn't thank me yet," Caleb warned.

"Why?" Hallie asked.

"He lied to us the other day when we came to ask him about your research. You were right all the long, there is something going on," Kiara explained.

"You lied?" Hallie looked surprised, which wasn't what he was expecting from the usually fiery young woman. "Didn't think you had it in you."

"I can't tell if that's a good thing or a bad thing."

"A bad thing," Kiara said.

"Meh, I dunno," Hallie countered. "I'd shrug my shoulders, but they've pretty much committed me to this 'mummy' look for a little while."

If she could crack jokes when she was this messed up, Caleb was pretty sure that she was going to be just fine.

"How can you be so cool with it?" Kiara asked her.

"This is Caleb we're talking about here, babe. If he lied, he had to have a good reason. He's one of the best people that I have ever known."

Caleb wanted to be touched by this, but he knew Kiara was still angry.

"Besides, even if he did lie, he didn't tell us to climb up a 100-foot bridge after a rainstorm. We're the ones who did the dumb thing. I'm just happy that I still get to see both of your pretty faces after what we pulled."

Kiara had been holding onto the dishonesty part so hard that she hadn't really gone there. He could tell because of the way she teared up.

"No, I wasn't supposed to make you cry," Hallie said.

"Why did we think that was a good idea?" Kiara tried to wipe her eyes, but the tears kept on coming.

"Brave stupidity. But it's okay, we learned our lesson. From now on only you get to do that sort of shit, I'll stay way out of it."

Kiara nodded her head. They all knew that was for the best. No one wanted to see Hallie this badly hurt ever again.

"Now you, explain," Hallie told Caleb. "So I can sit back and listen."

Caleb went over some of what Lily covered with Kiara, explaining how everything worked. Kiara chipped in here and there, including why she hadn't been found by the Guardians in the first place and why everything had spiralled out of control.

"I'm so sorry about your Dad, babe," Hallie said to Kiara.

"I know, I wish I'd got the chance to know him."

"You can always talk to Master Mahmid about him. I'm sure he won't mind once he knows who you are," Caleb suggested, figuring that the man might have a soft spot for her if what Lily had said was true about her Dad and Master Mahmid being close.

Kiara looked like she took that on board and that she was starting to warm up to him again. She would have to if they were going to train and work together.

"How did you become a Guardian?" Hallie asked him.

"My aunt had some of my Mom's old journals stored up in her attic, they had research in them that she had done into all of this when she was a teenager. I delved deeper and decided to head out to the Citadel to find out more."

"Citadel?" Kiara said.

"It's where all Guardians go to live and train when they're not travelling with their Chosen. The Elders also preside there, watching over all of us."

"Is Master Mahmid an Elder now?" Kiara continued prompting him.

"Yes, he has been for a while now, but he still mentors me from time to time. Or berates me in this case. I lied to him too and I think it's going to take a lot of hard work to gain his trust back."

"If anyone can do it, it's you," Hallie said from the bed.

"Thanks."

"Do Guardians run in the family too?" Kiara asked him.

"They used to, apparently, but then a Guardian broke the rules regarding when they could tell their child about everything to do with the order and it was forbidden for Guardians to have families," he explained. "I never knew either of my parents, they both died when I was young. My Mom could have been one, but I think Master Mahmid would have told me. It's more likely she didn't get any further than the research written in her journals."

"I didn't realise we were both orphans," Kiara said.

"Well, my story isn't quite as dramatic as yours. It's part of the reason I kept all this from you, I figured you had been through enough in your life without this secret order piling on a whole load of responsibility. I know it was wrong now but-"

"I don't know, actually," Kiara said, cutting him off. "I think if Hallie hadn't gone looking into reasons why all of this stuff was happening, yours and Lily's plan probably would have worked, and my life would have been much less scary for it. But then, I never would have known that I had family left or that there was a way to do something more meaningful with my life before I die. I don't like the way all of this happened, but I'm starting to understand it."

This sounded a lot more like the reasonable Kiara that he had come to know over the last several months. Everything was beginning to fall into place.

"What happens now?" Hallie asked.

"In a few days I have to report to the Citadel to explain what happened to the Elders. Now that we know you're going to be okay, I should be able to come back after that and start Kiara's training. So long as that's what you want, of course," he said, turning his attention to the redhead.

"I think so, yeah."

"Good, I think you can do some really great things once you're ready."

"Me too," Hallie smiled.

Caleb was really glad that they had got to talk. It would have been terrible if he'd had to leave with things still unresolved.

"I'll leave you two alone for a while," he said, pushing off from the wall.

"Caleb?" Kiara stopped him before he could leave.

"Yeah?"

"Can I have Lily's number?"

"Yeah, of course," he said, pulling the crumpled piece of paper out of his pocket and handing it to her. "I'm sure she'll be happy to hear from you."

"She can keep us company while you're gone," Kiara agreed.

Caleb nodded and smiled as he left the room. It seemed everything might work out after all.

One Month Later
Chapter Nine

It was chilly in LA considering it was the last month of spring. Usually it was in the mid to high 60s, so 32 was freezing by comparison. Diana was used to a warm climate, having been raised in San Diego. Her family moved there from Shanghai when she was seven, which made it harder for her to integrate than if she had moved as a baby. Now she appreciated it, as she was able to speak two languages from a young age, something she had built upon as the years went by.

Diana sometimes missed the crystal blue waters and bustling marina in the brief moments where her mind wasn't occupied with her mission. It would have been far more pleasant than being hunkered down in a rundown apartment in Anaheim with Will.

The Aussie was kicking around an empty beer can as they waited. Fidgeting when impatient was a habit of his as he preferred to keep his mind occupied, probably so he didn't constantly think about what he had left behind when he had agreed to help her.

Will had been a great find. As a Chosen, with a firm stature and a strong sense of determination, he had the skill set she needed to help her recruit people to her cause.

"Not falling asleep, are you?" Will said, distracting her from her thoughts.

Diana narrowed her eyes. "What are you inferring?"

"Just that we've been here a while with no sign of the target," he told her.

"Good, because the last time you cracked an old lady joke, you remember how much that hurt."

"I do. My shoulder still aches from time to time," he grinned.

Despite his cheeky quips, Will was as strong mentally as he was physically. He carried his burdens without complaint and was a powerful force to be reckoned with in terms of fighting. Diana didn't mess with him unless he needed the discipline.

"Has there been no movement at all?" she asked, picking herself up off the dusty floor so she could go stand by the window.

"Apart from a couple drunk folks in fancy dress, nada."

"Perhaps my source was wrong."

"Or these criminals are just late. They're not the most reliable people, eh?"

Diana looked up at him and smirked. "True."

"What? You didn't choose me just because of my looks."

"Your good looks?"

The 28-year-old was so full of himself.

"I've seen you give me the eye a couple of times, don't deny it."

"Do you want to keep flirting with me or do you want to go help catch those guys?" she asked him, pointing to the couple of vans that had finally pulled up outside the house opposite.

"Tough choice."

Diana shoved him towards the door, which elicited a quiet laugh.

The reason they were there was because an old friend of hers was supposed to be training a new Chosen and she knew she had a good chance of persuading him over to their side. Unless they were truly faithful to the cause, her story usually pushed them towards what she considered to be human decency.

"There's got to be, what, at least ten guys in those vans?" Will said as they made their way down the stairs.

"I'd say no less than twelve."

"Three each, nice and even."

"You sure about that?"

Will glanced back at her with a twinkle in his eye.

"After four years, you still want to keep score?"

"Of course, it's one of the many ways that I'm able to show you that experience trumps innate ability," Diana told him.

"You're on."

Will pulled the door open an inch, so he could hear what was going on across the street without having to strain his senses. He always found ways to make it easier on himself, Diana noticed. It was the sort of thinking that made him a better partner.

Once he was sure that the men had gone inside, he gestured for her to follow him. They clung to the shadows as they made their way across the street and into the alley, approaching the door they had tampered with earlier. Diana moved ahead of him at this point, carefully opening the door so they could slip inside unnoticed.

Where there had once been walls, there were now patches of plasterboard and piles rubble. The top floor had completely caved in. It wasn't the most comfortable place to do business, but the criminals didn't seem to mind. They had lumped a couple of sofas into one of the back corners, with an overturned crate for a table, which was littered with empty snack packets and beer cans.

Diana and Will crouched behind one of the pieces of plasterboard, able to see the gang of thugs through a small hole. They were milling about while they waited, a couple of them tossing a knife between them. Maybe they would take each other out, that would make their job here easier.

By Diana's count, there was fifteen of them, which wasn't a deal breaker.

It was a minute or so before Diana saw movement that didn't come from one of the gang. They were small and fast, keeping low so they wouldn't be spotted. Clearly, they were the Chosen. That meant that Aaren had to be around here somewhere, waiting for her to make her move.

And she did.

Aaren had trained her well, because they didn't see her coming. She struck out of nowhere, knocking two of them flat on their backs with one well-placed spinning kick. This was Aaren's cue. Tall and broad-shouldered, he slammed his fist into the face of one of the men at the other end of the group, splitting their attention in two.

Diana and Will's entrance would make it four ways.

To say mayhem ensued would be an understatement. The thugs were left scrambling by the sudden attack, which made it easier for Diana and Will to come in and intercept them as they tried to spread out. Diana had learned that the best way to fight people like this was to strike fast and show no mercy. It was the only way to ensure that friendly blood wasn't spilled, because criminals like this would always pull out whatever weapons they had to defend themselves if they could. Fighting effectively was made more difficult if you had to spend time dodging bullets.

Diana disarmed one by kicking his gun straight from his hand, then drove a fist into his gut. Winded, he dropped out of the way, so she was able to tackle a nearby woman head on. They rolled across the floor, Diana maintaining dominance as she peppered the woman's face with several quick punches, knocking her unconscious.

"Watch out!" came Aaren's voice from behind her.

Diana barely had time to duck her head down as another guy went soaring over her, smacking into the hard wall with a crunch.

"Brute force and ignorance?" she called to him.

"Every time," he replied with a smile, then nutted the nearest person in the face, shattering their nose.

Aaren distracting her had given Will a chance to get ahead, teaming up with Aaren's Chosen to wipe the floor with the remaining criminals. How quickly and fluidly they moved was something to behold, she never got tired of seeing it. It had been part of the magic for her, once upon a time.

After stamping on the last guy's face to make sure he was out cold, Aaren turned to Diana and said, "Long time, no see, Di. I thought you'd vanished off the face of the Earth after that bar fight in Morocco."

"I pretty much did," she admitted. It had been the day that she had told him all about the Guardians and Chosen, and the day that she decided to do something about her fortunes.

She hadn't expected him to sign up to be a Guardian, but now it might be something that could be turned in her favour.

"You were a lot scrawnier back then, I remember," she said, punching him in his tattooed arm. It was of a runic compass, a mark of his heritage.

"But I could still throw one hell of a right hook," he winked.

"I think some introductions are in order," Will piped up, approaching the pair of them with Aaren's Chosen in tow.

"Will, this is Aaren, an old friend of mine. Aaren this is Will, my partner."

"And a Chosen, if I'm not mistaken?" Aaren said, looking slightly curious.

"Yup. Been in the game a while now," Will confirmed.

"Well, this is Priya, my Chosen. One of the best I've ever trained."

Priya couldn't have been more than nineteen years old and was only five feet tall. Her green eyes stood out against her skin, something that was hard to miss.

"It's a pleasure," she said, her accent was thick, but her English was good. "Aaren has talked about you before, but I wasn't sure whether you were real."

"Why wouldn't you think she was real?" Will asked.

"Probably because I was drunk whenever I talked about her," Aaren offered.

"He only lets personal things slip when he's really wasted, so I try to liquor him up as often as possible," Priya said with a cheeky grin.

"I like her," Diana smirked.

"Yeah, yeah, of course you do," Aaren snorted. "Now, I know you didn't help us out of the goodness of your hearts. You had to have talked to an Oracle to even know we were coming here, so out with it."

Aaren usually got right to the point.

"I didn't tell you the whole story that night in the bar," Diana admitted.

"You know that rule about Guardians not being allowed to have families? How a Guardian's choice changed things for everyone else? I give you exhibit A," Will said, gesturing to Diana.

Diana rolled her eyes at him. She knew that he was sympathetic to her plight, otherwise he would have told her to screw off instead of following her. He was probably feeling cocky because of the four people he took out, when she only beat down two.

"That was you?" Aaren asked, surprised.

"Master Mahmid told me that a child got hurt," Priya added.

Diana scowled at Priya, which made her shrink back behind Will. "I wouldn't put much stock in what Ezra has to say. His words mean nothing."

"Oi, don't go off at her," Aaren told Diana.

Diana clenched her fists to help contain her anger towards Ezra. This was not the time or the place to rage about the man or what he had done, it would only alienate Aaren and Priya, which was counterproductive to what she was trying to achieve.

"Sorry," Diana said, as sincerely as she could muster.

"Now, explain," Aaren said.

"I had a son who was taken from me by the Guardians when he was only a young child. There was an accident, I made a mistake, but that didn't warrant tearing my family apart. He and his father died days after I was detained. That never would have happened if we had still been together."

"That's horrible," Priya whispered.

Aaren agreed. "I'm sorry, Di, I can only imagine that sort of grief."

Diana nodded her appreciation, she had accepted too many condolences in the last few years for it to be truly meaningful anymore.

"It doesn't answer my question about why you're here."

"I want to change the system. The way the Guardians work now is outdated and unfair. Oracles conscripted at birth, only to be used by the Guardians for their purposes. Guardians forbidden from forming relationships with anyone, from being able to live a normal life outside of their duties. You're even discouraged from getting close to your Chosen, something which I've found makes things more difficult in the long run. None of it makes any sense, they need an overhaul."

"How are the two of you going to achieve this?" Aaren asked, still uncertain.

"It's not just the two of us. We're a hundred strong and still rising."

This shocked Aaren. Apparently, the Elders had been keeping their missing numbers quiet.

"What are you going to do, storm the Citadel?"

"We almost have the power we need to do it. With the element of surprise on our side, and with most of the Guardians scattered across the world, we have what we need," Diana said.

Every question that he had, she had an answer. She had done this so many times before and every time, she won them over.

"What makes you think I'll join you?"

"Mari."

Aaren clenched his jaw and looked away.

"Who is Mari?" Priya asked.

"His childhood sweetheart. He would be married to her now if he could."

"You never told me about her," Priya said, looking up at Aaren.

"You never got me drunk enough," Aaren replied quietly.

"If you help me, we can change everything. We can make the Guardians better than they are right now. You can be with whoever you choose. And you can stop using drink as a way to have proper conversations with Priya," Diana said.

Aaren took a deep breath, exhaling through his nose. Diana could see that he was thinking about it. If he had known how the rules would come to dictate his life like this, he might not have chosen this path. Now Diana was giving him another choice.

"Can I get back to you?" he asked, not wanting to decide there and then. After all, she wasn't just asking this of him, it would be Priya too.

"Call me on this when you make up your mind," Diana said, passing him a burner phone. "Don't take too long."

"I'll see you," Aaren nodded, gesturing for Priya to come with him.

"Bye," Priya said as they left, waving at Will, who wiggled his fingers in return.

As the door swung closed behind them, Will looked at Diana.

"Do you think he'll come around?" he asked her.

"I'm pretty sure. The temptation will be too much to ignore."

Will didn't disagree. Instead, he nudged a nearby thug with his foot.

"What should we do about these guys?"

"We'll give the police an anonymous tip. I'm sure they can book some of them for something, once they've enjoyed taking their bloody and beaten mugshots."

"There'll be some cracking photos thanks to us."

"I only hope it was worth it."

Chapter Ten

"I haven't missed anything have I?" Lily asked, looking at the spread of snacks laid out across her coffee table.

"Are you kidding me? It's a FEAST!" Hallie declared, bouncing up and down with excitement from the sofa.

After a few weeks of bed rest, first at the hospital and then at home, barely able to do or eat anything, she was thoroughly looking forward to stuffing herself silly with all the delicious looking food spread out in front of them. Lily had been so good to her while she had been recovering. She was glad that Kiara had decided to get to know her. As someone who had a loving family, she knew how much it meant for Kiara to have a second chance at having one now her Mum had been gone for a couple years.

Caleb had got back a few days ago but couldn't start training with Kiara until she got the all clear from her doctor regarding her arm and ribs. The university was keeping him busy with work, so the girls were having a lot of fun together, as much as Hallie's improving situation would allow. The doctors were pleased with the progress that she was making so far. Apparently, it was much quicker than expected, which made her very happy. The sooner she could get back to normal life, the better.

To mark the last day before Kiara had to start her training and begin studying for her exams, they had decided to all go around to Lily's house for the night, bundle up in their PJ's and watch some of the cheesiest movies they could find.

Once everything was ready, Kiara popped the movie in and squeezed herself down between Hallie and Lily.

"Mmm, this is so comfy," she said, snuggling down for the long haul.

Hallie chuckled. "You might not be so pleased when I start breathing garlic all over you," she grinned as she picked up one of the slices of pizza bread.

"Not if I beat you to it!" Kiara said, lunging forwards to take a bite out of it before it could reach Hallie's mouth.

"Cheeky little!" Hallie tried to sound indignant, but she was giggling. So was Lily.

"That's why you looooove me."

"It is why I love you, but you still owe me a bite of whatever you eat next."

"Ooh, I don't know, you might have to fight me for it."

"You two are terrible," Lily said, finding it very hard not to dissolve in laughter. "It's wonderful."

Kiara leaned towards Lily to give her a quick snuggle. "I bet you've missed the craziness of having family and friends."

"Just a little," Lily admitted, which actually meant a lot.

"I would have thought it would be less lonely being able to poke around in people's heads," Hallie said.

"The opposite, actually. It always made me realise how much I was missing out on by having to stay in hiding. While I regret the way that we were brought back together, I'm not sorry that I have both of you here now."

Kiara hugged her even tighter. "We're not going anywhere. At least, not for now."

Most of the time they were able to breeze over the fact that Kiara was on a clock that was ticking closer to the end every day. It was still quite far away, and Kiara hadn't even begun training yet. But there was the occasional moment where it hit them all again.

Hallie pushed herself over so that it turned into a big hug pile, wrapping her arms around her babe.

"Yes, we're going to do our best to be the greatest family you've ever had," she agreed, trying to steer back towards sentimental.

Lily squeezed them both gently and smiled. "Are we actually going to watch this film?" she asked.

"I dunno," Hallie said as she pulled away. "You know me, I could happily talk all evening and still be entertained."

"She can. Once she kept me awake until five in the morning because she wouldn't stop," Kiara teased.

Lily chuckled. "What do you want to talk about?"

"When did you find out that you had abilities?" Hallie asked her as she grabbed a couple of gummy snakes and settled back into her spot.

"It was when I was five. My parents were called into see my teacher because they thought I was gifted and talented. It turned out that what I was doing was hearing the teacher say the answers in her head and then I wrote them down or spoke them out loud."

"I bet you wigged out some of the kids," Hallie smirked mischievously.

"Bullies certainly didn't bother me after I figured out how to control what I was hearing and seeing. I remember there was a kid in my Year 5 class that tried to steal my lunch from me. I'm ashamed to say that I threatened to tell the class about his love of Barbies, something I would never do now. It made him stop."

"Go little Lily," Kiara laughed.

"Don't be ashamed, girl, you did what you had to," Hallie agreed.

"Okay, okay," Lily giggled.

"What's the weirdest thing you've ever heard anyone think?" Kiara asked, curling her leg up and then propping her chin on top of her knee.

"Oh, you wouldn't believe the things that go through some people's heads. Just the other day I heard someone wondering what to dress their pet snake up in for its second birthday."

Kiara and Hallie looked at each other and burst out laughing.

"No way!" Hallie said, almost choking.

"Way. I had to duck down behind the counter for a minute to calm down before I could let them buy their healing bracelet and candles."

Kiara was flat out crying at this point, which was setting the other two off.

"Did they make a decision?" Hallie asked between bursts of hysterics.

"No, but they were leaning towards a top hat and bow tie."

This did nothing to stop the cackling that was coming from the other end of the sofa. Kiara was laughing so hard that she had to hold her stomach.

"It hurts… so much…"

Hallie patted her on the arm comfortingly, even though she was still chuckling. "There, there, it's okay."

"You're not helping!!"

Lily covered her face with a cushion to stop herself from falling apart over Kiara's shriek, but it didn't work.

It took them a little to calm down because they kept setting each other off again. All they had to do was catch another's eye or remember the image of the snake in the top hat and they started the loop over.

"Oh my gosh," Hallie said when they finally managed to get it down to wheezing and coughing.

"I'm sorry," Kiara breathed, still clutching her chest.

"I can't remember the last time I laughed that hard," Lily admitted.

Hallie couldn't either. She and Kiara used to get into giggle fits all the time, but life had snuck up on them and stolen away some of their joy with that prophecy.

"Maybe we should ask questions that are a bit more serious," Hallie suggested.

It didn't take Kiara too long to come up with one. "What was your favourite thing about my Dad?"

"Ooh, that's a tough one," Lily said, although she looked like she was glad to get
a break from all the laughter.

"Too much to choose from?" Hallie asked.

"Yes, but also, I was still only a teenager when he died, so I didn't get to know him as an adult. That would have added a whole different dynamic to our relationship. I used to love that he didn't treat me differently. My parents started walking on eggshells around me once they found out what I could do with my mind. He took it completely in his stride. In fact, he loved letting me put images in his head of the stories that we made up together. He was really great big brother."

Lily sighed. "I know that I shouldn't, because he did so much good, but sometimes I wish that he hadn't become a Chosen and that he was still around. The good that he could have done over an entire lifetime might not have measured up, but at least he wouldn't have missed everything."

"I used to wish that he wasn't really dead and that one day he would walk through the front door, sweep me up in his arms and tell me that it had all been a bad dream," Kiara said. "I still do sometimes."

Hallie looked at them both sympathetically. "My parents were better apart, so I can't really join in on this whole wishing thing."

"Don't you wish your parents had been better together?" Lily asked.

"Not really. I sort of preferred them apart, rather than together, because then I got to spend time with and know them each individually. Also, if my Dad had lived with us my whole life then Will would have missed out on having him around more and I wouldn't have wanted to take that away from him."

"Have you still not heard anything from him?" Kiara squeezed Hallie's hand.

"Nope, not a word. I wish he would just give me one quick call, let me know he's okay… Ha! There, I have a wish too."

Kiara snorted softly. "I know I've said this a million times already, but I'm sure that he'll show up when he's ready."

"I sure hope so," Hallie agreed. "Now, shall we actually do something other than sit here, gab and occasionally have a fit of hysterics?"

"Board game?" Lily suggested.

"It has to be Game of Life or I'm out," Kiara said.

"It's so she can marry me for the 50-something-th time. And she always wins."

"But it's a game of luck?" Lily said confused.

"Don't look at me," Hallie shrugged.

"Just break out the box and let's play!" Kiara grinned.

Chapter Eleven

Caleb was exhausted. A combination of his visit to the Citadel and all the essay marking he was having to catch up on had wiped him out. The latter had ended up being a mindless reprieve from the guilt, which had been amplified by his trip to Europe to be berated by the council. Ezra had already expressed most of his anger at the hospital, so he was on the defensive on Caleb's behalf to make sure that the Elders decided not to do anything rash. Caleb's job was spared, but they were going to be keeping a close eye on him for a while. He had to earn back their trust.

Once they had decided on their judgment, Caleb had been allowed to go straight back to London, but he decided not to go directly there. Instead, he took the long way back, driving through Switzerland and France before taking the channel tunnel to England. The time behind the wheel was worth it as it allowed him to clear his head of some of the negative thoughts, which helped him to start planning how he was going to approach training Kiara when she was well enough.

Supportive but firm seemed like the right stance, but he would have to adapt as they went along, as he did with all his Chosen.

Caleb gently tossed the last marked paper onto the nearby coffee table and let out a sigh. Thankfully, someone else was down to mark his student's exams, so he wouldn't have to do another huge pile of paperwork for a while. He could focus on more important things and return to the job he really loved, starting the following day.

He considered going to straight to bed, but his laptop pinged with an email and he realised he had forgotten to check his inbox in a couple of days.

From: Mee.lau68
To: cal-iforniadreaming
Date: Sunday, April 22, 2018 at 9:42 PM
Subject: Hello?

Nephew,

I have not heard from you in a while, so I'm writing to check in. Is everything going well with the job in London? How are your students? Do you think you'll be staying on after this year?

Not a lot has been happening here, except those frat boys got kicked out of the house down the street, at last! Also, my petunias are growing well this year. I have attached a picture, so you can see for yourself.

Hope to hear from you soon,
Love from your Aunty

PS: Have you found a nice girl yet?

Caleb smiled a little as he finished reading the email, then chuckled when he discovered that she'd forgotten to attach the photo. He'd tried to teach her how to use the computer properly a few times now, with little success. At least she could send emails, that was much easier than talking to her on the phone. Instead of replying right away, he decided to look through the other emails first.

From: kikikikiiiii
To: cal-iforniadreaming
Date: Saturday, April 21, 2018 at 11:23 PM
Subject: :)

Hey!

Just making sure that you haven't been buried under a landslide of essays.

You'll be happy to know that I got a 74 on my project. I'd say that it was mostly because of your help, but I think there were some pity marks thrown in because I looked like I had been hit by a bus :P

I'm looking forward to training on Monday. I can't wait to start doing good things and helping people. It'll be like being a social worker, like I originally planned, except I can also lay someone out.

Anyway, I hope you're not still beating yourself up too much and I'll see you Monday afternoon.

Kiara

From: byanyothername
To: cal-iforniadreaming
Date: Saturday, April 21, 2018 at 8:01 AM
Subject: Help!

I'm having the girls over tomorrow for a food and movie night and I have no idea what food to buy!

Also, hi :)

Lily x

    Oops, it was a bit late to reply to that one. Hopefully Lily figured out that she should buy everything in the supermarket. Hallie would eat it all without breaking a sweat.
    When Caleb saw the last email, he almost didn't open it, but then he reminded himself that he was supposed to be building trust, not being a chicken shit.

From: e.mahmid
To: cal-iforniadreaming
Date: Friday, April 20, 2018 at 12:12 PM
Subject: [No Subject]

Caleb,

I know that you're planning to start Kiara's training in the next couple of days and I wanted to wish you good luck. However terrible the bridge event may have been, it is not bad enough to break with tradition.

Keep me updated with your progress as often as possible.

E.

      Well, that wasn't so bad. Caleb knew that Master Mahmid and the other Elders wouldn't go easy on him, but it was good to know that he hadn't ruined his relationship with his mentor to the point where they lost all civility. Maybe, given time, he would see that more generous side of him again. The mere thought of it helped to send him straight to sleep for the first time in weeks.

Chapter Twelve

"Whoa, this place is cool."

When Kiara had turned up at the address Caleb had given her, she had been surprised to find that it was some run-down building in the middle of Battersea. For a Guardian safe house and training area, she had expected something a little fancier. However, when she pushed the fire exit open and made her way inside, it was like a completely different place. Sort of like stepping into the TARDIS, but without it being bigger on the inside.

The interior was seriously swish; bright and airy, with all the latest technology. There was a corridor off one end of the big training room, which she assumed was the 'safe house' part, for whenever Chosen and their Guardians needed to lay low in London. Apparently, there was no one staying there right now, so they had the place all to themselves. This was good, because Kiara was sure she was going to make an absolute fool of herself.

"That's what all the new Chosen say," Caleb smirked, beckoning her over.

She had dressed in her gym clothes, like he requested. He stressed that she needed to be able to move and be comfortable because they were going to be spending a lot of time getting her up to speed.

"Dump your bag over there and we'll get started. I'll show you where the kitchen and stuff are later when we take a break," he said.

"Okay, cool," she smiled, jogging over to the corner he pointed to in order to offload her stuff, then zipped back over to him.

"Am I right in thinking that you've had no other fight training?" he asked.

"Apart from a judo lesson I took at school which ended horribly, you're right, no training whatsoever."

"Good, that means we're starting with a blank slate. Sometimes it can help Chosen if they know how to fight, other times it can hinder them because it makes it harder to learn how to use their gifts."

"I get gifts out of this? Dang, why didn't you tell me sooner?" she grinned.

Caleb snorted and shook his head. "Have you always been this cheeky?"

"Yes, but usually only with Hallie. Now that we've been through a life or death scenario together, I think I can extend it to you as well."

"Consider me honoured."

Kiara was glad that she had decided to forgive him for the lies that he told, she would have missed out on having a friend for a teacher and that would have sucked.

"Where do we start?" she asked.

"We're going to start with some basics here on the mats. If you can get the hang of those, then maybe we can move onto something more complicated."

"Sounds good to me," she smiled.

Caleb took her gently by the arm and guided her into the middle of the square set of gray mats laid out on the floor.

"Place your feet a foot or so apart, find a stance where you feel comfortable and stable," he told her.

Kiara followed his instructions, planting herself properly before looking back at him for the next step.

"You good?"

"Yeah, now what?"

"Now look over there," he told her, nodding over towards the gym equipment that was lined up against the wall to her right.

As she was turning her head, out of the corner of her eye, she saw him move, but didn't realise what he was doing until it was too late. One moment she was standing and the next she was flat on her back with an amused Caleb standing over her.

"Hey!" she said indignantly. "That's not fair."

"No, it's not, but it's sort of a rite of passage for Chosen. What did you learn?"

"Not to let my guard down," she sighed.

"Exactly," he said as he stuck his hand out to help her back onto her feet.

Kiara took it, surprised at how easily he pulled her up. She wasn't sure why, based on how he dived into a river, completely unphased, from a bank that had to be at least fifteen feet high. If she thought about it, there had barely been any splash.

"How long have you been doing this for again?"

"10 years now," he said. "A year of training, then three Chosen. None of them had as long as you have to get this right."

"Well then, I'd better do them proud," she said with a determined nod.

Caleb looked pleased that was the attitude she decided to take. Despite her moments of worry and doubt, she wanted to make what time she had left as meaningful and as good as she possibly could, just like her Dad had done.

"Okay, your second lesson for today is that I can teach you everything you need to know about fighting, but it will do very little if you don't use it in tandem with your abilities," he said.

"What abilities?"

"Chosen gain heightened senses, quicker reflexes and become sturdier than the average human being when they are given their prophecy. You won't have noticed this in the last few weeks because you haven't been shown how to hone those abilities."

"Cool. How exactly do I hone them?"

"Focus."

"You make it sound simple, but it's not, is it?" she said, crossing her arms.

Caleb immediately pushed them back down again.

"You have to be able to clear everything else out of your head, like you would if you were practicing meditation," he explained.

"So, just empty my mind?"

"Yup."

"Can I close my eyes?" she asked.

"For now, yes. Obviously, you can't do that in the middle of a fight."

"*Obviously.*"

Pressing her eyes shut, Kiara kept her hands hanging loosely at her sides and tried to push all the thoughts floating around in there out of her head. Nothing about her butt still throbbing from where she hit the floor, or what they were going to be having for dinner tonight at Hallie's, or whether the weather was going to be good tomorrow. All of it had to go in order for her mind to be quiet.

"Ready?" Caleb asked.

Kiara nodded rather than say anything.

There was quiet for a few moments, then Caleb said, "What am I doing?"

His voice was much further away than it was before, she hadn't heard him move.

"I'm not sure…" she said, trying not to let her confusion cloud her empty head.

"Focus harder. Listen."

Kiara had to really think about reaching out to wherever he was in the room, listening out for any small sound, however quiet. It took her a little while, but eventually she heard something.

"Are you… playing with my bottle of water?" She could swear that she could hear the quiet sloshing of liquid moving back and forth.

"Open your eyes," he said.

When she did, she had to turn all the way round to find him over in the far corner, turning her bottle of water over and over in his hands. He was smiling.

"Well done," he said. "Now, catch."

Quick as a flash, he used a strong arm to lob the bottle like a rugby ball across the length of the room. Her first instinct was to panic, but that wasn't what he wanted her to do. She was supposed to be focusing.

Kiara followed the bottle with her eyes, letting her instincts take over. As she gave into them, it was like she was seeing what was happening in slow motion. Without even thinking about it, her hands went up and the bottle of water landed square in the middle of them. She didn't even stumble at the force of its impact.

"Whoa!" she said, looking at the water bottle then back up at him.

"Very good," he grinned as he came back over to her. "You're picking this up a lot quicker than most."

"I am?" she said, a feeling of pride washing over her.

"Yes, but we've still got a long way to go. Next you've got to learn how to use that focus to combat whatever I throw at you."

"Teach me, Sensei."

Time flew by as Caleb took her through some basic moves that she could use to attack him and defend herself. Trying to use her instincts while she fought him was tough because her mind was focusing on following the moves rather than reacting. It could be frustrating at times, but Caleb was patient and took her through it again and again if she needed him to, in order to make sure that she got it right. There was no way that he was taking her out into the world again unprepared, he'd made that perfectly clear when he'd come back from the Citadel.

"I think we should probably take a break," Caleb said after... well, Kiara wasn't sure how long it had been until she checked her watch.

"Two hours have gone by already?" she said, stunned.

"It might not feel like it now, but it'll catch up with you later," he warned, gesturing for her to follow him over to the corridor she had seen before.

The first door on the left ended up being the kitchen and it was exactly the same style as the rest of the place, very hi-tech. She wished her apartment came with half of the stuff that they had in there, she'd be able to make herself much better food than ready meals and beans on toast.

"Here, drink this," he said, tossing her a bottle full of green fluid with bits floating around in it.

Kiara pulled a face. "Well, doesn't this look... um, appetising."

"Don't judge it by its looks," he said as he grabbed one for himself and sat down at the white dining table in the center of the room.

Kiara plonked herself down too and took a tentative sip. Oh. "Mmm," she said, pleasantly surprised by its flavour. It was sweet, which she wasn't expecting.

"You see? It's really good for you, it'll help keep your strength up."

"I think this is a lesson that needs to be drilled into me, that things aren't what they seem" she said. "I never would have guessed that you were anything other than a nerdy history lecturer."

"Nerdy?" he pretended to look offended, which made her laugh.

"Yeah, you were pretty incognito with your brainiac level knowledge of most historical events. Did you swot up before every lesson or…?"

"No, actually, history was my major at college. I also read all sorts of non-fiction books, whenever I have the spare time."

"So, it wasn't exactly hard to assume that persona?"

"It's basically just me without the badass part," he smirked.

"You're badass alright. The way you jumped into the water to save Hallie and me? I'm sure if it hadn't been so scary, you would have made a quite a few women up on the river bank swoon."

It was Kiara's turn to make Caleb laugh.

"You think?"

"Oh yeah, for sure. If I wasn't a ladies-only sort of gal, I'd probably swoon too. Back when Hallie first started taking your class, she kept saying how cute she thought you were, it was funny. If I wasn't so secure in my relationship, I would have been worried."

Caleb smiled. "I don't think I've known anyone with a relationship quite like yours and Hallie's."

"We just… get each other. The first moment we met, we clicked. After that, as they say, the rest was history."

"I've never had anything like that," he admitted.

"Really? No girlfriends? Boyfriends?"

"I had a couple of girlfriends in college, but nothing stuck. Something just didn't feel right. And before you say it, no, it wasn't because they were girls. I'm a ladies-only sort of guy," he confirmed.

"What about Lily?" Kiara asked.

"What *about* Lily?" Caleb looked confused.

"You went way out on a limb for her with me and you'd only met her once? That's a pretty big thing to do for someone who's essentially a stranger."

Caleb shrugged his shoulders. "I knew she was your aunt, your family. It's a soft spot for me."

Kiara knew this already but was sure that there had to be something else there.

"Okay," she said, deciding to let it go for now.

"If I have start to have real feelings for anyone, I'm sure you and Hallie will be the first ones to know."

"I don't doubt it," Kiara smiled.

"Now, drink up. We should probably get back to it otherwise we won't get through everything before dinner."

"And we both know how much Hallie hates it when people are late."

~

They were late, all right. Caleb had been so encouraged by Kiara's initial progress that he had let the session go on far too long. They had ended up having to sprint from the tube stop up the street to Hallie's apartment. He wasn't sure that she would let them upstairs when they rang the buzzer. She did, but the silent anger on the other end of the speaker was palpable.

As Hallie opened her door and parted her lips speak, Caleb immediately stuck a finger in front of her mouth to stop the tirade before it even began.

"We're late, it's my fault, you begrudgingly forgive us. Can we eat now?"

Kiara burst out laughing behind him, which combined with Caleb's stunt, made Hallie stalk-hobble back into the apartment with a huff.

"What? I'm starving," he said, pushing through the door to find Lily already sitting down at Hallie's dinner table with her fist pressed against her mouth. It looked like she was trying to avoid garnering any of Hallie's wrath.

"Training is hard," Kiara agreed, kicking off her shoes. "And he refused to carry me here on his back as a reward for my hard work."

"I reminded her that I'm a Guardian, not a donkey."

"I can see where she got mixed up," Lily teased.

"Don't you join in."

"Hush, all of you, before this food gets even colder," Hallie commanded, pulling a big dish of lasagna out of the top oven.

"Mmmmm, oh God, that smells so good," Kiara said as she flopped into one of the chairs.

"That's not shushing," Caleb pointed out.

"QUIET, for goodness sake. It's like having a bunch of children around."

It would have been funny if Hallie had been the youngest, but if he remembered correctly, Kiara beat her out for that title. If only by a few months.

Caleb zipped his mouth closed and took a seat next to Lily, who provided him with an amused smile.

"Okay, here we go," Hallie said, placing the dish down in the center of the table.

"You made enough for twenty, as per usual," Kiara remarked.

"I figured you and Caleb could probably use the carbs," Hallie shrugged.

She budged her chair up, so she was seated right by her girlfriend.

"I'll serve, seeing as it's my fault we're late," Caleb said.

No one argued. They weren't in the habit of saying grace either, so they got to stuff their faces the moment the pasta hit the plate. There wasn't a whole lot of talking for the first few minutes, it was only once they started to slow down that Lily chirped up with a piece of conversation.

"You look like you're healing up really quickly, Hallie."

"Mmhmm, yup. The doctor actually used the word 'crazy' to describe how quickly I am getting back to normal. Usually, any one of these broken bones would have taken at least a couple of months to heal. I still ache, but otherwise, I'm pretty good."

As she filled her mouth with another piece of lasagna, Caleb and Lily both looked at each other. Were they thinking the same thing, Caleb wondered.

"It might not be so crazy," he said, getting her attention.

"I've been wondering too," Lily agreed.

Hallie and Kiara both looked at them curiously.

"What?" Hallie asked.

"As well as the Chosen, Oracles and all the rest of it, we also have healers," Caleb said.

"Healers? Like doctors?" Kiara guessed.

"Not really. Healers can physically heal a person who is sick or injured," Lily explained.

Hallie stared at her. "For real?"

"Yeah, I know a couple of them here in London."

"And there are several back at the Citadel. They're spread out all across the world," Caleb said.

"You didn't think to get one in here to give me a bit of a boost?" Hallie asked, looking disappointed that she had gone through all that pain when it could have been magicked away by some healer.

"We couldn't have one come into the hospital, someone would have noticed," Caleb told her.

"And besides, it's forbidden for healers to help anyone outside of the order and their allies," Lily backed him up. "They wouldn't have let one help you, even if Caleb asked."

Hallie still hrrrphhed at them, stabbing what was left of her dinner with her fork.

"Why do you think that Hallie could be one?" Kiara steered them back on topic.

"Healers naturally recover quickly when hurt, it helps them to do their job," Lily said, glancing at Caleb.

"We sometimes take them out into the field with us. They have to be able to bounce back from minor injuries in order to help others get out alive," he continued.

"Cool," Kiara said, then elbowed Hallie as she was still pouting.

"Yeah, cool. Do the powers come naturally or...?"

"You have to learn how to use them properly. I can take you to visit my friend Alastair, he'll be able to show you the basics, if you are really a healer," Lily said.

"He's still kicking about?" Caleb sound surprised.

"Every time I see him, he says he's getting 'too old for this shite', yet he won't give it up. I think he likes the gratitude too much, inflates his ego," Lily smiled.

"Sounds like a fun guy," Kiara smirked.

"I look forward to meeting him. Now, eat up, so I can clear away these plates and get the chocolate cheesecake," Hallie ordered.

Caleb shovelled the rest of his meal into his mouth and folded his arms across his chest. He tried to say, 'done,' but almost spit the food out all over the table and choked trying to stop himself.

Lily had to slap him a few times on the back before he could swallow.

"Serves you right," Hallie said, although he could see she was trying not to laugh through his blurred vision.

"I'll take some of that cheesecake now."

Chapter Thirteen

Despite everything that she had seen over the last few weeks, Hallie was still unsure about Caleb and Lily's idea that she was some sort of healer. She believed they existed, they wouldn't lie to her about something that cool. But her? A healer? Pfft. She was sure that this Alastair was going to tell her and Lily that they were completely mistaken and that they had traveled all the way out to Kingston for nothing.

"I didn't realise healing paid so well," Hallie said as they pulled into Alastair's driveway.

It was a gorgeous house, at least four bedrooms, well-kept with a red door in the middle. The flower beds around the garden were teeming with colour and life.

"Alastair used to be a surgeon before working for the Guardians, now he just helps out whenever needed," Lily explained. "Although, he was one of the best healers they ever had, so I can imagine they compensated him generously."

"Do healing powers extend to plants as well?" she wondered aloud.

"No, he's just got a lot of time on his hands these days," Lily chuckled as they both climbed out of the car.

The front door opened before they could reach it, revealing an older man with flecks of ginger in his greying hair and beard, wearing shorts, a t-shirt, and some tartan slippers.

"Lily? Is that your perfume I smell?" he asked in a broad Glaswegian accent.

"I'm surprised you can smell anything over all these flowers!" Lily said.

Hallie watched as Lily leaned in to give the man a kiss on the cheek, puzzling over why he had mentioned Lily's perfume first. Then she saw his eyes, a milky blue, staring right past Lily.

Alastair was blind.

"And who is this you have with you?" he said, sounding a little gruffer.

It didn't seem like he liked strangers.

"This is Hallie, my friend. I think that she might be a healer."

"It's nice to meet you," Hallie said to be polite.

"Hrrrrrm," Alastair replied, then gestured for them to come inside without another word.

The inside of the house must have been completely renovated in the last few years, because everything looked like it was part of a new build rather than a small 19th century mansion. Hallie assumed it was an accessibility thing. Everything was so open, with the furniture positioned carefully around the rooms. She also noticed a smart system by the front door that controlled the security, heating, and a host of other things.

"This house is awesome," she said quietly to herself.

"That's what people tell me," Alastair said.

"He has ears like a bat," Lily warned Hallie a few seconds too late.

"Should have known."

They went straight through the house to the back patio, which was the beginning of another stunning garden. It was so long, Hallie couldn't see the end. There were purely decorative areas, like out front, but there were also fruit trees dotted about and a vegetable patch. And, lying in the middle of the lawn soaking up the sun, a very happy Labrador.

Hallie let out a squeak of excitement and immediately went over to the dog, rubbing him behind the ears.

"Hello there, what's your name?"

"She's not psychic too, is she?" Alastair asked Lily as they both set themselves down on a couple of sun loungers.

"No, just cute."

Hallie grinned mischievously at Lily, glad that she was here to help deflect Alastair's grumpy comments.

"Her name is Sasha and I can guarantee she's still cuter than you," he said.

"No arguments here," Hallie replied.

The corner of the man's mouth quirked upwards, suggesting that was the right answer.

"So, why exactly do you think this young lady is a healer?" Alastair asked Lily.

"Do you remember hearing about the incident at Tower Bridge?" Lily asked.

Alastair nodded, then said, "She was one of the girls?"

He put two and two together very quickly.

"Yeah, the other one was a Chosen."

"She will have got off easy. They nearly always do."

Hallie didn't like the sound of the 'nearly always', but she didn't say anything. For once, she knew it was better to let them talk.

"Come over here," Alastair told her. "Let's see how your body is recovering."

As she got to her feet, Hallie wondered what this test entailed. Hopefully he wouldn't prod and poke too much, she was still a little tender in places.

"Your hand," he said, which she extended to him.

It turned out all he had to do was wrap his fingers around hers, then tilt his head back in thought. There was little point in him closing his eyes to concentrate, Hallie realised.

"You're almost completely healed, which is quite a feat for someone who fell from such a height," Alastair agreed.

"Is there a sure way to prove that I am one?" Hallie asked.

"Only one that I know of," he said. "Does either of you have a pin or something sharp?"

Lily routed around in her handbag, eventually pulling out a small sewing kit, which had a pair of scissors in it.

"What do you need it for?" she asked.

"I don't know about you ladies, but I'm not looking to break any Guardian rules today, so taking a stab at Lily or a jaunt to the nearest hospital is out of the question. The other way I know how to prove that a person is a healer is by trying to heal them."

"You want to stab me?" Hallie took a step back.

"A gentle poke, nothing so dramatic. If I can't heal you then that's proof."

"Healers can't heal other healers?"

"I didn't know that," Lily said.

"You never asked," Alastair pointed out. "I don't think anyone has ever been sure why that's the case, but it's how I lost a good friend of mine a few years ago."

Both Hallie and Lily fell silent.

"It's also the reason I lost my sight. My body couldn't repair the damage done and neither could anyone else."

It was cruel that there were people out of a healer's reach, not just because of some rules set out by an organisation either. Hallie couldn't begin to imagine how powerless he must have felt not being able to do anything to save his friend, as a doctor or a healer.

"Now, should I perform the test?"

"Okay," she said, placing her hand back in his.

Alastair carefully felt along her palm, making sure to find a place where he wouldn't cause too much damage. When he was certain he had found the right spot, he used the scissors to pierce her skin, drawing only a little blood.

Hallie hissed with pain and wanted to jerk her hand back, but he kept hold, so she wouldn't do anything dumb.

"If you're lucky, the pain will be gone in a moment," he told her.

Lifting his other hand over hers, a faint white glow shone from his palm, tickling her skin like someone was running a silk scarf over it. Alastair only persisted for a few seconds, quickly giving up when it didn't work.

"Not so lucky, then," Hallie said. "What does this mean for me?"

"My guess is that you'll end up picking up where I left off, after some training of course."

Hallie wasn't sure how she felt about this. Her plans for life were to finish her degree, go travelling, get married and figure it all out later. She knew that changed when Kiara became a Chosen and she was willing to go along with whatever she wanted. What she hadn't accounted for was being roped into it all herself.

"Ultimately, it's up to you. But based on the way you reacted to Sasha over there, I'm 99% sure you'll say yes to them when they ask."

Hallie looked over at Sasha and smiled. He was probably right.

"If I did say yes, would you train me?" she asked, which made him scoff.

"You don't want me as your teacher."

"What, the guy with the medical degree who has experience as a both a surgeon and a healer? I know slicing open my hand to prove a point isn't exactly orthodox, but at least you're honest. You also have to be likeable if Lily keeps coming back here. Even if it's only a little bit."

Alastair responded with a sigh.

"I think that's a yes," Lily laughed.

"It is, but we do this on my terms," he said. "Back here tomorrow, bright and early, and bring some shortbread for the tea."

"Yes, sir," Hallie beamed.

Chapter Fourteen

When Diana had been deciding where to set up the group's base of operations, she and Will had discussed a few places, but ended up deciding that it would be best if they set up somewhere not too far from the Citadel, so it would be easy to strike. As the Citadel was nestled near Italy's border with France, they chose a place across the border, on the Mediterranean coast. As they were camping out, it was important that it didn't get too cold during the winters when they were staying there.

Their camp was made of a group of Guardians, Chosen, and those who had been forced to leave the order for various reasons, whether that was because they had wanted a family more than fulfilling their duties or other issues. Some had done more serious things than others. Diana's opinion was that if she could be accepted after what she had done, then they could too. Will wasn't so sure but went along with it.

People tended to come and go throughout the year, running recruitment missions or picking up tips from their contacts about other work they could be doing. If they could ingratiate their way into powerful organisations now, before the coup, then they would find it easier to pick up where the other Guardians left off when the time came.

Will spent the vast majority of his time with Diana as they tended to travel a lot more than the others. When they weren't travelling, and he had time to himself, he tended to go off hiking around the local area. It was partly for his own enjoyment and partly to scout out the surrounding terrain in case the Guardians ever found out about them and tried to strike first.

Today, however, Diana had decided it was a good chance to get in some long overdue sparring practice. It would help them burn off the energy they had pent up over the long journey back from LA.

"That was a cheap shot," he said.

"Yeah, well, you remember the first lesson I taught you?" she raised her eyebrows.

"Don't let my guard down, I know, jeez."

Diana smirked, then tried again, springing forward to try and disable him. Will deflected her grab with ease, twisting her arm behind her back instead.

"I'm wise to your tricks now, it's been long enough," he said.

"Not all of them."

Diana tried to smack the back of her head into his nose first, but he dodged, knowing that move all too well. While he was laughing, however, she threw all of her force back onto him and he stumbled, sending them both crashing to the ground. Diana twisted herself out of his grasp and pinned him while he was still coughing at the dust.

"Do you yield?"

"We're only just getting started."

Their sparring matches quite often drew a crowd, as they were the most experienced pairing in the group. This time was no exception. As they traded blows, slowly getting tired and dirtier, Will thought he might be able to gain the upper hand, but he was distracted.

"Priy--OW!"

Diana punched him so hard in the face that he felt blood begin to trickle from his nose. His whole face was throbbing.

"Now that was a cheap shot," she admitted, coming up to him so she could check whether she had broken anything.

"It's fine, it'll add character," Aaren said from behind Priya, dropping his duffel bag onto the floor beside him.

"Diana didn't tell me you were coming," Will said, although it was difficult to talk with the blood, so he wasn't sure they understood what he said.

"Probably wanted it to be a surprise."

Will looked down at Diana, who shrugged innocently.

"I'd offer to show you around, but I think I have to start with a trip to our resident healer," Will said.

Eshe was very good, she would have him fixed up in no time. Possibly without a scar as well.

"You should," Diana said, carefully nudging him in the direction of Eshe's part of camp. "I'll clear up here."

Will covered his nose with one hand and motioned for Priya and Aaren to follow with the other. The camp was laid out in lines, which started from the community area in the center, the place they were just sparring. Most of the tents were where people slept, but on side nearest the ocean, they had some amenities, including the small area where Eshe and the younger Chosen liked to hang out.

"Over there is where we stockpile the supplies and weapons which aren't people's personal stashes," he said, gesturing to a shipping container that was locked up tight and guarded by at least one of their group, on a shift rotation.

"We also have bathrooms just through those trees, for a bit of privacy."

"Actual bathrooms not holes in the ground?" Priya said, sounding hopeful that she wouldn't have to squat between some bushes in order to relieve herself.

"Actual bathrooms. We didn't at first and you wouldn't believe the smell."

"I don't have to imagine," Aaren said.

"Oh yeah?"

"My family used to go camping all the time when I was a kid. My Dad, Mom and three older brothers. It wasn't pretty."

Priya screwed up her face. "Gross."

"Are your brothers all as tall as you are?" Will asked.

"They used to seem like giants when I was a kid, but I shot past them at eighteen, spent a couple of years hanging out at the local gym… They've looked puny ever since."

Will grinned. He had always wondered what it would be like to have brothers, although he had been overjoyed when Hallie had come along. Some days he worried about how she was doing, even thought about going to see her, but he knew if he did that there was a chance he would never come back. He couldn't abandon Diana, not after everything they had been through to get here.

"Who's that?" Priya asked, pointing at Eshe, looking mesmerised.

Will could hardly blame her. Of all the people here at camp, Eshe was the most beautiful, with her huge brown eyes and thick, black hair. They had come across her when they had been visiting one of Diana's contacts in Kampala. Will was a little ashamed to say that he had hit on her and it had ended badly, but Diana had managed to salvage things. They found out her Dad had been a Guardian who had committed suicide after being torn apart from his family, it wasn't difficult to convince her to join them.

"What happened to you?" Eshe sighed when she saw Will approaching.

"Diana."

"I should have known."

Eshe looked at the pair who were following him and offered them a friendly smile.

"I see we have another two recruits."

"This is Aaren and Priya," Will said as he sat himself down on one of the crates outside her tent.

Aaren nudged Priya gently with his elbow as she was still gawping.

"Oh, sorry, hi!" she said a little too loudly, then retreated into herself, embarrassed.

"It's okay, sweetheart. Nothing will ever be as embarrassing as the line this one tried to use on me the first time we met."

"I'm interested to hear this," Aaren smirked.

"Please don't. You tell everyone this story. Haven't I suffered enough?" Will said.

"I don't know, maybe I should make an exception for the boy with the broken nose?" Eshe said, looking at the other two, who both shook their heads.

"Oh, come on."

"The people have spoken!"

"Could you at least heal my nose first, so I don't have to suffer through the physical pain as well as the emotional anguish?"

"Fine."

Eshe held his chin steady with one hand and placed the other over his nose. The process was quick and painless, the bone realigning and the cut sealing up without any complaints from him. Other than the dry blood that was left on his face, he looked as good as new.

"That's amazing," Priya said, in awe.

"We've never had to visit a healer before," Aaren explained.

"Well then, you must be taking good care of Priya," Eshe smiled.

Will could almost see the spark between Eshe and Aaren. It looked like Mari might have some competition if Aaren and Priya hung around camp for long enough.

"Anyway, we should probably be getting on with the tour..." Will tried.

"You're not getting out of me telling that story."

Eshe grabbed his arm so he couldn't escape. She had a surprisingly firm grip for someone who healed with such a gentle touch.

"Please, no."

Eshe turned to Aaren and Priya, who were both keen to hear the story: "So, I was supposed to be meeting this friend of mine at her hotel. I decided to get a drink at the bar while I waited, when suddenly this guy swaggers over to me and says,

'There must be something wrong with my eyes, because I can't take them off you'."

Aaren groaned, whereas Priya immediately burst into a fit of giggles.

"My shame is never ending," Will despaired.

"We're friends now, but if Diana hadn't come over to save him, I probably would have eaten him alive."

"I don't doubt it," Aaren chuckled, looking between Eshe and Will, then his Chosen who was busy trying to control her laughter.

"I think we're going to like it here."

"Good," Will said.

It was always better if the people they recruited came to feel like a part of the community, it meant that there was a sense of solidarity between them.

"Now, let me show you where you'll be sleeping."

Chapter Fifteen

It had been three weeks since Kiara had started her training and she had been coming on in leaps and bounds. As soon as her exams were finished, she and Caleb started having sessions every day, all day if they could. She was pushing for progress as much as he was because she wanted to get out into the field as soon as possible.

While Caleb wasn't ready to take her on a mission just yet, he was willing to take her down to the MI6 building in Vauxhall to meet his contacts and see how it worked when they cooperated on missions.

When Hallie heard about this, she decided that she wanted to come too. She had been having lessons with Alastair on and off since their first meeting and she wanted to see what it was like to heal someone properly. Luckily for her, they did have people in recovery there who could do with a helping hand, so Caleb was able to convince them to let her come along. Lily too, to keep an eye on her.

Kiara had never been this close to the building before as she rarely wandered down this end of the city center, but it was intimidating. She couldn't see anything through the windows and there was no sign of life anywhere in the courtyard either. As they passed through the gate, she looked at the twisted, reinforced metal deterrents on top of the walls and squeezed Hallie's hand tighter.

If she hadn't been there with Caleb and the others, she probably would have backed out.

They were escorted into the building, where they were then scanned from top to bottom and thoroughly searched to make sure that none of them was going to try anything stupid.

Hallie normally would have made some sort of quip, but she kept her lips tightly shut so she didn't get herself arrested.

It wasn't until they stepped off the lift that the mood lightened up.

"Caleb!"

"Zoe," Caleb smiled, walking forward to meet the woman who was approaching them from across the office.

Kiara tore her eyes away from all the computer screens and found that Zoe was distinctly Latina, long brown hair with blonde highlights, brown eyes. The suit that she was wearing was all business, but she still found a way to work it.

The two of them hugged each other like old friends, a much warmer welcome than they had received downstairs.

"This must be Kiara, Hallie and Lily," she said, pointing them out correctly.

"How did you know?" Hallie gawped.

"I had to read all your files before I was allowed to give you access to the building," Zoe chuckled.

"Oh, that makes sense."

"I've gotta go over a couple of things with you before we can go on the tour," Zoe said, getting straight to the point. "It goes without saying that you should keep snooping to a minimum. The less you know, the better. That way if you happen to be targeted or taken hostage, you won't have to lie. Particularly you, Lily. I've never met one of your kind before, but try and stay out of people's head, it'll be better for all of us."

"Of course," Lily nodded.

"Don't wander off, stay with either me or Jack at all times. Jack will to take you ladies to the recovery suite, so you can visit some of our agents there. Caleb and Kiara, you'll be coming with me as we'll be visiting the ops center and the training area where I've got a couple of people who want to try sparring with a Chosen."

"Oh really?" Kiara said, raising her eyebrows at Caleb.

"I told Zoe she could put you through your paces," Caleb said. "I didn't want the trip here to be boring."

"Mmhmm, sure."

"And lastly, if you have questions, just ask us. We know what we can and can't tell you, so if you ask us something we're not allowed to answer, we'll shut that down straight away. Got it?"

There were general noises of agreement from their group. They were pretty simple rules to follow. None of them had any plans to wander off or get into trouble.

"Great. Jack!"

A young guy with jet black hair and sharp blue eyes stood up from a desk nearby, smiling warmly at them as he approached. He was wearing a shirt and tie but had left his jacket on his chair, so he looked a touch less formal.

"If you'd like to follow me," he said to Lily and Hallie.

"We'll meet back up with you later," Caleb promised.

Kiara gave Hallie a quick hug before she could disappear off.

"Have fun," she said.

"Go kick some agent butt," Hallie replied with a grin.

~

Hallie was being abnormally quiet, which probably hadn't gone unnoticed. It was mostly because she didn't want to accidentally cause a major incident, but she'd also learned to be quiet for long periods of time while she was having her lessons with Alastair. The healer could banter with the best of them. However, learning how to heal took a lot of focus. Neither of them could focus very well when Hallie was waffling on about her old family dog Fred and how he used to eat through shoes like they were part of a free buffet.

They had been out to visit a couple of old Guardians who Alastair had known for a long time. He was allowed to help them with any injuries and pains, so it was good practice for Hallie to heal minor complaints to get practice without breaking the rules. It wasn't very interesting, though, and no real challenge for her abilities. That was why she had been so eager to come along with Kiara and Caleb, because it would be a good way for her to see what she could do without straining herself.

"Where are you from, Jack?" Hallie asked him as they walked along the corridor, trying to make light conversation.

"The slight twang you're hearing is Irish, but I've been living over here since I was a little kid, so I don't sound like I just rolled off the boat from Dublin."

"Aha, thank you. I was sure I could hear something. I've been listening to a Scot barking orders at me all week, so I couldn't figure it out," she explained.

"Oh, are you talking about Alastair Dunn? He's been in here a couple of times since I transferred. Interesting bloke."

"Interesting is one word for him," Hallie snickered.

Lily looked amused too.

"He's always been a big softie with me," she said with a shrug.

"Who wouldn't be a big softie with you? Just look at you," Hallie laughed.

"I have to agree with Hallie. I think you'd be hard pressed to find a man in here who wouldn't treat you like a princess."

"It's the big hazel eyes, right?" Hallie said.

"And the cute skirt."

"Please, stop," Lily told them, blushing furiously.

"Sorry," Hallie said, even though she was not sorry in the slightest.

Hallie and Kiara had been working on a theory for a while now that Caleb and Lily quite liked each other. They always sat together at group dinners and could talk each other's ear off for hours if they were left alone. Any chance that Hallie had to build up Lily's confidence, she was going to take it.

"Here we are," Jack said, pushing open the double doors at the end of the hallway to reveal a decent sized room which was geared up to both treat patients and rehabilitate them.

On one side, there was hospital equipment, beds, medical supplies and a couple of nurses milling around tending to people. The other side had a couple of treadmills, some weights, and an area for people to sit and relax.

Hallie wondered how many people actually passed through this place. She imagined that quite a few injured agents and spies ended up in hospitals instead, as they were probably found by the emergency services first.

"Zoe told me that you were looking to try to heal someone?" Jack asked.

"If someone doesn't mind letting me," Hallie said. "I've been training with Alastair for a few weeks now and other than a sore hip and a bump to the head, I haven't had much to work with."

"I think we can find you something more exciting," he said.

They approached the first bed and pulled back the curtain to reveal a slightly older guy, who had an Eastern European look about him, and a bandaged left leg.

"Stefan, this is Hallie and Lily, the ladies I told you about earlier. Ladies, this is Stefan, one of our operatives who was badly wounded on a reconnaissance mission last week."

"I was lucky to make it back with my leg intact," Stefan told them, his English accent on the posher side. "It's a pleasure to meet you both. Jack tells me that one of you is a healer?"

The man looked at Lily first but had to turn his head when Hallie raised her hand.

"That would be me."

"Ah, you're very young," he said, looking a little surprised. "A lot of the healers I've met found out later in life."

"Why is that?"

Stefan shrugged his shoulders. "It's usually because they didn't have any family members who were healers or because their parents waited until they were older to tell them. It's a lot of responsibility."

"Well, that probably would have been the case for me too, but a few eventful weeks meant that I discovered what I was a lot earlier than usual."

It was strange to think of all the things that had to align in order for her to discover that she was a healer. Kiara becoming a Chosen, already knowing Caleb, finding Lily… If all those things hadn't have happened, then she would probably still be none the wiser.

"I see," he said. "I hope it doesn't take too much of a toll. Pace yourself in the beginning. You're going to see a lot of terrible things in your life because of the things that you can do, don't do too much too fast."

Hallie smiled a little. It was nice getting some advice. Alastair didn't tend to dole out helpful tips about how to handle it all, only what she needed to know.

"Thanks," she said.

"You're welcome. Now, do you want to have a go at healing this mess?"

Lily and Jack stood back to give Hallie some room. Hallie looked at the bandages and pursed her lips.

"I've never tried to heal through bandages before."

"So we don't scar everyone, I think it's probably best if we try to leave them on for now," he warned.

"I'll give it a try," she agreed.

Like Alastair taught her, Hallie extended her hands out over the part of the leg she wanted to heal. She found it went better if she could close her eyes, then she wasn't distracted by any of the things that were happening around her. Once she was ready, she said one word over and over again in her head.

'Heal, heal, heal…'

Her hands got warmer the more she said it and she opened her eyes to see that the pale glow was there, which was a comforting sign. As her senses began to connect with his body, she could feel the extent to which his leg was mangled. It gave her chills and almost threw her off, but she was able to rein herself back in.

The sensation she felt when she was repairing something was strange. It was like she was knitting everything back together in her mind's eye. The bones, the arteries, the muscle, the skin, anything that needed fixing.

Hallie could feel herself getting a little woozy as she persisted, trying to make sure that everything was completely healed before she stopped. Apparently, what was 'a little woozy' to her was actually her looking like she was going to pass out.

Lily came up behind her and carefully broke her connection with Stefan's leg, holding her up so that she didn't keel over.

"I wasn't done," Hallie said, blinking.

"Yes, you were," Lily told her. "If I'd let you go on, you would have fainted."

"Oh."

"I'll tell you what, I think you've done a good job, though," Stefan said, sounding a lot happier. "Jack, help me with these bandages."

Between the two of them, they were able to unwrap Stefan's leg. Apart from a few red patches and some bruising, it looked as good as new.

"Wow," Jack said, seriously impressed.

"I'll be up and about in no time, thanks to you," Stefan told Hallie.

"That's great," Hallie smiled, although she was still having to hold onto Lily for support, otherwise she was going to fall over. "Don't go flaunting your leg about too much, wouldn't the other folks in here to get jealous."

Stefan chuckled. "I'll be discreet."

"Ha, that's funny! Discreet, because you're a spy."

Usually she wouldn't have found that so funny, but the drowsiness was really starting to hit her.

"I think we'd better find somewhere to sit you down and get you something to eat," Lily said.

"We've got a canteen on the next floor down, we can go there," Jack said, stepping in to help Lily hold Hallie upright.

As they made their way towards the door, Stefan called, "I owe you one."

Hallie saluted in reply, thinking that a spy owing her a favour might come in handy someday. Now, if only she could walk in a straight line...

~

As they began to move about the floor, Kiara started to look less intimated and more intrigued, which was good because Caleb knew that she would have to get used to these sorts of surroundings. They would be visiting plenty of different agencies over the new few years, some scarier than others. He could admit that there were still times when he was a little unnerved, but once they got stuck into whatever mission they had agreed to take part in, his nerves usually settled down.

At MI6, Zoe's presence always helped. For someone who dealt with such serious issues, day in and day out, she was a very laid back and friendly person. It made her a great contact and an even better friend.

"This is incredible," Kiara said as they entered command ops.

It was wall to wall screens, with a large table in the middle that people could congregate around. There were a couple of people in there going over some files, occasionally pointing up at the screens, who ignored their presence. The screens showed all sorts of different things, from surveillance to intelligence. Caleb never looked too hard in case he gleaned something that he was better off not knowing.

"Our equipment here is always state of the art. Sometimes we use lower tech stuff out in the field as it can help us fly under the radar, but for the most part, everything around here is several years ahead of what the general public knows exists," Zoe said.

"Seriously, so cool," Kiara grinned.

"I was impressed when I came here for the first time too. My original plan was to join the FBI, but my boyfriend at the time got a job over here and I retrained with British intelligence."

"You're not still together?"

"No, it got too complicated," Zoe shrugged. "It's all right though, I've got a little something-something going on with a bartender who works not too far from here. She likes to keep things super casual, which is fine by me," she winked.

"Gotcha," Kiara chuckled.

"Zoe asked me out once," Caleb said, which elicited a very funny expression from Kiara.

"I didn't know about the rules, otherwise I wouldn't have bothered. I have always wondered, though, would you have said yes if you had been free to?" Zoe asked.

Caleb narrowed his eyes and pressed his lips together, like he was having to think hard about his answer.

"Hmmmm."

"Jerk," Zoe laughed.

"Of course, I would have said yes," he said.

"My ego is grateful. Now, should we move on to the training room? The guys there are probably wondering where we've got to," she said, elbowing Caleb as she passed him.

Kiara giggled.

The training room was down in the basement, which meant a quick ride in the elevator, back the way they came. It was sectioned off into rooms using plasterboard wall between the building's structural beams. The part they wanted was just around the corner, where two agents were already sparring.

The woman had her legs wrapped around the man's neck, his arm pulled out at an awkward angle so that he couldn't wriggle away or try to get the upper hand.

"All right, all right," the man choked as he tapped out.

She released him, although she looked very pleased with herself as she did.

"Oh, there you are," she said as she rolled onto her feet. "We were beginning to think that you weren't coming."

"We got caught up looking at the ops center," Zoe explained. "Kiara and Caleb, this is Maya and Todd, both field agents."

Todd was black and stocky, with big ears that stuck out from his head. He had a couple of piercings, one in his left nostril and another at the top of his right ear, as well as a nasty scar that poked out from the neckline of his top. Maya was long; long body, long legs, long blonde hair, which made her look taller when she was stood further away. In reality, she was still shorter than Caleb. Her ivory skin and round blue eyes gave her an innocent look, but she was missing part of her left eyebrow, which suggested she had been in just as many scrapes as Todd.

"It's great to meet you," Maya said, stepping forward to shake both their hands.

"We've heard a lot about you, Caleb, from people all around the building," Todd joined in. "What you were able to pull off in Costa Rica was impressive to say the least."

"Thanks," Caleb said.

"Wait, what happened in Costa Rica?" Kiara asked.

Todd and Maya both looked at Zoe for confirmation they could tell the story.

"Go ahead."

"Do you have to?" Caleb looked embarrassed.

"Don't listen to him," Maya told Kiara. "He's clearly just being modest."

"Caleb and his Chosen at the time got sent out there to bring back a rogue agent who had sold stolen intelligence to one of the region's warlords. Long story short, he ended up saving the Chosen, the rogue agent, and several others from a burning building that was about to collapse, all by himself. If he hadn't, we wouldn't have been able to recover all the information that was stolen, and it would have been a catastrophe for our government."

"He's considered a bit of a legend by the agency," Maya said.

"Oh yeah?" Kiara looked up at Caleb, amused.

"See? That look was exactly what I was afraid of," he sighed. "I've made more mistakes than I can count."

"Doesn't make the good you've done any less important," Zoe pointed out.

This conversation was not going the way he hoped it would. He didn't like to boast about any of the things that he had achieved because he was doing it all in the service of the greater good. Caleb also knew that if his ego ever showed signs of getting too big, Master Mahmid would quickly deflate it again.

"I thought you were both here to try your hand at sparring with Kiara?" he said, trying to shift the topic away from him.

"Yeah, of course. So long as you're game, Kiara," Maya said.

"I think so," Kiara said, tugging off her jacket and putting her boots to one side. "I've only been training for a month."

"That's plenty of time from what I hear," Todd nodded.

The three of them spread out across the mats, while Caleb and Zoe stood back against the wall, so they could watch.

Kiara glanced across at Caleb. "Any advice?"

"Just remember what I taught you and you'll be fine."

"Okay," she said, not sounding so certain.

This was going to be an interesting test for Kiara. Back at the safe house, while they were sparring, she had a safety net because she knew that he would never it take it too far. She had also got used to his moves, countering him had become predictable to a certain extent. Now, however, she was fighting not one but two people who she didn't know, each with their own fighting style. He wanted to see how the lessons she had learned so far stacked up against a close to real life scenario.

For a minute, it didn't look like anyone was going to make the first move, but then Maya decided to launch an attack. Kiara deftly dodged Maya's first punch, rolling out of the way of a spinning kick. Unfortunately, she sprung up right in front of Todd who was able to throw her over his shoulder like she weighed nothing whatsoever. She hit the mat with a slam that made both Caleb and Zoe wince.

"Shake it off," he called to her.

There was no way she was giving up after one take down.

As she got to her feet, he said, "Remember to use your greatest asset."

If she was going to win this fight, then she had to start using her senses. Anticipating their moves was the best way to figure out how to take them down.

Kiara had one of them on either side of her now, circling her as she slowly turned in the center, looking at each of them in turn to see if she could guess what they were going to do.

When she had her back turned to him, Todd made a run at her, but she bent down at the last minute and stuck her leg out, sending him flying. Maya was on her a moment later and tried to lock up her arm the way she had done with Todd earlier. Kiara wasn't having it though, twisting out of it before Maya could firm up her grip. She then turned the tables on the other woman, jabbing Maya in the face while her arm was immobilised, then letting go so that she could boot her in the stomach. As she fell over too, Caleb smiled.

"Good, that's more like it."

A few more moves like that and she might prove herself ready to go out into the field already, which would be a first for one of his Chosen.

The two agents came back with renewed determination, having been taken off guard by her speed. This meant that they wouldn't underestimate her again. It also meant that they knew they had to work as a team in order to make any headway, which was where it started to go wrong for Kiara.

At first, it wasn't so bad. Kiara was actually able to play them off against each other. But, as she learned, they adapted. They started to land more blows, disorientating her to the point where she got unsteady on her feet. Using one last big move, Maya was able to get Kiara to lose her balance. Todd caught her but flipped her around his body once before sending her soaring across the mats, landing in a heap against the far wall.

Caleb didn't think twice before sprinting over to her, carefully unfolding her so that he could see her face. Her eyes were closed.

"Kiara? Can you hear me?"

When she didn't respond, a guilty sounding Todd said, "I'm sorry, I got a little carried away. I thought she could handle it."

Caleb ignored him, holding Kiara's cheek in his hand. "Kiara, open your eyes. Look at me, please."

He waited, his heart pounding in his ears as he waited what seemed like an age before she coughed, then she peered at him through her squinted vision.

"Why are there three of you?" she asked quietly.

"You've got a concussion," he told her. "Don't fall asleep on me, okay? We need to get you to Hallie, she'll be able to take care of you."

"I'll find out where they are," Zoe said, pulling out her phone.

"Just stay awake," Caleb said as he scooped Kiara up into his arms.

"I'm sorry again," Todd said.

"Yeah, feel better soon, Kiara," Maya added, looking like she felt awful.

"Byeeeeeee," Kiara murmured as she was carried out of there, still managing to be friendly even though they'd just wiped the floor with her.

"They're in the canteen, this way," Zoe said, then ran ahead, making sure that the elevator was waiting for them when they arrived.

Hallie and Lily looked aghast when they entered the canteen, the former almost falling out of her chair as she tried to get up.

"What the hell happened?"

"Her sparring partners got a bit rough," Caleb said. "She's got a concussion."

"Head spinny," Kiara confirmed.

"Don't worry, babe, I've got you now."

Hallie laid one of her long hands across Kiara's forehead, looking at her with a concerned expression as her palm began to glow. It didn't long for Kiara to fully open her eyes, looking up at Caleb and Hallie.

"I think you can put me down now," she said, looking glad to be back on her own two feet.

"What would you do without me, eh?" Hallie said.

"Probably be on the way to the hospital," Kiara replied, giving her girlfriend a grateful hug. "The next time we got on an outing, can we keep fighting to a minimum, please?" she requested, looking at Caleb in particular.

"Of course, it'll be awhile before we try anything like that again," he said. "You did well though, considering."

"Yeah. A little more practice and I would consider pinching you from the Guardians," Zoe said.

"Thanks," Kiara said, although she didn't look convinced.

Caleb had hoped that this would boost her confidence, he would feel terrible if it had done the opposite.

"Sit, I'll go get you a slice of chocolate cake," Lily said, pulling out her chair.

"I'll come with you," Caleb said.

Once they were out of sight of the others, Lily turned to face him, stopping him in his tracks.

"You stop those thoughts right now," she ordered.

He was surprised by her forceful voice, he had never heard her speak like that to anyone before.

"Nothing about what you did today was the wrong idea. If Kiara is going to learn to defend herself, then she needs to take off her safety wheels. You had no clue that agent was going to go too far."

Caleb wasn't quite sure how to respond.

"You're right, but that doesn't stop me from feeling bad. I don't like seeing her get hurt."

"Neither do I. But sometimes it's a necessary step to a person learning the lessons they need to in order to be the best they can be."

Caleb let out a quiet breath.

"Have I mentioned how helpful it can be sometimes that you can read my mind?"

"No, but good. It makes it so much easier to know what you need to hear."

Caleb couldn't even begin to express how glad he was not to be going through all of this alone for once. Lily's support as Kiara's aunt and his friend was proving to be invaluable.

"You're welcome," she smiled.

"So helpful," he reiterated, which made her laugh softly. "What do you think about getting her two pieces of chocolate cake?"

"I think that's something you'll live to regret later when she's hyper on sugar."

"I think I can cope," he said, sounding sure of himself despite her doubts.

"Your funeral," she laughed.

Chapter Sixteen

Hallie let out a huge groan as she fell onto her bed, the metal frame creaking under the force of the fall. It had been a couple of weeks since their visit to MI6 and both she and Kiara were utterly wiped. Alastair was really putting her through her paces now that she had covered the basics, making sure that she built up the strength needed in order to be able to heal over long periods of time. This meant a lot of endurance training, which equated to Alastair being driven around on a motorbike by his carer while Hallie ran beside them for miles and miles around the countryside. Sasha sometimes kept her company, but only on shorter runs, usually when she did laps around the town. It was gruelling to say the least.

While she knew that this would be of great help to her in the long term, she couldn't help but feel like there was a lot of pain and no gain right now. Every night she came home aching from head to toe.

Kiara wasn't much better off. What happened at MI6 pushed her to do even more in order to prove herself. Because of this, they barely got any time to themselves anymore. They quite often had group dinners cooked by Lily, then when they got back to her place or Kiara's, they just fell asleep. Hallie missed the days when they had hours and hours to play games, watch movies and just hang out in the city.

"Do you think we can maybe stay awake for more than ten seconds tonight?" Hallie asked Kiara as her babe flopped down beside her.

"Oh, I don't know. I did a ridiculous amount of reps today. I'm going to start looking like a bodybuilder soon if we don't move onto something else."

Hallie tried to laugh, but she was so tired that it sounded more like a gurgle.

"Oh dear," Kiara said, leaning over Hallie so she could look at her properly. "How far did Alastair make you run today?"

"I lost count around mile 10, I've no idea how far it was after then. The only thing that stopped me from collapsing was the fact that he was following me around. I didn't want him to see me fall down, not when I've been working so damn hard all week."

"I know. You're doing great, I'm so proud." Kiara kissed her on the nose.

"Thanks, babe. I wish it was you making me jog marathons around Greater London, you'd be a lot more supportive."

"I probably wouldn't make you do it in the first place."

"This is true. There's not a mean bone in your body."

"Hmmm, not sure. Caleb might disagree with you about my elbows after I almost knocked him out earlier. It was dumb luck that I didn't break something."

"Whoa. If you can kick his ass, then surely you're ready to go out in the field?"

"Not yet. He says he's waiting to see what Master Mahmid thinks based on the reports that he's been sending him."

Hallie sighed. "I guess I don't blame him. He won't want to piss the other Guardians off again because of what happened with us."

"Yeah," Kiara said, but she looked a little upset that she wasn't ready yet.

"Don't worry. I'm sure you'll be out there soon enough, saving the world," Hallie told her, managing a small grin.

"If you believe it then it must be true," Kiara smiled.

Hallie twirled a strand of red hair around her finger, taking a moment to look at Kiara properly. She hadn't realised how much her face her changed over the last month and a bit. Kiara looked so fit despite being so exhausted.

"I've missed you," Hallie said.

"I've missed you too," Kiara replied, leaning in to brush her lips against Hallie's.

Hallie caught Kiara's bottom lip between both of hers, a long and slow kiss to suit their mood.

"You know what we need?" Hallie asked.

"If you say sex, I'm going to need to nap first."

"No, that would be nice, but I don't think either of us could manage right now without snoozing all over each other. What I was going to say is that we need a night out. Lily and Caleb too. We all deserve to have some fun after all the hard work we've been putting in lately."

"I agree."

"Then it's settled, we're having a proper Friday night out this week. All we've got to do is convince the two old fogeys."

Lily wouldn't be too hard, she figured. The woman didn't get out much, so this could be an exciting adventure. Caleb, however… she would probably have to let Kiara take care of that one. The worst he could do was say no.

~

"Where did you even find these clothes?" Caleb asked.

Kiara could hear him struggling to pull on the jeans she had chosen for him. They had looked pretty tight, even for someone with Caleb's stature.

"I found the jacket, jeans and shoes buried in the back of your wardrobe, and I bought the shirt to class the whole outfit up a bit."

It had taken a little persuasion to get Caleb to agree to go out for the evening with them. Lily had been game, particularly when Hallie had said they could go shopping and use her Dad's credit card. She knew that Caleb was worried about getting distracted, but she had been training so hard that giving him the big puppy dog eyes had eventually worked. It wasn't just her that needed a break, Caleb had to need one as well.

"I don't even remember buying these things."

"Just shut up and get dressed already."

While Caleb did as he was told, Kiara spent a few minutes wandering around the apartment. She had never been here before today and she understood why. It wasn't the fanciest place and he certainly hadn't made it a home. There were some things lying about though. Plenty of books, of course. But it was the trinkets that she was drawn to, the stuff that came from his past.

"Where is your family from again?" she asked, looking at the lantern and the bear. Obviously, his family was Asian, but she didn't want to be rude.

"My Dad was from Incheon, which is close to Seoul, but on the coast. Apparently, my Mom was originally from China, but my aunt doesn't like to talk about her. She didn't approve of her for some reason."

Kiara wondered why.

"Your aunt was your Dad's sister, right?"

It didn't make much sense for her to not approve of her own sister, although families could fall to pieces given the right tensions or tragedy.

"Yeah. If my Mom has family that are still alive, I haven't been able to find them."

Kiara felt a little sad for Caleb because she knew how lonely it could be to have such little family. Who knew what could have happened to him if his parents survived?

"Do you ever go back and visit your aunt?"

"I do when I can, but it's hard lying to her about what I do."

Kiara could understand. She was lucky that Hallie had been there from the beginning and that Master Mahmid had let Caleb loop her in on everything. She couldn't imagine lying to Hallie, it would have torn their relationship apart.

"All right, how do I look?" Caleb asked as he opened his bedroom door.

"Ooh, very nice," Kiara said, grinning from ear to ear.

She took a few steps closer, so she could straighten his collar.

"I told you that you'd look good in the shirt. It doesn't hide this like all your other clothes do," she said, poking his rock-hard abs.

"And yet it makes me feel naked. Not as naked as you though."

Her plunging neckline made his eyebrows practically shoot off his head when he opened his front door to her earlier.

"At least my sexy legs are covered," she said, referring to the pleated trousers she'd purchased for herself.

"I don't know, I'd much rather see sexy legs than breasts."

They both looked at each other and ended up laughing.

"Why are we even having this conversation?" he asked.

"I don't know, you were the one who used the word naked," she said.

"My bad." He zipped his lips closed to show her that he was done.

"I think we're almost ready to head out. One last question though."

Kiara picked up the bear and held out one of its paws, the one with the bracelet.

"What does this symbol mean?"

"It's the Chinese symbol for love."

"That's sweet," she smiled.

"Do you want it?"

Kiara looked taken aback. "What? No, it's got to be from your Mum or something."

"It was hers, but it's too small for me," he said, taking the bracelet from the bear's paw so he could undo the clasp.

"Caleb."

Gently, he pulled on her hand so that her arm was extended, then reconnected the clasp. The bracelet fit perfectly; leaving enough wiggle room so that it wasn't tight but didn't slip.

"I know that I train you really hard, and that we're exhausted most of the time we spend together outside of the safe house, but you're becoming a really good friend, as well as a skilled Chosen. I never thanked you for forgiving me for the lies, but I am now."

Kiara pulled Caleb into a tight hug, squeezing her eyes shut so that she wouldn't be overwhelmed by the moment.

"There's nothing to forgive."

She felt Caleb smile against her shoulder.

"Now, what do you say we go shake some booty on the dancefloor?"

"If you wanted me to do that, you shouldn't have dressed me in these jeans. I can barely move my legs, let alone my ass."

Kiara grabbed his hand and laughed her way out the door.

~

Caleb was still fidgeting when they rocked up to the club a little later than planned. It was the damn pants. They must have been left over from college, back when he was practically skin and bone. Stupid muscles. *Stupid pants.*

"Would you stop?" Kiara smacked him in the arm. "They're here."

If it had just been Hallie she was referring to, then it probably wouldn't have made a difference to his behaviour. She would have found it funny and he wouldn't have minded. What stopped him dead in his tracks was Lily.

Her everyday wear was always lovely, skirts and dresses, cute sweaters, flat shoes that helped make him feel tall. But she'd had the full Hallie makeover treatment in preparation for their evening out and… well...

"Wow."

"You can say that again," Kiara said as she scooched over to the ladies. "I told you that dress was going to look so cute on you!"

It was pink lace with cream underneath, pulled in at the waist and came to stop well before her knees. Caleb was probably paying far too much attention, but they'd already covered his weakness for legs.

"I still don't know," Lily said, trying to tug the hem down.

"I've had to tell her to stop fussing so many times on the way over here," Hallie said, exasperated. "I wouldn't let you go out in public looking ridiculous."

"It doesn't stop me from feeling ridiculous."

"I think you look beautiful."

They all looked round at Caleb when he spoke, Lily's cheeks flushing a pale shade of pink.

"You think?" she asked.

"Without a doubt," he smiled.

"Oh, so you'll take it from him?! FINE!" Hallie pretended to act like she was offended, but she was clearly enjoying herself.

"I think we both did a fine job," Kiara said. "Celebratory kiss!"

Hallie couldn't say no to a celebratory kiss.

As the other two were busy congratulating themselves, Caleb moved in to offer Lily an arm as she didn't look entirely steady in the heels she was wearing.

"Shall we?" he asked.

"Yeah," she said, leaning into him as they made their way into the club.

Caleb wasn't sure what to expect as most of his nights these days involved reading at home, hanging out with the girls, or training. He didn't go to bars and clubs unless a mission called for it or someone wanted to meet there. It appeared Lily was the same, because she ended up looking around in awe as they walked into the main bar area. It was lot more upmarket than he was expecting from the outside, which had been two metal doors to a brick building with the club's name above the door. He hadn't got a chance to read it, he'd been too distracted by Lily.

The theme appeared to be opulent, with blacks, golds and reds, velvet covered seats and loungers, and a spectacular bar covered in fairy lights which twinkled through the darkness. His doubts about how the night would go started to fade and he found himself making for the bar before he even really knew where his feet were taking him.

"What does everyone want to drink?" he asked, not having to yell too loudly.

"SHOTS!" Hallie bellowed over everyone.

"Shut up, we're not starting with shots," Kiara laughed.

"We are if it'll make Lily stop messing with her dress."

Lily quickly hid her hands behind her back and looked innocent.

"That's just proof!" Hallie decided, flagging down a bartender.

"Hallie--" Caleb tried.

"No! You get to be Mister Bossy Pants most days of the week. Tonight, I'm in control and I say two rounds of Bazookas for the four of us, if you please."

Caleb stared at Kiara with a look that said, 'Help!' but she just giggled at her girlfriend. They all knew deep down that there was nothing they could do when Hallie got something into her head. Tonight, that meant getting drunk.

The bartender returned quickly with a tray full of brightly coloured shots. Caleb didn't know what they were going to taste like, probably burning.

"To us!" Hallie beamed as she lifted up her glass.

They all followed suit, raising their drinks to each other before tossing them back. Lily almost choked.

"Holy shit," Caleb coughed, placing the empty glass back on the bar top.

Hallie was completely unphased. In fact, she was bouncing up and down on the spot, totally psyched up.

This unfortunately meant that they had to do the second in quick succession, which made Caleb's throat feel like he was giving it an acid bath. How had he been able to cope with this sort of thing in his early 20's? And enjoyed it?

"To the dancefloor!" Hallie told them, wrapping an arm around Kiara's waist so she could steer her away.

Caleb took a step forward to follow them, but Lily caught his hand so that she could hold him back. At first, he wasn't sure what she was doing, but then he realised that Hallie and Kiara were so hyper that they hadn't even noticed they weren't following.

"Clever," he said, looking back at her with a smirk.

"It'll be a little while before they realise. Shall we find somewhere a little quieter?"

"I think I can see somewhere," he said, linking his fingers with hers.

There was a spot at the back that was secluded, the sofas creating a sort of barrier between the seating and the rest of the club.

"This is better," he said as he fell back onto one of the couches.

Lily followed him, not letting go of his hand once she was comfortable. He didn't move to either, because it was nice, even if he knew they couldn't be more than friends.

"So, I know how I got roped into this evening," Caleb said. "How about you?"

"The girls made it sound like so much fun, but that's probably because they're young and to them, this is a blast."

"I know, I feel so old. The rest of them are having the time of their lives and all I can think about is how suffocating these pants are…"

"They are pretty clingy."

"Right? I might as well be wearing denim coloured tights."

This made Lily laugh.

"I like the shirt though, Kiara was right thinking it would look good on you."

"Yeah, well, she's allowed to be right about some things, I guess."

"Funny."

"How do you know I'm not just being a jerk?" he chuckled.

"We talk a lot about her training sessions because she's curious to know how she compares to her Dad, but we nearly always end up on tangents to other things. One thing she always comes back to is how much she's enjoying herself getting to learn how to fight and to focus. I know that's because of you."

Caleb didn't know what to say.

"I also spotted that bracelet on the way in, couldn't have come from anyone else."

Sometimes he forgot how perceptive she was, even without her abilities.

"I think she deserves to be treated like royalty, you all do. It helps that you all make it so easy," he said, turning the compliment around.

"Apart from when one of us is barking 'SHOTS!' at you from across the bar."

"No, even then. Royalty all the way."

Caleb was impressed with how long they were able to hide away from the girls, chatting amongst themselves. It took a couple of beers for Kiara to come bounding over, immediately seizing Lily's hand.

"You cheeky buggers! You're supposed to be dancing!"

"But we're having so much fun here," Lily protested.

"Nope, if I don't come back with you now then you'll get a super drunk Hallie hunting you down instead. She'll drag you along the floor if she has to," Kiara said.

"I'd like to see her try," Caleb replied, but relented anyway.

He was sure that Hallie's expression, when they appeared from the crowd, would have been one of scorn if one of her favourite songs hadn't just started blasting from the DJ booth.

"Oh my God, this is perfect!" she jumped up and down on the spot.

Kiara held a hand out to Hallie, who took it and spun herself into the redhead's arms with flare, attracting the attention of those around them. That didn't help Caleb feel any less self-conscious.

"Come on! I know you know how to move those hips," Kiara encouraged him.

"Yeah, in a fight," he said.

"Just feel the music, move to the beat, it's easy," Hallie instructed as she pressed her body against Kiara's, the pair of them making him sweat.

It was Lily who decided to act, pulling Caleb round so that he couldn't see the girls anymore.

"Don't look at them, focus on me."

It was a smart move on her part, as it was much easier to relax when they weren't trying to coerce him.

"One dance. We can manage one dance."

"I think we can do a little more than manage," he said.

Fixing his eyes on her big hazel ones, Caleb enveloped her hand in his and placed it on his shoulder, letting his hips and torso begin to shift from side to side in time to the Latin beat. Lily smiled softly, her moves falling into sync with his as he secured a hand at her waist, their other hands finding each other without them having to look. The more natural it felt, the easier it was for them to lose themselves to the music.

As the song built to the chorus, Caleb felt confident enough to change positions, twirling her round so her back was flat against his chest. It was like they were being carried by the guitars and drums, which were overwhelming all the other noises in the room, including the whoops of excitement coming from Kiara and Hallie.

They slowly dissolved into the crowd, others following their lead as the floor came alive with passion. Caleb wasn't sure he had ever felt this way before, so completely absorbed in another. The way Lily was looking at him made him feel like he could dance like this forever. And he probably could have if an angry cry hadn't brought him back to earth with a thud.

~

Hallie hadn't been sure that they could convince Caleb and Lily to have any fun because of how uptight they were being about their outfit choices. But seeing them steam up the dancefloor restored her faith in both of them. All it took was a little, gentle nudging…

Honestly, she'd been having a whale of a time all evening. The drinks were delicious, her babe looked smoking hot, and the music was old enough to be fun, but not too old to be disco. It was shaping up to be a pretty perfect night. Until some douchebag thought that it was okay to cut in.

"Oi!" she growled, thrusting his meaty hands away from her. "Can't you see that I'm with my girlfriend, jackass?"

"You've got a mouth on you, haven't you?" he said, trying to make another grab for her, but Caleb stepped in.

"You heard her, she said no."

"Piss off, yank, I didn't ask your permission."

The guy tried to shove Caleb out the way, but he held fast, like the guy had just tried to push over a mountain.

"Leave her alone or I drag you out of here myself."

Hallie had never seen Caleb act this way before. It was like he was suddenly two feet taller, the most imposing guy in the room. She had no doubt that he could wipe the floor with the idiot, but then six of his friends appeared to back him up.

"Ah crap," she muttered.

Two of them came at Caleb at once, but he stepped back out of their reach, watching as they bumped into each other. This only angered them further. Kiara made a move towards the guy who had tried to come between her and Hallie, swinging her fist right at his face. He grabbed her hand and twisted it behind her back, forcing her forwards towards the fire exit.

"Let's take this outside, shall we?"

Despite their protests, the four of them were manhandled out the back of the club and tossed to the floor. Hallie had no idea where the bouncers were, but she hoped someone fired them.

"Get back," Caleb told Lily and Hallie as he got to his feet.

They knew this was going to get ugly fast and they were no match for seven Londoners all looking for a fight. Hallie helped Lily up and they both ran over to the nearest trash container to give them some cover.

Hallie knew that Kiara had been training so hard, but after her defeat at MI6 the other week, she wasn't sure that her girl was ready for a fight on this scale. Apparently, she was wrong.

Fierce as a lioness, Kiara wasted no time engaging the man closest to her. Her moves were so quick that Hallie had trouble keeping track of them. A kick to the stomach sent one stumbling back, but the next was immediately upon her, earning himself a nasty left jab.

Caleb was just as fast, tight pants be damned. He slammed an arm so hard into one of the men's chests that it looked like he had run into a metal beam, falling straight onto his back with a crash.

The pair of them worked in tandem with each other, sending the brawlers this way and that way. At one point, Kiara even rolled across Caleb's back to slam her foot into one of their faces.

Meanwhile, Hallie was just standing there with her mouth open, Lily holding onto her arm tightly because of the tension.

"Enough!" McGropey spluttered as Kiara stood over him, ready to give him a second black eye to match his other one. "We've had enough."

"Good," Kiara said, kicking him in the ribs for good measure. "Maybe you'll think next time before butting in."

"I doubt it," Caleb said as he wiped some blood from his mouth.

"Let's just get out of here, please?" Lily called to them, probably worried that someone might have called the police.

Hallie would have if she'd seen four people so outnumbered.

Not wasting any more time with the idiots lying on the floor, they all hurried for the nearest tube station, not really caring which lines it had. They had a choice of places they could retreat to; the train would take them to one of them.

Once they were safely bundled onto one of the carriages, Hallie was finally able to take a deep breath.

"You wiped the floor with those guys," she said, impressed.

"Right?" Kiara grinned as she mopped some sweat from her brow with the back of her hand. "And in heels, too!"

"You've really come on in leaps and bounds since your last fight," Caleb agreed.

"That uppercut to that guy's jaw," Hallie shuddered.

"I thought I heard his teeth break," Lily chimed in quietly.

"Not quite what you had in mind for an evening of fun, huh?" Caleb said.

"Everything else was good," Lily smiled up at him. "Although, I think this dress is ruined," she added, showing them the streak of mud up the side of it and her leg.

"I know a great dry cleaner who will be, admittedly, very confused, but will get that out no problem," Hallie said.

"I think she was trying to get out of wearing it again," Kiara snickered.

"No, we're not going back to that conversation," Hallie told them, drawing a line under it with her hands.

"What do you want to talk about then?" Caleb asked.

"I don't know. Socks!"

"Socks isn't steering us very far away from outfits, now, is it?"

"Oh, sweet baby Jesus…"

Chapter Seventeen

Downtime between recruitment missions was usually a busy time for Diana. There was a whole camp to check on, relationships to maintain, supplies to collect. But now that they were nearing the numbers they needed, she could afford to spend a little time taking a breath and regrouping mentally before they made their final move.

A large part of the camp had gathered in the center for a big barbecue to celebrate one of their birthdays, she had missed whose. It didn't matter too much, so long as they were enjoying themselves. Sometimes there could be disagreements between the people here, which had ended in bust ups once or twice. She would have to keep an eye out to make sure no one got too drunk and decided to pick a fight.

After collecting a veggie burger from the barbecue, Diana found Aaren and Eshe sat away from the main group, talking among themselves.

"I'm not interrupting, am I?" she asked, looking down at them.

"No, of course not," Eshe smiled.

"Actually… Nah, I'm just kidding," Aaren said, making room for Diana next to him.

"Always the joker," Diana shook her head.

Usually there was some truth behind the 'jokes' that people made. Diana had seen the way that Aaren was looking at Eshe as they spoke, she had definitely interrupted something.

"What is that?" Aaren asked her, looking at her food.

"I'm a vegetarian," she said.

"I never knew that," he said.

"That's because we've only ever drank together."

"True."

"Diana loves my shakshuka," Eshe told him, which made him choke.

Diana kicked him in the leg. "Such a dirty mind."

"I'm sorry," he cleared his throat. "What's shakshuka?"

"It's poached eggs with tomatoes, chillies and spices. Definitely not for the faint of heart or weak stomach," Eshe explained. "My mother used to make it for me, and her mother used to make it for her, and so on."

"My Mom used to have a recipe like that too, but it was for tosca cake. It couldn't make you breathe fire, but it could crack a tooth if made wrong."

"Sounds like the perfect combination," Diana commented.

"Ah, see, she cracks jokes too," Aaren said.

"They're just a lot subtler than yours," Eshe smirked.

The sound of a shriek drew their attention, all of them quickly looking round to try and find the source. It turned out that Will had thrown Priya over his shoulder and was spinning her round and round, making her burst out laughing.

Diana let out a quiet sigh of relief.

"They seem to be getting along well," Aaren said.

"Will gets on well with everyone," Eshe told him.

"Where did you find him anyway?" he asked Diana, pulling her attention back.

"Brisbane. I had been looking for a Chosen to help me in my endeavours. Will hadn't been picked up by the Guardians yet. He was anxious, afraid of what the prophecy meant for him. I told him everything and he chose to come with me."

"There are quite a few people who wouldn't be here if it weren't for him," Eshe added. "If they're not entirely swayed by Diana's words, then it's usually his big heart that gets them."

"I can see that," Aaren said.

Diana didn't always give Will enough credit for the part he played in all this. If she was honest with herself, she wouldn't have been able to get this far alone. Eshe was often the one who reminded her. Even though Eshe loved to tease Will mercilessly about their first meeting, she was also his biggest champion.

"How did Priya take it when you made the decision to come here?" Diana asked.

"She was the one pushing me to say yes, actually," he admitted. "I think she really likes the idea of us all being free to be who we want to be."

This was good. It was better if people didn't feel forced to be here, it meant they were more likely to follow through when it was time for the final push.

"How long does she have?" Eshe asked him.

"Less than two years. It'll be on her twenty-first birthday."

Eshe reached across to squeeze his hand comfortingly. It was hard to know that someone so young got such a short time. The youngest Diana had ever seen was sixteen, but they had seven years to grow into everything. This meant that they had so much time to fulfill their destiny, however, that it must have been hard for their Guardian to let them go when the time came. There were very few blessings that came with this job. The Chosen made it worth it.

"Once we take the Citadel, you'll be able to make every second of what life she has left count," Diana told him.

"I sure hope so," he said. "How much longer before you intend to make your move?"

"I'm waiting on word from a contact of mine about another Guardian who might be open to our cause. After that, I think we'll be ready."

"Good, because I'm not sure how much longer I can stand sharing that toilet."

Diana rolled her eyes.

"I'm being serious!"

For such a big man, he sure could be a big baby.

~

Will found it easy to talk to most of the people at camp. There were a lot of people who had been separated from their families, felt like they couldn't go back to them, or who had never had a chance at one. So, they all had quite a lot in common. Some could be terse, but they kept to themselves or didn't spend a lot of time at camp. Priya, though, was turning out to be a ton of fun to hang out with while everyone else was busy chatting or eating. They had left Eshe and Aaren to their own devices; if they were going to hit it off then they needed some alone time.

After playing around and making a lot of noise during dinner, Will took Priya down to the beach so they could sit near the shore and watch the waves lap up by their feet.

"It's so beautiful here," Priya said, looking at the fading colours of the setting sun.

"Yeah," he agreed. "The water and the temperature remind me a little of home."

The house his parents had owned when he was little wasn't anything to shout about; it was quite small and about as far away from the ocean as you could get. When his Dad's company took off, though, he bought a beautiful house right on the coast. All Will had to do was look out his bedroom window and there was the ocean, beckoning him to come and surf, swim, or muck about. His friends at school came over to his house all the time because it was so cool. His Dad was proud of that fact.

"When was the last time you were back there?" Priya asked.

"Just under four years ago. I'd just come back from a trip to see my sister in the states and was basically still packed. I went out to get a pizza when someone in the street dragged me to one side to tell me my future. I wouldn't have believed them, but I almost got killed that night trying to get home. Then Diana found me before the Guardians could. I haven't been back since."

Will wasn't sure what would have happened if the Guardians had found him first. His life would probably look a lot different right now, maybe he would still have been in touch with his family.

"Do you miss it? And your family?"

"Of course. I miss my parents, even though me and my Dad were in a fight before I disappeared."

"What about?"

"He wanted me to join his business, whereas I wanted to travel. He threatened to cut me off if I didn't do as he said. I have no idea if he ended up doing it, I never checked."

"I'm sorry," Priya said, looking sad for him. "Parents can be difficult."

Will and his Dad used to get along so well when he was a kid. He always said that Will was his mini-me. They used to go down to the beach or the park whenever his Dad had free time and play football or softball. Things got more complicated when his parents separated and then his Dad met Hallie's Mom, but it wasn't until Will started to become an adult that things between them became fraught.

"What are yours like?" he asked.

"My mother died when I was young, so that made it hard. I don't think my father knew what to do with me. He remarried and left it up to my stepmother and stepbrother, but they never really understood me either. I spent a lot of time alone. Aaren coming along, with the Guardians, was sort of a blessing in my case. I was completely lost, then the Oracle gave me my prophecy and suddenly my life was full of people whose focus was all on me."

His family had always been so close knit that he couldn't begin to imagine how lonely that must have been for her. Somehow, she had got through it and come out stronger for it.

"It's weird, the different ways and places in our lives that fate finds us," he said. "I freaked out at first. There had always been so much time left for me to find my feet. Having all that time suddenly taken away almost broke me. It probably would have succeeded if it hadn't been for Diana."

"I didn't have much time to think," Priya said. "Aaren was there with a solution to all my problems mere hours after the prophecy. I welcomed it with open arms."

"You've come to terms with your death already?" he asked.

"Yes. There is no greater calling than being a Chosen in my eyes. Whatever I do here will only mean more in my next life."

Will smiled. "That's an interesting way to look at it."

"Do you have a religion?"

The blonde shook his head. "Neither of my parents believed in anything religious. Hallie's Mum was a Christian, but Hallie didn't go to church. We put our faith and trust in each other rather than a God."

"That's interesting too. Aaren tells me old tales about the Norse Gods sometimes, I find it all so fascinating."

Will found that was the best way to be: open to other people's beliefs. If you could accept that their belief was real to them, then it caused much less animosity.

Priya shivered as the cool evening breeze started to blow in from the sea. Will tugged her closer, wrapping an arm around her shoulders to keep her warm.

"Thank you."

"I always used to do this for Hallie when she got cold, which was a lot because she's always been skinny as anything. You remind me of her a bit."

"Because I'm tiny?"

Will laughed. "Not so much. She's a lot taller than you, for starters."

Priya would look like a dwarf standing next to his sister.

"It's because of your joy. She always saw the bright side of things and wanted to do what was best."

Priya smiled softly and rested her head on his shoulder.

"Have you thought about going to see her? It's not too late to check in."

"I don't think I can. Besides, I wouldn't know where to find her or how to contact her. She could have gone to college anywhere in the world."

"Sounds to me like you're chicken."

Will nudged her. "I'm no coward."

"Not when it comes to fighting for what's right. But what about fighting for what's important to you?"

She had a point. Hallie was very important to him. But this was too.

"How about I make you a deal? When this is all over, I'll go find her."

"Promise?"

"Promise."

They pinky swore to make sure that he would keep his word. And he would. His only worry was whether he would live long enough to fulfill it.

Chapter Eighteen

"Hey, eyes on me. If I'd known that Hallie being here was going to be so distracting, I would have said no," Caleb said.

Kiara looked a little embarrassed. Hallie had wanted to tag along with them because Alastair had cancelled her lesson for today and she didn't want to be stuck at home, bored. What she hadn't realised was that Hallie would end up sitting in the corner of the room, pulling faces behind Caleb's back.

"My bad, my bad!" Hallie said, rightfully taking the blame. "I'll stop, so long as you stop to have a five-minute break and drink some refreshing water with me. Ehhhh?"

Caleb looked at Kiara, who shrugged her shoulders.

"I am a little thirsty."

"Fine," he sighed.

Kiara ran over to Hallie and was immediately greeted by a big bottle of water and a grin. Caleb followed at a much slower place, eventually coming to a stop near the treadmill so he could lean against it.

"Soooooo, how did things go last night when you dropped Lily off at her house?" Hallie asked Caleb innocently.

"What do you mean?" he narrowed his eyes at her.

"Just that it looked like you and Lily were getting pretty close last night before that rude interruption."

Caleb shook his head. "We're just friends."

"But whhhhhhhyyyyyy?"

Kiara couldn't help but giggle quietly. It was like Caleb was suddenly having to deal with a two-year-old.

"Because of the rules. Do you remember what happened the last time I didn't follow the rules?"

"I broke practically every bone in my body, but that's not the point."

"What's the point?"

"You like her. That's all that should matter."

Caleb rubbed his forehead and groaned.

"Would you please help me here?" he asked Kiara.

"I'm on her side with this one," Kiara told him. "What's the harm in trying? It's not like you're getting married tomorrow, it might not even come to anything."

"It might ruin a perfectly good friendship."

"You're both mature adults, you won't let that happen," Hallie said.

Caleb looked between the pair of them, only seeing their stubborn determination to make something happen.

"You're going to keep bugging me about this until I relent, aren't you?"

"He's learning," Hallie stage whispered to Kiara, who snorted.

"One date, that's all I'm guaranteeing."

"That's all we're asking," Kiara replied. "If it doesn't work, it doesn't work."

Hallie pulled Caleb's phone out his bag and thrust it towards him.

"Here you go. Call her."

"All right, but not in front of you two," he said wisely.

Taking the phone from Hallie, he strode off to the kitchen to do his thing. Hallie offered Kiara a high five, which she met with enthusiasm.

"He'll thank us someday," Kiara said.

"Shall we go listen at the door?" Hallie asked cheekily.

Kiara nodded, the pair of them having to stifle giggles as they scampered to their feet and sprinted across the room to the kitchen. Caleb had left the door open just a crack, so they could see him pacing, waiting for Lily to pick up.

"Please don't answer, please don't answer, please don't answer..." he muttered over and over to himself until... "Oh, hey, it's me. By me, I mean Caleb."

There was the obvious pause where Lily spoke, then Caleb let out a goofy laugh.

"Yeah, should have realised you can probably recognise my voice by now. Anywho, about the other night-- ... Yeah, I really enjoyed myself too. ... I was, uh, wondering if you wanted to go out again, but just the two of us. ... Yeah, sort of. ... It'll be a surprise. ... Okay, I'll come by and pick you up later. ... Bye."

As Caleb put his phone away, he smiled softly to himself. Despite what he had said to both of them, he looked like he was excited for his date, which was sweet.

Sweet enough to make Hallie "aww" out loud.

Kiara shot her a look as she covered her mouth, realising her mistake.

"Were you two spying on me?"

"No," Kiara tried, but it wasn't going to work.

"Run," he warned them. "Run now."

Both of them screamed as he whipped the door open, lunging for Kiara who was just about able to dodge his hands. As she got away, he went for Hallie instead, managing to wrap an arm around her waist as she tried to go for cover behind a nearby rowing machine. He lifted her up, which made her squeal and then cackle when he made a fart noise in her ear.

"Laugh all you like, but you're next," he told Kiara.

Kiara grinned.

"Only if you can catch me!"

~

Caleb wasn't 100% sure why he had agreed to do this. The concerns he had voiced to the girls were valid. However, what truly scared him was when he and Lily inevitably ended up having a great time, they would want to do it again, and things would start to get complicated. Everything between them was so simple and good that he didn't want to mess it up.

His only solution to this was to make sure that the night was going to be fun and easy going, nothing overly romantic, in the hopes that they wouldn't go too far. There were plenty of things to do in London, from clubs and bars to bowling and skating, all of which could have worked. But he had something else in mind.

"Namco Funscape, really?" Lily laughed.

"Yeah. The cool kids tell me it's a hip place to hang out."

Caleb grinned as she continued to giggle, struggling to form a witty comeback.

"'Hip'? I didn't realise I was on a date with an old man."

"You've seen me in my glasses. Hadn't those given me away?"

"They are pretty thick. Like you're looking out through a fish tank."

"Ohhhh, low blow."

"You were the one who started it," she smacked him in the arm.

"Now she's turned violent!"

Lily absolutely creased up.

"Stop!"

"Okay, okay," he said. "Why don't we go inside, continue laughing in there?"

"I would love that."

Caleb had been to arcades as a kid, but this place was absolutely massive. They had all sorts, from retro games to more recent releases, air hockey and even bumper cars. This had been a great idea.

"Where do you want to start?" he asked. "We can race each other in the Batmobile or see who can whack the most moles?"

"I actually really love air hockey. When my Dad and I used to go to the local bowling alley, we used to spend more time playing it than bowling."

"Are you trying to intimidate me?"

"No…"

Lily looked too innocent for that to be true.

"All right. I'll try not to let my pride be too badly wounded when you kick my ass."

Putting a pound coin in the machine, Caleb pushed her striker towards her and grabbed the puck.

"Guess I get to start."

Caleb licked his lips in concentration, focusing on his aim, making her wait. Just when it looked like he was about to pull off an amazing first move, he slipped and hit the side of the puck by accident. It ricocheted from side to side across the table, where Lily caught it and smacked it straight back, scoring immediately.

"Ah, damn it," he said.

"Rookie mistake, you'll do better next time," she said.

Except that he didn't. Her next three goals were all flawless, with him flailing about all over the place to hit the puck back.

"This is embarrassing," he said.

"I want to tell you that it's not…" She didn't actually finish her sentence because she was too amused.

"Maybe I should just give up now and call you the winner?"

"Nooo, that would be a waste of money. Let's keep going. You might make a comeback, you never know."

"Yeah, yeah."

Caleb lined up the shot again, although this time he looked defeated. With a sigh, he flicked his wrist and hit the puck straight into her goal. It was like he put no effort into it at all.

Lily's mouth fell open.

"What was *that*?"

"I believe that was what people used to call my signature move."

"Have you been hustling me this whole time?"

"Maybe."

"Yoouuuuu!"

She shook her striker at him menacingly but ended up looking ridiculously cute.

"That's adorable."

"It's not supposed to be adorable! You fiend!"

"Seriously, I can't even right now."

Lily looked like she was struggling to decide whether to laugh or growl.

"You're going down, Lau," she told him.

"Right back atcha, Shaw."

The next five minutes made up the most furious game of air hockey he had ever played. They were batting the puck back and forth so violently and making so much noise that they actually drew a crowd.

It came down to one last point, which could go either way. Caleb was psyching himself up for the win and he could see Lily doing the same across the other end of the table. He hadn't realised this was going to get so competitive so fast. How this ended could set the tone for the rest of the evening.

"Ready?" she asked him, placing the puck on the table.

"Hit me," he replied.

Lily used the old false start to try and throw him off before she put the puck into play, but it didn't work. Each time one of them was able to bounce the puck back, the crowd went 'oooh' or 'aaah'. They were having to do some spectacular leaps and reaches in order to keep it going, until eventually, one last slip up meant…

"YES!"

Lily threw her arms in the air to raucous cheers and did a small victory dance, bouncing and twirling on the spot.

"Your trick didn't work! I still won!"

"Yeah, yeah," he said, waving her off.

Lily took a victory lap of the crowd, giving and receiving high fives, before coming to a stop beside him.

"You're not going to be a sore loser, are you?"

Caleb gave her his best pout, sticking his bottom lip out as far as it would go.

"Aww," she said, reaching across to kiss him on the cheek. "There there."

A smile spread across his face, unbidden, the touch of her lips making his skin warm. Or maybe it was the blushing.

"I think I'll survive," he decided.

"Good," she said.

"Should we do something that maybe we're both bad at next?" he suggested.

"If it'll make you feel better."

The rest of their evening was a ton of fun. They moved from game to game, whatever they felt like doing when they were done with the last one, until they got too hungry to keep going. They shared a couple of meals between them at one of the big fast food restaurants outside, then decided to walk home through the city, enjoying the cool night air.

"This was nice," Lily said when they stopped outside her apartment door.

"Yeah, I think… that was probably the best night out that I've had in a long time."

"Better than the club?"

"Oh, miles better than the club."

"Great, because I happen to agree."

"I'm glad we're on the same page."

The two of them smiled at each other. Everything had been so wonderful up until this part. If this was a normal date between two normal people, Caleb would have leaned in to try to kiss her. But this wasn't a normal date, and they weren't normal people.

"I should, uh, probably go," he said.

"Yeah, right. I should, uh…" she pointed upstairs.

God, this got so awkward so fast.

"I'll see you tomorrow at Hallie's, okay?"

"Yeah, I'll see you then."

"Goodnight, Lily."

"Night Caleb."

Chapter Nineteen

When Kiara had realised that Caleb wasn't going to be arriving any time soon, marking the first time *he* had ever been late to one of their training sessions, she had laid down in the middle of the mats and closed her eyes. Thanks to Caleb's training, she found it very easy to quiet her mind these days. It helped when she was trying to get to sleep because it shut down all the thoughts of the day and allowed her to nod off with little trouble. In this case, it was nice to just catch her breath before another several-hour-long session of exercises.

Kiara was able to drift so far away from the room that she didn't notice that there was anyone else there, so the 'hello' came as a surprise.

Her eyes flew open to find Master Mahmid standing over her, a small smile tugging at his features. His hair was more gray than black, but he still had a thick head of it. The stubble on his face wasn't what she expected from someone who headed up such an important organisation, but then she hadn't known what to expect really considering how little Caleb actually spoke about his mentor. She had seen him once before, yes, but she had been drugged to the gills and very confused.

"Hi," she said, remembering her manners somewhere in the middle of her thoughts. "Caleb didn't mention you were coming."

"To be fair to him, he didn't know."

Master Mahmid offered her a hand up, which she gladly accepted.

"I wasn't expecting you to…" he trailed off, suddenly looking unsure of himself.

"Be lounging around on the floor when I should be training? Noooo, It's not usually like this. Usually it's all go-go Chosen-ness," she said, making a punching motion with both of her hands one after the other.

Master Mahmid let out a soft laugh. "I was going to say that I wasn't expecting you to look so much like your father."

"Oh. Um, yeah, that would have made more sense."

"It's the hair, more than anything."

Kiara ran her fingers through her red locks, looking at it with a smile.

"I didn't find that out until recently, when Lily showed me her old pictures. I have his smile too, big and goofy."

"Joyful," Master Mahmid said as an alternative.

"Yeah?"

"Yes. No matter how bad things got, Peter could always see the positive side in everything. He didn't experience life in half measures, he made every second count."

Kiara was grateful every time Lily talked about him, because she got another glimpse into the man who could have been her Dad from a little sister's perspective. Master Mahmid had a completely different one, that of a student and maybe a friend?

"I'm trying to do the same. Training makes it hard at times, but I fit in fun wherever I can."

"With Caleb?"

Kiara wasn't sure how to answer that question. Caleb felt like he was on a very tight leash after hers and Hallie's near-death experience. The ominous silence from the Citadel hadn't been helping. Kiara didn't want to get him into trouble. But then, her silence might give it away.

"You can say yes," he told her.

"I just… he works so hard, I don't want you to think that he doesn't. He's such a good teacher, I can't imagine going through this with anyone else."

"I've known Caleb a long time. I know he puts everything into what he does, you don't have to worry."

"Good," Kiara sighed with relief.

"And all of his reports have been promising, I just wanted to make him squirm a little after the stunt he pulled."

Apparently Master Mahmid had a bit of a crafty side.

"Is it different mentoring other Guardians to Chosen?" she asked, curious. She wondered how his methods differed watching over someone like Caleb compared to someone like her Dad.

"Chosen are much more likely to listen, because they know that their life hangs in the balance. Guardians in training can be harder to handle. It depends on their temperament."

"What was Caleb like when he first turned up looking for training?"

Master Mahmid pursed his lips in thought. "Enthusiastic. Quite a lot of recruits that we see know or have known a Guardian, whereas Caleb came armed with his research and a lot of questions. I haven't mentored anyone else who is as eager to learn and to be the best they can be."

"You see, it's funny, because even when I'm not getting things, he's always so calm and patient with me."

"That's because he's trying to be the best teacher for you. Sometimes others need a different style. His second Chosen, Eduardo, was full of fire and could barely sit still. It took a lot more management to get him to do as he was told. Caleb learned the hard way with that one, but it made him a better mentor in the long run."

"Hallie can be a bit like that sometimes. No wonder he takes her in his stride in class," Kiara smiled.

"Your girlfriend was how you and Caleb met?" Master Mahmid asked.

"Yeah, the class overran because Hallie would not stop asking questions. I snuck into the room, so I could watch them going back and forth, it was great. Hallie wasn't very focused throughout her first year of classes, so to see her grilling him like that was as cool as it was funny. It was like a game of verbal tennis. She introduced me after the rest of the class managed to escape. I think Caleb and I have quite a lot in common, we just didn't realise that until all of this happened."

"Hmmmm. Caleb has always been more involved with Chosen than he should be, but knowing about your history, I can see why you connected. I don't begrudge him the friendships he makes, but the closer you get the harder it is to let that person go when the time comes."

Kiara nodded. She didn't know how to comprehend how difficult it was going to be when that day arrived, when she had to let go of everything and everyone she held dear. However hard it was for her, it was going to be worse for those who had to go on without her.

"Becoming an Elder was an easy choice from that perspective."

"You don't have to carry that burden around with you anymore," Kiara said.

"I still do to some extent. Nine Chosen over the course of nearly three decades was bound to take its toll. However, I can now pass that experience and wisdom onto others to help them cope. Sometimes they listen, sometimes they don't."

The more she talked to Master Mahmid, the more she could see how he had influenced Caleb. Whatever relationship Caleb thought the two of them had, it was clear to her that Master Mahmid cared for him more than he would ever admit aloud.

"Do you still remember all your Chosen?" she asked.

"Every detail. The situations that you are put into as Guardian and Chosen mean that, even if you are able to stay emotionally unattached, you still form an immense bond. You spend so much time with them that they become impossible to forget."

That made sense. If she was in Caleb's shoes, and him in hers, she knew that she would never forget him.

"What was my Dad like as a student?"

"Attentive and determined. There was a lot to pick up very quickly and he took it all in his stride. He was willing to do anything so long as it meant helping others. My only regret is that I didn't realise that he had a family beyond his parents and his sister. I would have urged him to spend more time with your mother while he still could."

If Master Mahmid had said that at the beginning of the conversation, Kiara would have been surprised. But now she was starting to see that there were a lot of layers to the man standing before her and he very purposefully only let people see the surface.

"I'm sorry I'm late," Caleb banged in through the door, bringing their chat to a sudden end. It took him a moment to realise Kiara wasn't alone. He'd clearly been in a rush because he was wearing his glasses.

"Oh, hey." He stood up a little straighter when he saw Master Mahmid. "You didn't call ahead?"

"It wasn't a planned trip. I thought I would come meet Kiara for myself, seeing as you've been singing her praises."

"I see that you have… Met her, I mean" Caleb said, unsure as to what had happened since Master Mahmid arrived.

"You never told me how cool he was," Kiara said, to ease some of the tension.

"Cool?"

"You don't have to sound so skeptical," Master Mahmid said.

Kiara knew that he was teasing, but Caleb laughed nervously.

"We were just talking about Guardians and Chosen, a little bit about my Dad. Master Mahmid was imparting his wisdom, which was very helpful."

"See? Nothing to be concerned about," Master Mahmid confirmed.

This did seem to help a little. Caleb started to look a less awkward.

"Now, let's you and I have a chat," Master Mahmid told Caleb, gesturing for them to go back outside.

Before they did, he looked back at Kiara and offered her a hand to shake.

"I'm glad I got to meet you," he said.

Kiara smiled as she grasped his hand. "Me too," she said, truly meaning it.

~

Considering what happened when Caleb first became Kiara's Guardian, Ezra had been concerned. It wasn't possible for Caleb to detach himself from the people he mentored, whether he was with them for a matter of months or a couple of years. For him to have befriended his Chosen beforehand was unheard of in their order. The unprecedented situation had almost got him removed, but Ezra had used all the pull he had to make sure that didn't happen. He could see now that had paid off.

Kiara had flourished faster than anyone Ezra had ever seen come through their doors. It was their bond that allowed them to be such a good team and to help Kiara progress at such a magnificent pace. But it was also Caleb's skill as a teacher.

Ezra appreciated the fact that he had got to speak to Kiara before Caleb had arrived. It had been insightful, in more ways than one.

"So?" Caleb asked, looking up at his mentor as he waited for Ezra's judgment.

"Like father, like daughter," Ezra smiled.

"That's a good thing, right?"

"I'm not in the habit of assigning favourites, but Peter was one of the most agreeable and determined Chosen that I ever met. It seems the apple doesn't fall from the tree."

Any lingering tension faded, allowing Caleb to look pleased.

"I don't say this enough, but you're a fine teacher, Caleb. You've proven our decision to let you stay as her Guardian right."

"Thank you," Caleb said sincerely as he adjusted his glasses. "And I would never usually say this, but your approval means a lot to me."

"I know," Ezra smirked.

"You couldn't just take the compliment?"

"I saw an opportunity and I seized it. They don't come up very often with the company I usually keep."

"Hmm, yeah, the other Elders seem like a hoot," Caleb said.

"A laugh a minute," Ezra agreed.

He had missed having conversations like this with Caleb. They didn't happen much, but when they did they were always memorable. Their relationship had been particularly strained these last couple of months, hopefully all that would change.

"Now that you've convinced me that Kiara is ready, what would you have her do next?" Ezra asked him.

"I think it's time for her first mission."

"I'm inclined to agree."

"My contact at MI6 says that she has something that could prove to be a little challenging but should go smoothly so long as we stick to her plan," Caleb said.

"The risk is yours," Ezra told him. "But I trust your judgment."

Caleb reached up and squeezed his mentor's shoulder appreciatively.

"I guess I should go back inside and tell Kiara the good news," he said. "Want to join us for the rest of the session?"

"I'd be honoured."

Chapter Twenty

"Are you shaking?" Caleb asked.

"It's cold outside," Kiara said, making excuses.

"Not that cold," he teased.

"Shut up, you're just making me more nervous. I've never been to an event like this before, I don't know how to act fancy."

"You want to know a secret?"

Kiara nodded her head.

Caleb leaned in a little closer and whispered in her ear, "Neither do I."

Kiara laughed and linked her arm with his, smiling across at him.

Caleb was glad that he was able to put her at ease. This wasn't usually the sort of thing that they would do on a first mission as it required a little undercover work. However, when Zoe asked him if they were up for it, Caleb felt confident enough to say yes. Stealing encrypted information was a good test of Kiara's senses, as she would have to be alert at all times. There was also only a slight chance of conflict, something he would prefer to avoid.

He gave the names that Zoe told him to use at the door. They didn't have to pose as husband and wife. There was a little too big of an age difference to believe that was true, so they stuck with friends.

"Let's go over to the bar," he suggested, knowing that it would be a good place for Kiara to wait around while he sorted out the security.

"Free booze, me likey."

"That is definitely the sort of low class jibber jabber that will get you thrown out of here," he said, pretending to be patronising.

Kiara snorted loudly, then hid her face in his shoulder.

"Oh God."

"You'll be fine," he promised as he guided her over to a free spot at the bar.

"I'll try to keep those sorts of noises to a minimum."

"Good."

Caleb ordered them a couple of virgin cocktails, so they could stay focused. To others it would look like they were as tipsy as everyone else.

"Now, do you remember the plan?" he asked.

Kiara took a sip from her glass, looking pleased that he had remembered her tendency towards fruity drinks.

"I wait here while you go and tap into the security system, try not to attract too much attention. That might be difficult in this dress."

Caleb chuckled.

"When you let me know over our cool new earpieces that you're ready, I sneak upstairs to the Emerald Suite, you let me in. I plug the memory stick into the guy's laptop, grab the information and go. You will warn me if anyone is coming my way."

"Perfect. And what's the first rule if something goes wrong?"

"Don't panic."

Caleb smiled. "You got this."

"Yeah, I do. Go do your thing," she said.

"Yes ma'am."

Caleb squeezed her hand before slipping away into the crowd. So long as nothing went horribly wrong, they could be in and out in an hour and no one would be the wiser.

~

The confidence that Kiara had been buoyed with by Caleb's pep talk slowly started to fade the further he moved away. This was the first time she had been all alone since they started her training. Like Hallie had told her before she left the apartment, she was allowed to be a little nervous. She would need the adrenaline to get her through this without a hitch.

Kiara decided to focus on polishing off both hers and Caleb's drinks, so that she didn't catch anyone's eye. It would be better that way as she wouldn't actively invite anyone's attention on herself. She didn't know how long it was going to take for Caleb to hack into the system, so she had to remain alert.

"Is this seat taken?"

"There aren't any--" Kiara cut herself off, realising that was just a line.

When she looked up, there was a tall, suave man dressed in a very expensive suit grinning down at her. He was tan, definitely some sort of Middle Eastern influence in his heritage, but something else as well that she couldn't place. Despite this, he spoke with a smooth American accent.

"Very funny," she said in effort not to be flustered by him catching her off guard.

"I thought so," he said, clearly very pleased with himself.

It seemed like the sort of self-assurance that might get tiresome after a while.

"I'm Noah," he said, holding out a hand for her to shake.

"Kiara," she replied, taking it and shaking firmly once.

She really wanted to tell him to buzz off, but she didn't want to cause a fuss.

"Are you a donor or a guest?" he asked.

This was probably a way of finding out if she had someone with her that could come back at any moment and spoil his fun.

"Guest," she said.

"Ditto," he said, which surprised her. "My date insisted I wear this, he didn't think jeans and loafers would fit in with this crowd."

He. Kiara wasn't expecting that either. She *seriously* had to stop assuming things. It was doing to be the death of her.

"Why aren't you over there with him?"

"Him and his friends are talking business, I've never been very good at handling that side of things."

This sounded like something that could lead into a deeper conversation if she asked the follow up question, but she didn't have time to chit chat. She should probably try to escape.

"What does your donor do?" he asked.

"He's a, uh… life coach."

"Oh really? I didn't realise life coaches made that much money."

"They do if they're as good as he is."

Kiara really needed to get away before he found another way to continue the conversation. She was in the middle of concocting an excuse to escape the bar when she saw someone in the crowd who she recognised, but it wasn't Caleb. It was a face she had only seen in pictures, but she was sure it was him.

"Excuse me, I've just… I've got to go," she said, completely distracted.

Kiara didn't look back in case she lost the other guy in the crowd, so she wasn't able to see the expression on Noah's face as she disappeared into the sea of people on the dancefloor.

She did, however, hear a faint, "See you around."

No, she wouldn't.

The guy she was following was fast, almost disappearing out of her sight a few times before she spotted him again. It looked like he was looking for someone too as he moved about the room, head turning left and right.

As they neared the edge of the crowd and Kiara closed the gap between them, she called out to him to try and stop him from vanishing before she could talk to him.

"Will!"

Kiara wasn't sure how he heard her over the din that was going on around them, but he did, slowly turning his head in confusion. He had a beard now, and a lot more muscle, but it was definitely him.

It was Hallie's brother.

~

Caleb always spent time studying the blueprints for a mission if they were available. It was good to have other escape routes if things went wrong, but it also helped him to figure out which were the best places to tap into the hotel's systems. Hitting the security room was never a good option, not unless you had no other choice. This time his plan was to access one of the terminals in the server room and go from there. He had to take a roundabout way of reaching the room, though, so the hotel's security didn't figure out where he was going right away.

Cutting through the kitchen, Caleb skirted around the busy hotel staff, careful not to make eye contact so they were less likely to remember his face. Everything smelled so good, it made his stomach rumble. He should have grabbed one of the hors d'oeuvres on the way past.

Caleb left the kitchen and turned down a passageway to reach the service elevator, which needed a staff passkey. It was a good thing that Zoe had given him one earlier. He used the elevator to go up to the top floor, then made his way quickly down the corridor to the left, away from the suites, to the server room.

Using the pass on the door again, Caleb stepped inside and shut the door silently behind him. He was ready to turn around and start tapping into the nearest terminal, but when he spun on his heel, he discovered that there was someone else in there with him, and she already had access to everything.

"Who are you?" he asked, making the woman jump.

The woman was around average height for a woman, slight of build, and dressed head to toe in black. Her head whipped round to reveal her face, which was when he saw that she was Chinese and… if he wasn't mistaken, sort of familiar to him.

She looked struck by his presence, and not because she hadn't been expecting anyone to walk in on her hacking the hotel's systems. Her face suggested that she was shaken, right down to her very core.

"Caleb?"

It was his turn to look taken aback.

"How do you know my name?"

The woman closed her eyes and tried to calm her shaking hands.

"This can't be real, you're supposed to be dead."

"What do you mean I'm supposed to be dead? Who *are* you?" Caleb demanded, feeling his own nerves begin to fray with the anticipation.

The woman opened her dark eyes and looked directly at him, so the seriousness of her words couldn't be doubted.

"I'm Diana Yu, but my married name was Lau. I am your mother."

The silence that followed the revelation was deafening. Caleb began shaking his head without realising that he was doing it. She took a step towards him, but he also took a step back, slamming backwards into the door by accident.

"No, both my parents died," he stammered.

"I thought the same about you and John, it's what I was told by the Elders after you were both taken from me."

"The Elders? Taken from you? What?"

Caleb was so bewildered by all of this. If what she was saying was true, then there were people who he loved who had been lying to him for almost his entire life. It wasn't something that he could easily accept.

"There was an accident. I took you on a scouting mission when I should have left you at home, but your father wasn't around, and you begged me to let you come. I thought it would be harmless enough, but then I was spotted. We got into a chase and I crashed the car. You hit your head on the dashboard. It took me so long to get you to a healer that they thought you might not make it."

Caleb reached up to touch the small scar under his hairline.

"Aunt Mee told me there was a car accident that killed my Mom, but I survived. That was how I got the scar." It was supposed to have been bad luck that his Dad died so soon.

"She lied. Everyone lied."

Everyone lied.

"What happened then?" he asked, but he could hear his voice shaking.

"I broke the order's rules by letting you know that Guardians existed, but the accident made them and John furious. They said I was a danger to you and that I wasn't fit to be your mother, so they locked me up for long enough to take you away. I was told that you both died in that plane crash."

Caleb frowned.

"You're the reason that no one can have families?"

"Everyone always places the blame on me, but they were the ones who made the decision to rip ours and everyone else's families apart. We could have found a way to make it work, changed the rules, but they overreacted, as always," she said, her temper starting to flare.

"You almost got me killed and you think—" he stopped mid-sentence, too upset to continue. "You know what, no, I don't have to listen to this."

Caleb turned to open the door, but Diana reached past him and held it shut. The expression on her face was intimidating as all hell.

"I lost you once," she told him, her face barely an inch from his now.

"I'm not going through that again."

~

Diana had told Will that this would be easy. It was the same as always, find the Guardian and Chosen, convince them, and get out. The difference this time was that they knew that they would be here, but not what they looked like. Her plan was to tap into the security, see who moved to complete the mission, and catch them before they left. But, of course, things were rarely that simple.

Particularly when someone he swore he had never met before called out his name in the middle of the ballroom.

Will approached the red-head cautiously, stopped in front of her and looked down.

"Do I know you?"

"No, but I know your sister. I'm Kiara, Hallie's girlfriend."

Hallie? She knew Hallie?

For her to be able to pick him out of a crowd, she had to have seen pictures of him, and only three people in his life had those; his parents and his sister. It could be a trap, but… One look at her hazel eyes and he could see that she was sincere.

"Come with me," he said, placing a hand on the small of her back so that he could guide her into one of the small function rooms. They needed privacy.

"Is Hallie here?" he asked, once they had closed the doors.

"No, she's back at her apartment, probably wondering how I'm doing. She would freak out if she knew that you were here too," she said, sounding excited.

"Is she okay? How's everything been for her?"

"Yeah, she's great. There's a lot of stuff that's been going on recently, but she's been studying here at King's College, which is how I met her. She misses you so much, so, so much, I can't even begin to…"

Kiara stopped when she realised she was babbling and looked up at him again, tilting her head when she saw the expression on his face.

"Where have you been?" she asked.

"I can't tell you," he said.

"Why not? What have you been doing all this time that's been more important than your family?"

His guilt flared up again hearing someone who cared a lot about his sister angry that he hadn't even called Hallie to check she was okay.

"You couldn't even begin to understand."

"Try me."

Will couldn't do it, not this close to him and Diana achieving everything she had ever wanted. Not this close to--

"Caleb?" Kiara said suddenly, pressing her fingers to her ear like she had some sort of earpiece in.

Wait, was she the one here for the mission?

"I'm coming," she told him, suddenly looking panicked.

"My friend's in trouble, I'm sorry, I--"

"No, let's go," he said, ushering her towards the door.

Will knew this wasn't exactly what he was here for, but if she ended up being the Guardian or the Chosen, then helping her was bound to win him points when he tried to convince her to join him and Diana. Her already having a strong connection to his sister would too.

Both of the lifts were being used, so they took the stairs instead. Kiara had to ditch her heels at the bottom, but once she did, they sprinted up them, Will following behind to make sure that she didn't trip on her dress and fall.

They were racing so fast that he hadn't even realised where they were going until they reached the door to the server room and Kiara threw herself against it to send it crashing open.

Oh no.

Diana and a man, presumably Caleb, were both standing in the middle of the room, looking overcome with emotion. Kiara darted to Caleb's side, grabbing his arm and looking up at him.

"What's happening? What's wrong?" she asked.

Will moved to stand beside Diana instead, his confusion clear.

"This is him, this is my son," Diana told him, looking back at Caleb.

"I thought you said your Mum was dead?" Kiara said.

"It turns out that a lot of people lied to me about my family too," he said.

Will couldn't believe this was happening. Obviously, it was great that Diana's son wasn't dead. But the fact that he was the Guardian that they were trying to recruit, and his sister's girlfriend was the Chosen… It was exactly the sort of drama that they didn't need right now.

"Why are you both here?" Kiara asked Diana and Will, fuming over the fact that Caleb was so upset.

"We can't do this here," Will said before Diana could start speaking. "Someone will have seen us both running up to the room, we have to go before security comes."

Diana knew he was right. She looked directly at her son.

"I need you to come with me, so I can explain everything."

Caleb shook his head. "I'm not going anywhere with you."

"And I'm not leaving without you."

Will lunged forward to try and seize Caleb, but Kiara blocked him and drove her fist into his face in retaliation.

"Don't you dare lay a hand on him!"

Will shook off the surprise and grabbed her by both shoulders, so that he could lift her off the ground.

"I'm sorry," he said as he threw her onto the floor, where Diana pinned her.

Will made another move towards Caleb, but he had pissed off the Guardian as well by hurting his Chosen. It seemed that hadn't been a wise idea, because even with his heightened senses and his training, he could barely block the flurry of attacks that came his way. Fist and foot, and knee and fist… It seemed like it would never end. That was until Will finally saw an opening and was able to catch one of Caleb's wrists, twisting it hard enough to make a cracking sound before flipping him over onto his back.

"Stay down," Will told him, but was distracted by Diana crying out.

He thought that she would have been able to cover a fledgling Chosen, but Kiara had somehow got the upper hand and was laying into her with enough fury to cover both her and Caleb combined.

Will tried to stop Kiara, but she saw him coming. A swift knee to the balls was all it took to make him slump to the floor in blinding pain.

"Get after them!" he heard Diana shout, but he was paralysed.

Through his blurred vision, he watched as Kiara hoisted Caleb up off the floor. The pair of them bolted for the door and didn't look back.

Chapter Twenty-One

Caleb had said he needed some time alone, but he didn't know why. The last thing he needed to be was alone after what he had just discovered. Kiara had fussed over him all the way back to Hallie's apartment, where she and Lily were waiting to find out how it had gone. They were worried too, but he hadn't been able to handle all of them trying to tell him that it was going to be okay. Now that he was standing outside in the cold night air, he realised how ungrateful he had been up there.

Loosening another button on his shirt, he took a deep breath to prepare himself to go back inside, but a voice stopped him.

"Caleb."

Caleb shook his head and looked round at his Mom, standing there in the shadow of the building.

"Did you follow me?"

"I put a phone in the pocket of your jacket when I stopped you from leaving."

A quick check of his tux proved that she wasn't lying.

"I just want to talk," she said.

"I thought I made myself very clear back at the hotel."

"You didn't give me a chance to explain," she told him.

"It's hard to keep listening to you when you're the reason that I grew up with no parents," he shot back.

"You have no idea how much it hurt me to not have you in my life," she said, only increasing the tension between them.

"No idea?! I was four years old! I've had to live the last three decades with no idea about my heritage, no real parental guidance, can you imagine how hard that must have been? Do you think maybe I understand how much it hurts to be separated from my family?"

Diana shook her head. "It's not the same as a mother losing her child."

"No, you do not get to play that card. You do not get to play any cards with me. If you had been a good mother to me, then you wouldn't have let me go along with you in the first place. None of this would have happened. All of that pain would be erased."

"You weren't there, you don't know what it was like," his Mom said, frustrated.

"I don't care. I don't want to hear it. I want you to leave me the fuck alone."

This time Caleb strode away, but she still chased him. She darted in front of him, barring his access to the door.

"Don't make me hurt you," he warned.

He was prepared to do it if it meant getting away from her.

"No," she said, holding firm. "You have to hear me out."

"I don't *have* to do anything."

"I want to tell you how I'm going to change everything for the better."

"You can't," he said.

"I want to try. The way things are now at the Citadel, the strict regime that the Elders have for the way this world works, it's not fair. If they had given me a second chance, then we never would have been in this situation in the first place. Now all they do is keep secrets and put their people down."

"You're exaggerating," he said.

Caleb knew that they were stern, that things had to be just so, but they had their reasons. If the whole word knew about what Chosen, Oracles and healers could do then everything would change, not for the better.

"Oh really? You think they haven't told you lies?" she said. "Do you know Ezra Mahmid?"

Caleb frowned. "He's my mentor, what's he got to do with this?"

His Mom laughed bitterly.

"Ezra was there in the hospital with me the day you were born."

"No," Caleb said, unable to take another earth shattering revelation.

"Yes," she continued. "He was my sparring partner, my confidant, my best friend. We gave you a Hebrew name so that you would always have a connection to him. Yet he's been lying to your face this whole time."

"No," Caleb murmured.

"Listen to me," she said as she seized his head in her hands, forcing him to look at her. "Things have to change. I have an army of people at my back and I'm going to tear the old regime asunder to make sure that nothing like what happened to us ever happens to anyone again. It would mean everything to me if you were by my side."

Caleb looked into her eyes, which were his eyes. The fire she held inside her was burning so brightly that it was blinding. Many would have crumbled in that moment, but he had been taught better.

"I'm part of that old regime," he said. "I can't let you hurt the people I care about just to prove to the Elders that they're wrong."

"Caleb, please…"

He secured her wrists, pulling her arms down so that he was in control.

"You're coming with me."

For the briefest of moments, Caleb could see the devastation in her eyes before it turned into determination.

"No, I'm not."

If what happened next was any indication, she had been taking it easy on them earlier. Despite the warning, his Mom was able to twist out of his grasp, elbow him hard in the stomach and throw him back against the door. His eyes watered as he struggled for breath, slumping over onto the cold concrete.

"Don't get in my way," was her final warning as she disappeared into the night.

~

"Do you think he's going to be okay?" Lily asked, pacing back and forth across the living room.

Poor Caleb hadn't been able to get out of the apartment fast enough once he had made sure that Kiara was safely home. They all knew he hadn't gone far but were worried about him all the same. Kiara most of all. She had been there moments after his world had got turned upside down. The pain that he was feeling had to be overwhelming.

She had only managed to get bits and pieces out of him on the long walk to Hallie's apartment, all of which she told Lily and Hallie as soon as he went outside. Hallie had grabbed a bowl of warm water and a towel and was busying herself tending to Kiara's busted lip, making sure it was clean before she healed it.

"I don't know," Kiara admitted, then winced when her wound stung.

"How hard did you bite his Mom?" Hallie asked.

"Hard enough to get her to let me go," Kiara said quietly.

"She tried to take on the two of you by herself?"

Hallie was obviously trying to get everything straight in her head. Unfortunately, what Kiara had to tell her wasn't going to make any of this any easier.

"No, she had someone with her."

Hallie looked confused. "Who?"

"Will."

"My Will?"

Kiara nodded.

There were plenty of different ways that Hallie could have reacted, but she wouldn't have put her money on dead silence.

"How?"

"I can only assume that he's been with Caleb's Mom all this time."

"But why?"

"His reflexes were fast. If I had to guess, I would say that he's like me."

"A Chosen?"

"Yeah."

Hallie ran her fingers through her messy hair.

"Why would he be hanging out with her though?"

"I don't know, I didn't get a chance to ask."

They might never get a chance to either if Will and Caleb's Mom went back into hiding.

Hallie started to ask another question when the door banged open and Caleb stumbled through it, clutching his stomach and wheezing.

"Oh my God!" Lily exclaimed.

She and Kiara both bolted over to him, each taking an arm, so they could steer him to the sofa and place him where Kiara had just been sitting.

"What happened?" Hallie asked, forgetting all about their conversation for now.

Caleb gestured to his pocket instead of speaking. Lily pulled out a phone.

"She tracked us," he coughed.

"Your Mum?"

He nodded at Kiara, then looked across at Lily who stroked his face gently with her hand. She was probably feeling everything that he was feeling, because of her abilities and their bond.

"What did she say?" Kiara looked to either of them for an answer.

"She's planning an attack on the Citadel," Lily said for him.

"An attack, why?"

"Diana blames the Elders for splitting up her family. She wants to take everything apart so that she can build something new in its place."

So that was what she had wanted to talk about back at the gala.

"She can't do that," Kiara said. "What about the collateral damage?"

"She doesn't seem to care so long as it gets her what she wants."

Lily wiped away a tear from Caleb's cheek, leaning in so that she could hold him in her arms. He had been through so much in such a short space of time. This had to have hit him like a ton of bricks.

"Screw that," Hallie said, taking charge. "I don't care if she's your Mom, we can't let her have her revenge, not at the expense of others. Get that Mahmid guy on the phone right now, I'll tell him what's up."

"They need time to prepare," Kiara agreed. "Your Mom showed her hand, if she doesn't move fast then she loses her chance of striking altogether."

"I'll tell him," Caleb managed, wrapping his arm around Lily. "Just give me a minute."

Caleb and Lily had given Kiara all the time she needed to adjust after she found out the truth about her family, the least they could give him was a few minutes.

~

Will watched anxiously from the bathroom doorway as Diana proceeded to tear apart their hotel room. He had been able to tell that her talk with Caleb hadn't gone well by the thunderous look on her face when she came through the door, but he had retreated when she had begun throwing things in an effort to sate the emotions that had to be eating her from the inside out.

He had never seen her become this unhinged before. Will could count the number of times they'd had meaningful conversations about family on one hand. He had suspected, but never experienced, how badly what happened to her son had been affecting her. But this was different. Now she knew he was alive and he still didn't want her in his life.

After several minutes of chaos, Diana let out one final cry and collapsed to the floor, losing her face in her hands.

Will waited a moment before approaching her, kicking some of the debris away from her with his foot so he could sit down behind her and pull her against his chest. She resisted at first, but gave in when he wouldn't relent, crumpling into him.

"I couldn't make him see," she said, her voice hoarse from all the noise. "He doesn't want anything to do with me."

"I'm sorry," Will said quietly, holding her even tighter.

It must have felt like she was losing her son all over again.

They stayed there like that for a while, Will sitting quietly as Diana muddled through everything in her head and steadily calmed down. When she eventually pulled away, she looked a lot more like her composed self again.

"I'm sorry, you shouldn't have had to see me like that," she said.

"Don't worry about it," he smiled. "I think after four years by your side, I can survive one break down."

Diana snorted, although she didn't look to be in a laughing mood.

"What do you want to do now?" he asked her.

Surely finding out that Caleb was alive and that he was a Guardian would affect her plans. She wouldn't want to put him in harm's way. He was worried about Hallie and she wasn't actually involved in any of this, not directly.

"We make our way back to camp, get everyone ready to mobilise."

Will couldn't help but look surprised.

"Nothing's changed," she said. "Now there's even more reason to overthrow the Elders and their regime. Once they're out of the way, Caleb won't be under their influence anymore and he'll see how much better this life can be without them."

"Oh, okay."

"What's wrong?"

Will shook his head. "It's nothing. I assumed, but I should have known that you wouldn't give this up now."

Diana didn't look like she believed him 100%, which meant that her intuition was as sharp as ever, but she didn't pursue it.

"Get a couple of hours sleep, we'll leave on the first flight out," she told him.

Just like that, it was all back to business for her. Will wasn't so sure he could do the same.

One Week Later
Chapter Twenty-Two

Everything had begun to move very quickly after Caleb told Master Mahmid what had happened the night of the gala. It was clear that an attack was imminent, so they had to start calling back the Guardians and Chosen who were still loyal, which included Caleb and Kiara. Hallie had been adamant that she was going too. There was no way she was watching either of them go off to fight and staying behind so she could fret. Lily had much the same reaction, except calmer. They were all going, there was no changing their minds.

It was the night before their flight to Italy and Hallie was almost ready to go. There had been a lot of running around getting all the stuff she and Kiara needed for an extended stay in Europe. They had imagined travelling across the continent together after they had both graduated, but life had a funny way of messing with your dreams. If they made it through the ordeal ahead intact, they were taking a vacation afterwards. They deserved it after the last few months.

Hallie had left Kiara sorting out the last of their clothes to take out the trash. She didn't want her apartment reeking of banana peels and half eaten chicken when she returned. That would be gross.

She had just lifted the lid on the building's big, plastic rubbish bin when she heard footsteps approaching behind her out of the darkness.

"Back off!" Hallie cried out, brandishing the trash bag in the lurker's direction.

The person immediately raised their hands in surrender, stepping into the light so that she could see his face.

"Will?"

She let out a huge sigh of relief.

"God, I thought you were going to murder me."

"I think that would have been--"

He didn't manage to finish his sentence because suddenly he was being slapped across head with a dirty sack of old food.

"Where the hell have you been?!" she demanded, switching from relief to pissed beyond belief in under five seconds.

Hallie had every reason to be angry with him. It had been almost four years since any of their family had seen Will alive, they were all worried sick. She still wouldn't have known anything if Kiara hadn't seen him at the gala with Caleb's Mom.

"Just let me--"

Will caught the bag with his hand when she raised it to smack him again, throwing it to the ground. They squared off, only a couple of inches between them in height. It was like they were kids again and Will had just stolen Hallie's toy car.

"Didn't your girlfriend explain?"

"Well, yuh. But I want to hear it from you, the jerk who abandoned his entire family without so much as a word."

Will looked wounded, but she wouldn't take it back. She hurt more.

"I had to leave. I couldn't stick around knowing that I was going to die. It would have been such a burden on all of you."

"Don't you think we deserved that choice? Instead of sparing us pain, you only caused more of it! I've been worried about you every day since you left, wondering where you were or if you were even still alive. That wasn't fair."

"I wasn't..." Will stopped and started again. "It would have been worse if I stayed."

"How are you supposed to know what would have been worse? I've been going through all of this with Kiara and sticking together is what has made it bearable," she said. "You just don't want to admit to yourself that we're not the reason you left."

"Oh yeah?"

"Yeah. You were scared, you freaked out, you didn't want to be the cause of our pain and so you ran. It was all about you, Will, not us. We love you so much that we would have taken anything just to be able to spend this time with you. But you took that away from us."

Will started to look guilty.

"These last four years we could have been visiting all the places on your list, eating ridiculous amounts of junk food, spending time as a family. All that time you stole, we can't get back. It's gone. How were you expecting me to feel about it?"

It didn't look like he knew.

Will slumped back from her, becoming smaller physically and figuratively.

"I didn't think," he said.

"No, of course you didn't. If you had, then none of this would be happening right now. We wouldn't be on opposite sides of a stupid fight about stupid revenge."

"No, wait," he went to defend Caleb's Mom, but a sharp laugh from him cut him off before he could really start.

"Don't you dare. If you had seen how heartbroken Caleb was after what happened that night, you wouldn't bother trying to protect her."

"Caleb wasn't the only one who was heartbroken that night."

This took Hallie by surprise.

"*You* didn't see Diana when she came back from trying to convince him to join her, she was an absolute mess. I've never seen her fall apart like that before."

Hallie opened and closed her mouth.

"Does this mean that she's reconsidering?"

Will shook his head. "If anything, it spurred her on."

"Well, there's goes my sympathy," Hallie said.

"How can you still stand beside her when you know how many people could get hurt by this, including me and my friends?"

"I..." Will faltered. "I don't know."

Hallie looked at his face, seeing the confusion there. He had been committed to Diana for who knew how long, but one argument with her and his resolve was crumbling. The Guardian hadn't been able to break his loyalty to his family, not really.

"You don't have to follow her to the end of this road. You can change your mind."

"Hallie..."

"You want to tell me it's not that easy, but it is, Will. Diana was doing this because she thought her son was dead, but he's not, he's alive. She should be able to take anything else up with those who wronged her, she doesn't have to attack a Citadel full of people to get what she wants. You have to see that she's being unreasonable."

Will rubbed his forehead the back of his hand, taking a moment to hide behind his arm as he considered what she was saying.

"I can, but…"

"But what?"

"I've been at her side all this time. If I turn on her now, then it'll be like I'm betraying her as badly as Mahmid and the others did all those years ago."

"That's not your problem."

Will didn't look so sure.

Hallie reached out to him and took his hand in hers, squeezing it gently.

"Will, please. We've spent so much time apart. I don't want whatever time you have left to involve us fighting."

He looked into her pleading brown eyes, the same eyes that had ended so many of their arguments over the years, then linked his fingers with hers.

"I want to say yes, but I can't do anything without talking to her."

Hallie's fingers began to slip away from his, but he kept a hold of them.

"I know how dumb I've been. I'm going to try and make this right. Can you at least believe that much?"

It took her a moment, but she nodded.

"Thank you."

Without asking for permission, Will wrapped her up in a bone crushing hug. If she wasn't so tired of missing him, she might have protested, but the truth was that she'd forgotten how good it felt to be smooshed under his big, strong arms.

"I love you," he said. "Whatever happens, that's never going to change."

"I love you too."

Hallie would have usually followed that with some sort of insult or quip, but she didn't want to ruin the moment in case this ended up being the last time she ever saw him.

Will eventually pulled away, putting a little distance between them, she assumed so that he wasn't tempted to stay.

"I'll see you around," he said. "Stay out of trouble, Trouble."

"Right back atcha, Big T," she replied with a tight lipped but genuine smile.

A couple of steps back and, just like that, her brother was gone.

Hallie didn't know where exactly he was headed, or how his talk with Diana would turn out, but she hoped that she would see him again. After all, parting was supposed to be sweet sorrow. It wasn't supposed to suck.

Chapter Twenty-Three

Will felt sick. His stomach had been churning the whole overnight train ride back from London, worrying about what was going to happen. Hallie hadn't been gentle with him, which was probably what he had needed. He had spent so much time in his head assuming how it would go that everything had got twisted. She brought him straight back to reality. He had been selfish and stupid, he knew that now. However, knowing that he had her to go back to wouldn't make talking to Diana any easier. He wanted to see her get what she wanted because her ideas, when you boiled them down, were the direction he believed the Guardian order should go. But he couldn't stand by and see his sister get hurt when he knew he could have stopped it and he certainly couldn't be the one to hurt her anymore.

"There you are," Diana said.

The woman had been waiting outside his tent, no doubt wondering what was taking so long. All he had said was that he had one more thing he had to take care of before the siege, he hadn't told her that thing was seeing his sister.

"Yeah, hi."

His voice was strangled, that wasn't how it was supposed to come out.

"What's wrong?" she asked, instantly knowing that something had changed.

Will looked around, they weren't exactly alone right now.

"Can we go somewhere a little more private?"

Diana motioned for him to lead the way. She was probably wondering why he was leading her so far out of camp, but he didn't want to cause a massive fuss in front of everyone, especially if this went badly.

"I didn't know we needed *this* much privacy," she remarked when they came to a stop, looking at him with a raised eyebrow.

"You'll understand why in a moment."

Diana looked puzzled. "What are you talking about? What's going on?"

Will took a deep breath, knowing that what he said next was going to change everything between them.

"I'm leaving."

Diana actually laughed.

"Is that a joke?"

"No," Will replied quietly.

Her expression shifted from disbelief to serious as the realisation that he was being honest settled in.

"Where were you the last couple of days?"

"I went to see my sister, Hallie. I couldn't resist the opportunity, not after I found out that she was in London."

"How did you find out?"

"Caleb's Chosen, Kiara, she's dating my sister."

It was such a massive coincidence that he couldn't ignore it.

"So, she'll be fighting for the other side," Diana deduced.

"Yes."

"And your conscience can't take it."

"Exactly."

It seemed like Diana was being understanding, but then he saw it in her eyes, how wounded she was by this.

"So, you're going to abandon me too?"

If Will hadn't been upset, he probably would have noticed how she was loading her language.

"I don't want to, but--"

"Then don't. What if I promised that no harm would come to her?"

"You can't make that promise. There are a hundred people here. The fight is going to be out of control once it gets inside those walls, she could get hurt regardless."

"I'll order them to--"

"No. There's too much of a risk."

Diana could see him slipping away, her anger and panic making it hard for her to form words.

"If you give me some time, I'm sure we can figure something out," she said.

"Something that doesn't involve violence?"

"You know they won't respond to anything but, we've gone over this."

"Then there's nothing to figure out. You've been the best mentor and friend that I ever could have asked for, but I have to choose family over everything else. I can see how choosing the opposite is tearing you apart, I can't do that to myself or my sister."

"I'm doing that because I know that it will provide a better future for the both of us," she told him, her voice getting louder. "Why give up on this now when we're so close to getting everything that we want?"

"Because if someone who I recruited to this cause hurts even one hair on Hallie's head, I will never forgive myself. The end does not justify the means."

Diana snapped her mouth shut and turned away from him. It looked like she was about to explode.

"I…" he tried, but he saw her clench her fists.

"If you're going to go, then go," she said harshly. "Get out of my sight before I do something that I regret."

"Diana."

"GO."

Will knew that the only reason he wasn't being beaten to a pulp right now was because of the connection they had. Anyone else would have been pinned down and locked away so they couldn't cause any more trouble.

"Goodbye," he said softly, before turning on his heel and putting as much distance between them as quickly as possible.

Will sprinted back to the main camp, ripping open his tent so that he could throw all of his stuff quickly into a duffel bag. If he didn't leave right now, people would start asking questions.

Too late.

"Will?"

It was Priya, poking her head into his tent.

"What's going on? Where are you going?"

"I can't stay," he said, not looking at her. Instead he focused on packing everything in as tightly as possible so that nothing got left behind.

"Why not?"

"I saw my sister."

"Oh."

Will turned his head and saw the understanding but disappointed expression on her face. Zipping up his bag, he crawled over to her and stood up.

"It turns out that she's going to be right in the thick of it when the siege goes down and I can't--"

"Will, you don't have to explain it to me. I know how much you love her."

He scooped her up in a grateful hug and she squeezed him hard, not wanting to let go. In truth, neither did he.

"Take care of yourself, okay? If we're lucky, when we see each other again, we'll be on the same side," he said.

"I pray we are."

Will put her back down on the ground and took a step back.

"Tell Aaren and Eshe to keep an eye on Diana for me, will you? I don't want her to spiral completely out of control, so many more people could end up getting hurt."

"I will, I promise."

Will smiled.

"I'll see you around."

"Good luck," Priya called after him, but he was already gone.

Chapter Twenty-Four

Kiara had never flown in a private jet before. It had been a surreal experience going to London City Airport and not having to go through the usual long wait, security checks and the awkward hour of boarding where everyone queued for ages, then walked onto the plane at a snail's pace because they were all faffing with their hand luggage. They walked straight through a part of the airport she'd never seen before, had a few quick checks and then they were off. Hallie kept giggling at the expressions on her face as she looked around in wonder or bewilderment, depending on what was happening.

Caleb was with them, but he was very focused on what lay ahead. This was going to be his first time back at the Citadel since he discovered everything about the accident and the cover up with his Mum. He was certainly going to be having words with Master Mahmid, Kiara imagined.

Lily had flown out a couple of days ago with a couple of Guardians and another healer that she knew who lived in London. They wanted to help get everything set up as they were going to need regular medical supplies, as well as their healing hands. Anything that wasn't life threatening was going to have to be bandaged up and dealt with after the battle was over.

The plane wasn't very big, but the inside was very cosy. Cream leather seats, proper carpet, food and drinks provided. They weren't sipping on champagne or anything, but the can of lemonade and packet of crisps tided her over until they touched down on Italian soil.

She and Hallie spent most of the flight talking about Will and what to expect at the Citadel. For Hallie's sake, she really hoped that Will came through. It would be great for her to spend some time with her brother, try to make up for what they had lost.

In keeping with the same theme as the safe house, the Citadel wasn't much to look at on the outside, other than the fact that it appeared to be an old 14th or 15th century castle, which was pretty cool. It had a boundary wall and a gate, where a member of security let them through when they pulled up in Caleb's car. They drove up a dusty road which wound its way up the hill to a large courtyard of cobbles. The car bounced along as Caleb veered off to the right towards a ramp which she hadn't noticed at first. It turned out it led to an underground car park where there were plenty of cars of all shapes and sizes, from all over the world.

Hallie whistled when they parked up next to a very flashy car.

"Someone here is weal-*thy*," she said. "One of my Dad's friends has one of these. He makes a shit ton of money and he still says it cost him an arm and a leg."

"That's Master Talbot's car. He's been a Guardian for close to five decades," Caleb explained. "He trained Master Mahmid."

"Dammmmmn," Hallie said, still looking at the car approvingly.

"I didn't realise you earned that much money," Kiara said.

"We keep a decent living," he replied. "We've built up lucrative deals with agencies around the world, then there's rewards. Some Guardians take up second jobs when they don't have an assigned Chosen, it's how they make the big bucks."

"Man, I'd become a Guardian if I wasn't already rich," Hallie said.

Caleb chuckled. Hallie was the only one who had been able to make him laugh over the last week.

"This way," he said.

They grabbed their bags from the boot and made their way over to a lift which said it was for the east wing.

"How many wings are there?" Kiara asked.

"Three; east, north and south. The west side of the building collapsed a couple of hundred years ago, no one ever tried to rebuild it."

Kiara began to wonder why but didn't get much time to think as the doors pinged open to reveal the building's lobby. It was so shiny that she had to blink a couple of times for her eyes to adjust to the amount of light streaming in through the glass ceiling. They were in one of the castle's towers, from what she could tell, as there was only one floor. The others had been removed so you could look straight up at the sky. The walls were the original brick, but they had been fortified with metal beams that ran up and around the inside of the tower.

"I'll go find out which rooms you're in. Wait here," he told them.

Kiara wasn't really listening, she was too busy taking in her surroundings.

"This is *so* cool," Hallie said.

"Yeah, imagine the sound in here when it rains," Kiara agreed.

"God, I hope it rains while we're here, that'd be amazing."

"What about snow? That'd be so weird, looking up and seeing a layer of white powder snow on the ceiling."

Hallie snorted, the sound echoing throughout the room. "Whoops!"

This only made them laugh harder. For a moment, the forgot why they were here.

"Enjoying the acoustics?" Caleb asked when he returned.

"Something like that," Hallie replied.

"Okay, they had enough common sense to put you in rooms next to each other, up on the third floor. Do you want me to show you or are you okay finding them yourselves?"

Kiara and Hallie looked at each other. Under different circumstances, Caleb would have shown them regardless, but he probably wanted to go catch Master Mahmid before things got too hectic.

"Yeah, of course. We'll go find Lily and meet up with you later," Kiara said.

"Great, thanks," Caleb squeezed the piece of paper with the rooms on into Kiara's hand as he left.

"I think Master Mahmid might be about to get an earful," Hallie said.

"I was thinking exactly the same thing," Kiara nodded. "All right, rooms or find Lily in the infirmary?"

"Let's ditch our bags and head straight back out. Lily can give us the grand tour."

"Sounds like a plan to me."

~

Caleb wasn't sure exactly where he would find Master Mahmid. He had been thinking a lot about this and what he was going to say to him on the flight over, while Kiara and Hallie had both been gawping at the view out of the window. It wasn't going to be an easy conversation, that was for sure.

After checking the training room and the main communal areas, Caleb made his way across to the north wing to the Elder's offices and came across Master Mahmid walking the other way. Both men stopped in their tracks and locked eyes with each other.

"Can I have a word?" Caleb asked.

"Yes, of course."

Master Mahmid had to know that this was coming. Caleb had refrained from talking to him about it over the phone because he had wanted to do this face-to-face. Their relationship, however far it truly stretched back, deserved that much.

Once they were both shut away inside the privacy of Master Mahmid's office, his mentor turned to him and said, "Before you say anything, I want to apologise unequivocally for the lies that I have told."

His words were so sincere. The fear of losing Caleb must have been palpable.

"It probably means very little to you now, but they were all designed to protect you," Master Mahmid continued.

"I know a little about lying to protect people," Caleb said. "I see now why you were so angry at me for not telling you about Kiara. It must have hit close to home."

Caleb didn't see the need to blow up at Master Mahmid. He had already done enough of that with his Mom.

"Too close," Master Mahmid agreed.

"Can you explain everything to me?" Caleb asked, settling himself into one of the arm chairs in front of Master Mahmid's desk.

"All of it?"

"From the beginning," Caleb nodded.

Master Mahmid took the armchair next to Caleb, rather than sit on the other side of his desk. It would have put extra distance between them had he done it, which wouldn't have helped things.

"I was one of the first people to meet your mother when she arrived here. Master Talbot thought that I could be a good influence, show her the ropes, so to speak. We became fast friends, then we became something else."

"You two were…?"

"Together? Yes, for almost a year. We never told anyone, except your father and my wife when they each came into our lives. It's strange to think now that we all managed to be friends, despite our past. Particularly considering what made everything fall apart."

"The accident," Caleb deduced.

"I'm not sure whether Diana and John were fighting before it happened, I've come to think that might have been the case. It would better explain your father's blinding anger following the crash. You came within an inch of death. It shook us all to our very cores. John sided with the Elders when they passed their judgment and decided you would be safer away from Diana. It was agreed that you were never to know anything about this world as we didn't want you getting hurt again. Your mother was furious that I didn't do anything to stop them, but I was more afraid of you being put in danger again than her fury. She never forgave me."

"So, the plane crash?"

"A fluke accident which never should have happened. The Elders decided that it would be easier to tell Diana that you had both died so that she didn't go looking for you. I think that was probably the most terrible lie of them all."

Caleb hadn't been able to piece together all the lies yet, but he would be inclined to agree if they hadn't also lied to him.

"Was I always supposed to end up with my aunt?"

"No. When you were born, your parents asked me to take care of you if anything ever happened to them. But, following the crash and the fallout from your accident, I couldn't fulfill that wish."

Wow.

Caleb wondered what his life would have been like if Master Mahmid had been his guardian instead. Probably not terribly different from how it was now, just... more informal.

"You mentioned a wife?"

"Anya. She was seven months pregnant when the accident happened. Shortly after, the Elders forbade anyone from having families and I had a choice to make. I chose duty over love, something I have been doing ever since."

"Why?" Caleb asked, unable to see what sort of motivations would have kept him here over being with his wife and child.

"You know how important it is, the work that we do here. I didn't want to give it up, not after making the decision to go against Diana. It would have made losing her seem pointless. That was my reasoning at the time, anyway. After a while, I couldn't change my mind. Too much time had passed. Anya wouldn't have let me back into her life or our child's."

Caleb had to admit, this was already a lot to wrap his head around. But hearing it all from Master Mahmid was making it easier to understand.

"So, when I turned up here after college, why did you lie to me then?"

"When I realised that you didn't recognise me, I didn't see what good it would do to dredge up the past after everything your aunt had done to hide it from you. The chances of you ever meeting your mother were virtually non-existent. It also would have affected who you became as a Guardian if you had that hanging over your head. I wanted you to have your best chance at being exceptional, like I always have done."

"I always thought you were cold and distant because of the rules," Caleb said.

"I didn't want to give anything away," Master Mahmid admitted.

Sinking further into his chair, Caleb rubbed his eyes and took a moment to sift through his thoughts.

"I thought I would be angrier, but I'm more sad than anything else."

"Why?" Master Mahmid asked.

"Well, for one, I'm upset that one stupid decision screwed up my entire family and put my Mom on a path to revenge. I'm not sure how to deal with that crap," he said honestly. It was going to take time, time that wasn't available to him.

"But the other thing I'm sad about is that I had another family member out there all this time, someone who could have completely changed my life, and he chose duty over family."

There was a deep well of sadness and regret in Master Mahmid's eyes which he had never let Caleb see before. The truth had shifted their relationship entirely. No longer were they mentor and student; they were equals, and they were both hurting.

"If I'm expected to be honest with you, then you now have to be honest with me. We can't go forward lying to each other, none of us can. Not with this threat looming over us," Caleb said.

"Agreed. I'm sorry it's come to this," Ezra said.

"Yeah, me too. But so long as she's threatening to hurt the people here, to hurt you, I have to stand against her."

Ezra answered with a somber nod.

"I should go unpack and check on Kiara and Hallie," Caleb said, deciding that they had talked enough for now.

Ezra didn't argue with him, he had a lot to think about as well.

As Caleb made his way over to the door, he heard the other man take a breath and briefly glanced back.

"Caleb?"

"Yeah?"

"If I had to do it over again, I would have chosen family."

"I know."

Chapter Twenty-Five

"How is your room so much nicer than both of ours?" Hallie asked Lily as she sprawled herself across the double bed.

"Just lucky, I guess."

The three ladies had just had dinner together in the main hall for the first time with Caleb, who had gone out to get them pizza. Boy, did that make everyone else jealous. It smelled so much more delicious than whatever pasta they were eating, and the pizzas had the best base that Hallie had ever tasted! Which was crazy coming from someone who lived a stone's throw from New York most of her life.

As they didn't want to go to sleep yet, they all retreated to Lily's room to hang out for a while. Caleb seemed a little lighter after his talk with Master Mahmid, which had gone well considering all the secrets the man had kept and the lies he had told. Hallie understood why it might be easier to forgive him rather than his Mom. Master Mahmid had been a constant, strong figure in his life these last ten years, he had apologised straight off the bat, and he wasn't threatening to hurt everyone and everything Caleb held dear.

Hallie probably would have forgiven him too.

"Eh, I don't know about luck," Kiara said, looking at Caleb and wiggling her eyebrows suggestively.

"Nope, nothing to do with me. Someone else here must like you," Caleb said.

"The guy on the front desk was being a little flirty," Lily remembered.

Hallie could see Caleb trying not to have a visual reaction, but Lily must have heard whatever went through his head because she hooted with laughter.

"Don't worry, he was terrible at it. A fish could have done a better job."

"Ooooooooh," Hallie declared. "Snarky Lily has made a comeback. I love it."

"Snarky Lily?" Caleb questioned.

"Well, back at school, she--"

Caleb suddenly started buzzing and held up a finger.

"Hold that thought," he said as he pulled his cell from his back pocket and checked the text. "Master-- uh, Ezra wants us all to come to the lobby."

"Master uh Ezra?" Hallie teased.

"Just shush and follow me," he said.

On the elevator ride down, Hallie leaned against the mirror at the back, pondering what could be so important that they all had to come. It quickly became clear why the moment they entered the room.

"Will?!"

Hallie had hoped so hard that he would be able to make it. Although, knowing how difficult it would be for him to leave Diana, she had started to believe he wasn't coming.

Sprinting the length of the lobby, she pushed past the guards who were standing just in front of him and threw her arms around his neck.

"You made it."

Will's hands were bound, otherwise he would have hugged her back. Instead he had to make do with leaning his head against her shoulder.

"I did."

"They found him skulking around the lower grounds, trying to find away in," Ezra said. "He said he knew you, I wanted to be sure."

Ezra motioned for the guards to uncuff Will so her brother could give her a proper squeeze.

"How did you get away?" Caleb asked, the rest of them all crowding around Hallie and Will.

"Your Mum let me go," he replied, which caused a ripple of shock. "I know, I wasn't expecting it either."

"How did she take the fact that you were leaving?" Hallie asked.

"Not very well. I tried to explain that there was no way that I was risking you for her agenda, I think that was hard for her because of…" he trailed off, looking at Caleb.

"Because she wouldn't do it for me?"

"Yeah, that. I'm sorry, mate. I wish I could have convinced her."

"It's not your fault, I'm not sure anyone can at this point," Caleb said.

Hallie glanced at Ezra, who was looking thoughtful, but she didn't say anything.

"We're glad you're here though," Kiara said.

"Yes, it was very brave of you to stand up to her," Lily chimed in.

"I'd do anything for Hallie."

Hallie smiled at him, so happy that he had pulled through.

"Can we find Will a room and get him settled in?" she asked Ezra.

"I have some questions for him first," Ezra said. "You have a lot of information that will be useful to us, like numbers and who is fighting on Diana's side."

Will looked a little hesitant.

"I know it's hard to break her trust, but whatever you can tell us could help us end this fight quicker, with less casualties on both sides," Caleb said.

Hallie wasn't sure how Caleb was remaining so calm and reasonable considering who was involved and how this affected him. She admired his ability to do it. And him.

"Okay," Will said. "I'll see you soon and we can finally catch up," he told Hallie.

"Of course, we'll be waiting right here."

As Ezra and Caleb escorted Will away, Kiara wrapped her arms around Hallie.

"I'm so happy for you," she said.

Hallie kissed her on the head. Despite how it looked, Ezra and Caleb taking Will away, they all knew that this was a good thing. He was proof that there was a chance they could win this thing. It gave her hope for what things could be like after the battle was done. One thing she knew for certain, now that he was back in her life, she was never letting him go anywhere ever again.

Chapter Twenty-Six

Ezra knew that if anyone found out what he was doing, they would try stop him. This was the reason he chose to wait until nightfall. Everyone else was sound asleep back at the Citadel after a long day of preparations, they wouldn't notice that he was gone. If they did, it was doubtful they would have any clue as to his whereabouts. He had almost talked himself out it, but he needed to do this. For Caleb, if no one else.

Will had told Ezra the location of Diana's camp under strict confidence. He had no plans to mount a counter strike. If they all ended up coming to blows, it was better that they do so in the Citadel which they knew well rather than in unknown territory. However, he was hoping that he might be able to stop all of this in its tracks. It was better for everyone if there was no fighting at all.

Diana's camp was much larger than he expected. He had to use a car to get close, then left it on the outskirts so his approach wouldn't be heard by any of the residents. Keeping to the shadows, he navigated his way around the edge of camp, searching for any sign of Diana. Will said that she didn't usually sleep well, which would probably be compounded by the argument that the two of them had earlier. It must have hurt her for the person closest to her to choose to leave her. She had a fair amount of experience in betrayal and heartbreak, which evidently hadn't eased over time.

Ezra was considering entering the camp itself, which could prove to be dangerous, when he finally spotted her. She was outside the camp, through the tree line, throwing knives at a battered old tree trunk. This was not an ideal situation, but he hadn't come this far to be scared off by the threat of being stabbed.

"Diana," he said quietly, but clearly, appearing from between the trees.

Diana froze.

"You," she growled as she turned, throwing a knife directly at his chest.

Ezra only just managed to dive out of the way, the knife bouncing off a nearby rock. If Diana hadn't used all the knives already, he probably would have had to move again pretty sharpish.

"How dare you come here!" she said, unleashing her words instead. "How dare you ever show your face around me after what you did!"

"Diana," he said, dusting himself off. "Please, just let me speak."

"No! You already took everything from me, you're not getting anything else."

"No, I... Diana--" he tried, flustered.

He hadn't been expecting a warm welcome, but the knife had thrown him off.

"Get out of here now, before I wake everyone else up. I know some other people here who wouldn't mind a piece of you."

"Your threats don't scare me, Diana. I know I have a lot to answer for, but I'm not here to talk about the past, I'm here to talk about you having any chance of a future with your son."

Diana faltered for a moment, but only a moment.

"Caleb already made it very clear where his loyalties lie."

"That's because Caleb is practical and is choosing what he knows, as well as the people he cares about," Ezra said. "If Caleb knew you, if you knew him, things would be different."

Diana shook her head.

"The Elders took away any chance of reconciliation when they sent him away and told me he was dead. There's no coming back from what has been done."

"That's because you don't understand…"

"I don't understand?! You're the one who doesn't understand! You have no idea what it's like to be separated from your only child!" she spat.

Ezra had forgotten that they never got the chance to tell Diana that Anya was pregnant. They were going to do it when he came back from his mission, but it was cut short by Caleb's accident, and everything fell apart from there.

"You're wrong. I have a child somewhere out there in the world who doesn't even know I exist. I don't know their name, whether they're a boy, girl or somewhere in between. I don't know what they're like, who they like, where they live, what they do. At least you got to know your son for a little while and at least you have a chance of getting to know your son again now."

Diana didn't look like she knew what to do with this information. She was still beyond furious, but she hadn't stopped to consider what had happened since she had been gone, what she had put in motion with her own decisions.

"You can't put that on me."

"It was my decision, yes, but your recklessness has spoiled so much of your own life. Why are you prepared to continue down this path when you know that it will only bring you more heartache?"

"Because this can't go on. Guardians and Chosen are vital to the survival of life on this planet, but the rules they live under are archaic," she said.

"I understand, and I want to talk."

"The other Elders won't," she still sounded so certain.

"It may take some coaxing…"

"No, Ezra. These are the same people who took my son away from me and banned all Guardians from having families after one accident. They are not amenable to reason and they won't listen to words. It has to be a show of force or they have to be removed."

Ezra could feel himself losing grip on this uphill climb. It had been too long, Diana was far too set on this course of action.

"You won't even consider doing this for Caleb?" he asked.

Diana pressed her lips together but didn't make any other motion.

"It's impossible," she said, sounding sad now rather than angry. "I'm the unstoppable force and he's the immovable object. There is no way we get a happy ending in these circumstances."

"I don't believe that to be true," he said.

Diana shrugged.

"It doesn't matter. Your opinion doesn't matter to me anymore."

Ezra stared at her, unable to discern whether or not she truly meant those words. There was too much history between them now that he couldn't tell.

"Now, I won't tell you again. Leave or I'll let them at you and it won't be pretty."

He knew that much to be true.

Before he took his leave, he glanced back at her standing there, hands on hips, her stern expression wavering as she thought he wouldn't see.

"Whatever happens, I want you to know how remarkable Caleb is as both a person and a Guardian. He's better than anyone I've ever known, and I've done my best to protect him and care for him as if he were my own family. It's torture watching him, knowing that he thinks you've made him the sole reason for your entire crusade. Consider that before you make your final decision," he said.

Ezra didn't wait for a reaction, him staying wouldn't help change her mind. Hopefully what he said would touch what was left of her broken heart and maybe, just maybe, they could find a peaceful solution that would suit everyone.

Chapter Twenty-Seven

Caleb had decided to take some time alone to clear his head. Preparing the Citadel for battle was tiring work and kept him distracted for the most part but worries kept creeping back in whenever he wasn't preoccupied with chores. There were more general concerns about the Citadel at large and everyone who lived there, who would end up fighting there. Even with Will on their side now, there were going to be casualties. Their limited number of healers meant that some might even die.

But then there were more specific worries too. Lily and Hallie were both defenceless without someone protecting them and he didn't want to see either of them hurt. Then there was the fact that this was Kiara's first big fight. The guys at the bar were going to seem like nothing in comparison to well-trained Guardians and Chosen. He knew she couldn't get killed, but that didn't stop her from getting badly injured. She wasn't immune to everything.

Finally, he was scared about what would happen if he ended up coming face to face with his Mom in the middle of it all. He knew how vehement he'd been with her back in London, but it was different when there was a chance that they could come to blows.

Caleb kept trying to push this all from his mind, knowing that it would only make things worse for him when the battle began. It was difficult, though, even now that he was away from everyone else.

His phone ringing startled him. He thought that it might be Lily or Kiara telling him to come back inside, as he'd ended up wandering quite far from the Citadel, but it was a blocked number.

"Hello?"

"Caleb, it's me."

Caleb almost dropped his phone. It was his Mom.

"How did you get this number?"

"It doesn't matter. Just, don't hang up."

Caleb probably would have if there wasn't something different about her voice. He could tell that something had changed.

"Okay."

There was a small but grateful sigh.

"Ezra came to see me last night."

"He did?"

This conversation was full of surprises already.

"Yes, and he took his own life in his hands to do so, as I almost skewered him on sight," she said.

It was a good thing she hadn't otherwise they probably wouldn't be talking.

"What did he say?"

"A lot of stuff that I didn't want to listen to at first, but I've been walking around the camp all morning thinking about you and the people whose lives I'm putting in danger by doing this and... "

And?

"I've decided that I want to stop everything for long enough to talk to the Elders. If there's a way that we can solve this without fighting, then we should at least try."

Caleb felt himself trembling.

"Really?"

"Really."

He didn't know what exactly Ezra had said to his Mom, but it had to have been some powerful stuff to make her consider doing this.

"Thank you," he said.

"Don't thank me yet. I still have to convince everyone else that pressing pause is the right decision here. It's difficult to know how many will be willing to try diplomacy after all the promises I've made."

She was right, this was far from over. Relief could wait.

"How do you want to do this?" he asked.

"I'll call a camp meeting this afternoon and let them know of my decision. If that goes well, then I will meet you at the border at seven this evening and I'll come with you back to the Citadel to have a sit down with the Elders. If I'm not there, then…"

"I'll assume the worst."

Caleb hoped that her people would be willing to listen, he didn't want to think that they would turn on her when she was trying to be reasonable.

There was silence, neither of them knowing what to say.

"Be careful," he said eventually.

"You too, Caleb."

~

At the time, Diana hadn't wanted to listen to Ezra's words, but they had stuck with her anyway. The man was a pain in her ass. She had been fully prepared to go ahead with her plan, even after Will left, but then he came waltzing in with his wisdom and put her head in a spin. In the end, she hadn't been able to reason away her doubts anymore. She had to try to peaceful way.

She called a full camp meeting in the middle of the afternoon that she could see going one of two ways: either most would be accepting of this new plan and she would be able to meet Caleb later, or it would go down like a lead balloon and all hell would break loose. She honestly had no idea which it would be.

Once everyone had gathered together, Diana climbed up onto one of the benches to give her a better vantage over the crowd. People slowly quietened down until she had almost complete silence.

"First of all, thank you to all of you for coming. I know it was short notice asking you all to make your way from your respective locations, but I thought we were going to have to make a move quickly once the Elders discovered our plan. As it turns out, we've been offered an alternative."

A wave of murmurs broke out, but quickly died back down. Aaren, who was stood near her with Priya, looked intrigued.

"I've spoken with Ezra Mahmid and he has told me that he is willing to listen. It seems the Elders want to avoid a fight at all costs. This could work in our favour."

"You once told me that you would never consider an offer from the Elders, that whatever they gave us would be nothing in comparison to what we could achieve if we overthrew them," someone called out from a couple of rows back.

"Things have changed since then. Will has left us to be with his sister, who is at the Citadel, and I've discovered that my son is there too."

This earned some gasps and more noise, which didn't quiet down.

"Why didn't you tell me?" Aaren asked.

"I didn't want to be talked out of my plan because Caleb chose them over me, but now I know that there's a chance for peace, I must try."

Aaren nodded. She knew that she could count on him to have her back.

The others, however…

"So, you're just going to give in to them because they have leverage?" Ricardo asked, looking displeased.

A lot of people were starting to look annoyed.

"My son isn't leverage. He was the reason that I started all of this, if I don't try to work things out then I risk losing him forever."

"That's great for you, what about us? We've already turned our backs on the Elders and they know it. Do you think they'll be forgiving?" he continued.

"We haven't made a move against them yet," Aaren said, coming to her aid. "That's got to count for something."

"You're being naive. The other reason we started this was because of their lack of forgiveness, the cold-hearted way they treat those in their order."

"Please, everyone, if we reject this offer now then there truly is no going back," Diana said.

"We already accepted the danger when you recruited us. We won't back down because of a moment of weakness on your part," Ricardo told her, brandishing a finger in her direction. "Who is still for the original plan?"

There was a roar from behind him, the majority of the camp falling in line with their new leader.

"Ricardo, listen to me, you can't--"

"Get her down from there. She can't be trusted to lead us anymore."

A couple of people tried to make a grab for her, but Aaren stood squarely in their way. "If you want her, you have to go through me."

"And me," Priya said.

"So be it."

It was astonishing how quickly everything turned nasty. As the camp surged towards them, Diana hopped down from the bench and stood in a semicircle with Aaren and Priya. She wasn't going to be silenced that easily.

Diana threw a punch at the first person who tried to strike her, knuckles connecting with jaw. As they stumbled backwards, Diana had to bend out of the way of Aaren tossing someone right across her, watching them as they crashed into a nearby tent. She had forgotten what Aaren was capable of when he was angry.

She floored someone coming up on Priya, then spun and decked another camper right in the neck, which made them collapse instantly, writhing on the floor as they gasped for oxygen.

"Watch out!" Priya said just a moment too late, leaving Diana unprepared for fist to the gut.

Another person moved in, the two of them surrounding her as she clutched her stomach. Priya helped fight them off, but there were too many of them closing in fast.

"Go! Run!" Aaren growled, throwing another of the group away from them.

"We're not leaving you here alone," Diana told him, pushing him out of the way of a bullet so it grazed his arm rather than pierce his chest.

There was no way that he could take on a hundred of them by himself.

Aaren swung out with his arm and it connected with a man's torso, but he was immediately overwhelmed by three more.

"Aaren!" Priya shouted as she was jumped from behind, but he was powerless to do anything to help her because he was being beaten to a pulp.

Diana let out a war cry as a distraction, however, it was too late. Despite her attempts to resist them, a blinding pain seared across the side of her head and everything went dark.

~

"Uhhnnn."

Diana groaned in response to her throbbing head, briefly wishing that she was still unconscious. She didn't know how long it been and she couldn't open her eyes quite yet, just thinking about doing it made it hurt more.

"Diana?"

"Priya, is that you?"

"Oh, I'm so glad you're awake. I was beginning to think that you might not come around at all, the blood on your head…"

"It feels worse than it looks," Diana grumbled.

Forcing her eyelids apart made her senses start to adjust to her surroundings. There were muffled voices outside, which meant they were likely in a tent. Her hands and legs were both tied up, so she couldn't escape, and she could now see that the light outside was beginning to fade.

"How long has it been?" she asked Priya.

"A couple of hours. Aaren is here too, but he's out cold. They beat him for a while longer after you passed out, he's barely breathing."

That wasn't good. If they didn't get Aaren proper medical help soon then he might not survive, especially if he had internal injuries.

"Is there a way to get out of these bindings?"

"Not without a knife and they stripped us of all our weapons."

"Calling for help isn't an option, we don't know who we can trust," Diana said, going through their options out loud. "I was supposed to be meeting Caleb soon. There's a chance that when I don't show, he'll try to come get us."

"Will Aaren last that long?"

"I don't know."

This was dire. What they truly needed right now was a miracle. Life hadn't been inclined to give her any slack before, why would that change now?

"Diana?"

"Eshe?"

Someone up there must have heard her.

"Are you all okay?" Eshe asked, pressing her ear to the back of the tent so she could hear them without them having to shout.

"Priya and I are coping, Aaren is in a bad way."

"I saw the end of the fight when I came back from the market and had to question a couple of people to find out what happened. I'm so sorry, Diana. If I had been here, then…"

"You would have got lumped in here with us," Diana said. "You're not the one to blame."

"Neither are you. You tried to do the right thing, their animosity towards the order is not all your doing."

"I stoked the fire."

"Erm," Priya interrupted. "Aaren is getting worse."

Diana could hear him wheezing now every time he breathed.

"Eshe, I need you to go to the border and get my son. Caleb's waiting for me there. If you can bring him back here, then he can help you get us out."

"Then what?"

"We'll seek refuge at the Citadel. The healers there will be able to sort out the worst of Aaren's injuries in no time. It's the only good plan we have if he's to live."

"I'll go straight away. Just, hang in there."

"We will."

Diana watched Eshe's shadow disappear as the woman ran for the camp's parking lot.

"Diana?" Priya said.

"Yeah?"

"Do you mind if I pray for Aaren?"

"Go ahead."

Diana knew that Aaren needed all the help he could get, and it gave her time to figure out an escape if her current plan didn't work. This wasn't going to be the day that any of them died, she would make sure of it.

~

Caleb never expected to be this concerned about his Mom's well-being, mostly because for the last three decades, he thought she was dead. Now that she was alive and risking everything to try to find a way to peacefully resolve her fight with the Elders, he had even more reason to tap his fingers nervously against the steering wheel as he waited for her to appear. Every minute that ticked by only made him more anxious. When she was half an hour late, he considered trying to figure out a way to ring her back on the blocked number but told himself that she might have got held up by traffic. After an hour, however, he was starting to conclude that the worst had in fact happened and that he needed to get back to the Citadel as quickly as possible before the camp launched an attack.

Sliding the car key into the ignition, Caleb was about to start the car when another car screeched up and parked in front of his, so it blocked him in. A black woman jumped out and ran around to his window, motioning for him to wind it down.

Caleb went one better and opened the door.

"Are you Caleb?" she said, wanting to be sure.

"Yeah, what's wrong?"

"Your mother's in trouble. She tried to convince the camp that talking to the Elders was the best way forward, but they turned on her. She and a couple of others are injured and locked up, we need to go rescue them."

Caleb didn't even bat an eyelid.

"You drive."

Jumping into her car, the pair of them shot off at speeds that Caleb was sure were illegal in both Italy and France. Whoever this woman was, she cared deeply enough about his Mom and those who were hurt to risk a police chase. Hell, if they attracted the attention of the police, maybe they could arrest whoever had mutinied.

They managed to make it all the way back to camp without getting arrested, so they hopped out and took cover. It had gone dark while they were driving, so that helped to hide them from anyone walking by.

The place was still bustling with people, preparing for their attack in the morning. It seemed like whatever they did now, they couldn't stop this battle from happening. The most important thing was getting his Mom and her friends out of the camp alive so that they could live to fight another day.

"Over here," the woman whispered, skirting around the back of a couple of tents before coming to a stop at the edge.

"See that tent over there?" she asked him.

It was obvious which one she meant as there were two guards outside.

"Yeah."

"I'm going to circle round and get behind the guard furthest away from us. When you see me move, you take out the other one. We can't be heard or else we won't make it out of the camp."

"Understood."

The woman vanished, leaving him crouched behind the tent. He couldn't see any outlines of people in the tent in the lamplight. All he could do was hope that they were still in there and that they managed to take down these guards silently, as the woman planned.

It took a few minutes, but finally Caleb saw her start to rise out from behind a crate, prowling like a tiger out of the long grass. He moved quickly, keeping in the guard's blind spot as he snuck up on him and covered his mouth, restricting his arms so he couldn't flail. Eventually, he fell unconscious.

The woman hadn't been so gentle, electing to knock the other guard out with a blow to the head. Other than a crack, they made no noise whatsoever.

Caleb pulled open the tent's zipper to find three very sore looking people all lying on the ground with their hands tied behind their backs and their feet bound together so they couldn't escape. The man was unconscious, but his Mom and a young Indian girl both looked at them when they entered.

"Eshe!" the girl exclaimed but was immediately shushed by all of them.

"Caleb, thank God," his Mom said quietly, closing her eyes for a moment.

The open wound on her head must have been throbbing.

Part of Caleb wanted to turn back around and go kick some camper ass for what they had done to these three, but he knew that wouldn't do any of them any good. Instead, he pulled a pocket knife from his jacket and began to cut their plastic bindings.

"Aaren?" Eshe murmured as she crouched over the unconscious man, gently touching his cheek. "Aaren, wake up."

"They beat him long after Diana blacked out. I don't know how he's alive," the girl whimpered.

"We'll get him back to our healers, he'll be fine," Caleb told her.

It looked like she needed to hear something hopeful in order to get her through their escape, so he decided he could do that for her.

His Mom squeezed his hand when he set her free. He reached up to get a better look at the gash at her hairline.

"I'll be alright," she said. "At least now we'll have matching scars."

Caleb would have snorted if the situation hadn't been so serious.

"Eshe and I will get Aaren, you two make sure that the coast is clear."

"Of course," his Mom said, nudging the girl towards the opening.

While they were peeking outside, Caleb moved in to help Eshe get the big guy on his feet. It felt like they were trying to lift a horse.

"All right," he grunted. "Let's go."

When his Mom was sure that there was no one else in sight, they made a break for the trees. They needed to be hidden as quickly as possible, as carrying Aaren wasn't exactly inconspicuous. The man had to be at least six-foot-two and he was twice Eshe's size, which made moving him a difficult task.

They pegged it as fast as they could, almost making there, but then they heard angry cries coming from the camp behind them.

"Move, move, move," Caleb called out, trying to pick up the pace.

As they rounded a corner on the path, the parking lot came into view, but lights were starting to flicker from behind them as the campers gave chase.

"Someone get in the driver's seat," he said as he did his best lumping Aaren into the back seat.

His Mom did as he asked, the young girl waiting by the passenger seat. They managed to position Aaren so that his head was in Eshe's lap and his feet were tucked inside before Caleb slammed the door shut. Running around to the front, he climbed into the passenger seat and pulled the girl in with him, sitting her in between his legs. He just about managed to close his door before his Mom gunned it, tyres screeching against the road as they zoomed as far away from the camp as quickly as possible.

Once they were sure that they weren't being followed anymore, his Mom asked, "Everyone okay?"

"Just drive," Eshe said. "I'll do what I can to help keep him alive, but it'll take more than just me to heal these wounds."

Caleb hadn't realised that Eshe was a healer, but he knew she was right. If Aaren was going to make a full recovery, then he needed all the healers they could provide.

As he twisted his head back round to focus on the road ahead, he realised the girl in front of him was shaking.

"Hey," he said, wrapping his arms around her to comfort her. "What's your name?"

"Priya."

"Everything's going to be fine, Priya."

"How can you be so sure?"

"Because when we're united, we can do anything."

Caleb briefly looked across at his Mom and found that she was smiling.

"My son is right. Whatever happens now, we'll get through it together."

"Together," Eshe agreed.

Priya leaned her head back against Caleb's chest and whispered, "Together."

Chapter Twenty-Eight

Will had never thought he would see the inside of the Citadel, not like this, not as an ally to those he had been helping to plot against. Without Hallie, he wouldn't be here. They had taken the opportunity to catch up after Ezra and Caleb finished questioning him. It was 3am by the time they went to sleep. They had barely even scratched the surface, but it had to be enough for now.

Everything was up in the air. If all went to plan, then there would be no fight, according to Caleb. But they had to continue on preparing until they knew either way.

He had volunteered to help Kiara with whatever she was up to because he wanted the chance to talk to her properly. Hallie loved her so much, he wanted to understand why.

They had ended up in the armory, locking away all the weapons so that they couldn't be used against them. All that was spared were stun guns, to help protect those who hadn't been trained to fight or weren't yet ready to take on people in hand to hand combat. Apparently, they had several new recruits come in recently who all needed extra protection. This wasn't the sort of welcome they had been expecting.

"Here, let me take that," Will said, pointing to the particularly big box of ammo she was about to attempt to lift. "Can't have you blowing out your back."

"Wouldn't that be ironic?" she snorted.

"Yeah, I'll spare you having to explain that to Master Mahmid."

Once it was safely stowed away in the underground locker, with all the rest of the stuff that they had moved so far, he said, "Time for a break?"

"Yeah, I could do with a moment to breathe."

The pair of them sat down on a bench near the door, passing a bottle of water between them. Kiara flapped her loose t-shirt around, trying to cool down.

"Hallie told me that you only found out that you were a Chosen back in March?"

"Yeah, it's been a bit of a whirlwind adventure," she said, looking up at him.

"The gala was your first mission?"

"Mmhmm. I was promised smooth and easy, it was sort of anything but."

"No kidding."

"I know what happened that night was awful for Caleb, but the fact that it led us here, to you being with us and his Mum possibly on her way too, I can't help but be grateful that it happened. Family is so important."

"I agree," Will said. "If I hadn't bumped into you, then I probably never would have seen Hallie again."

"And she would have been much worse off for it," she said. "Seriously, she's so happy that you're back, Will."

"Me too," he smiled. "But I don't think she would have been as happy as she has been the last couple of years if she hadn't had you around. You should hear her gush about you, you'd never stop blushing."

"Oh, believe me, she does it when I'm around. I wasn't very good at handling it at first, but I got used to it."

"Why weren't you very good at handling it?"

"I guess because it was just me and my Mum for the longest time. My Mum loved me, and I loved her, but she was never very good at showing it. I didn't know why until I found out about all this. The secrets she felt like she had to keep put this distance between us, because she was always lying. So, when Hallie burst into my life, all hugs and kisses, I was a bit 'whooaaa' at first."

"Understandable."

"But I love it now. I've even got better at doing all that with other people."

"You should try going around to Hallie's Mum's house on a holiday like Easter or Christmas. They get the whole family round, from all over the world. You walk in the door and it's just hug after hug after hug. When I was a kid, I used to be all 'bleehhh' about it, as nine-year-old boys do. But it became my favourite part of spending time over in the US."

"I'll have to get Hallie to finally take me home for Christmas," Kiara laughed.

"Do it, you won't regret it."

"Maybe it'll even be the three of us?" she suggested.

"If we're lucky," he nodded.

"Have you talked to any of your other family since you arrived here?" she asked.

"No, not yet. I haven't been able to work up the nerve."

Will wasn't sure what her response was going to be, but she looked at him sympathetically.

"I can't tell you how they're going to react," she said. "When I found out that my Aunt Lily had been missing from my life all these years because of a promise she'd made to my Mum, I was angry at first. But Hallie made me see that it was better to forgive her than to not have her at all. If I was your parents, I'd want to be put out of my misery, because whatever you've done to them, they still love you and want you back."

It hadn't taken long, but Will understood now why Hallie loved Kiara. They were perfect for each other.

"You're right," he said.

Kiara looked pleased.

Reaching behind her, she pulled her phone from her pocket and offered it to him.

"There's no time like the present."

Will stared at it for a minute before taking it, clutching it in his hand.

"I'll give you some privacy," she said.

His eyes trailed after her as she left. It was crazy that someone so young could be so wise, but then he supposed that circumstance had made her that way. He briefly considered not doing it and just sitting there for a while, but if he could be brave enough to turn his back on Diana for Hallie, then he could certainly handle one phone call to his Dad to let him know he was okay.

With each ring, Will began to think that the man wasn't actually going to pick up. Instead he would have to leave a message. Should he leave a message? Would he have the time to try again later?

"Hello?"

Oh.

Will's words suddenly got caught in his throat, which meant that all his Dad heard on the other end of the line was silence.

"Hello? Is anyone there?" he asked, impatiently.

"Yeah," Will choked. "Yes, Dad. It's me."

The line crackled in the absence of any speech. Waiting for a response was torturous.

"Will, is that really you?"

"Yeah, it is."

"How do I know that this is not just another hoax?"

They'd had hoax callers? Jeez, some people were absolute shits.

"Uhhh," he had to come up with something only him and his Dad knew. "On my eleventh birthday, we went out to Victoria Rock, just the two of us, to go camping. The last evening we were there, we lay out under the stars and you told me that having Hallie and I was the best thing that you had ever done in your life."

A soft sob from the other end of the line made his own eyes sting with tears.

"Will, it's you."

"Yeah, it's me," he said, barely keeping it together.

"I'm so sorry, son. Whatever I said or did to make you think that you weren't wanted, I'm so unbelievably sorry."

"No, Dad, I'm the one that needs to apologise. I should never have disappeared like that and made you all worry. I can't even--"

"Will, stop. It's okay. I'm just... I'm so happy to hear your voice."

"Yeah, me too."

Their heavy breathing filled the quiet before his Dad spoke again.

"I don't know where you are right now or what you're doing, but son, come home," he said.

"I can't yet, I have something really important that I have to do, but as soon as it's over, I'm on the first flight. I promise."

"I'll hold you to it."

~

Hallie let out a massive sigh when she placed the last box of medical supplies down in the back corner of the infirmary. She and Lily had been shifting stuff around all afternoon in an effort to make sure everything was ready. Caleb had come by earlier to tell them about his call with his Mom, but they couldn't take any chances. If Diana wasn't successful, then it was likely that her camp would make a move immediately. They had to be prepared for all sorts of injuries. While those residing in the Citadel had been told to disarm, and disable if necessary, her camp wasn't going to be fighting fair.

She hoped that the training that Alastair had been able to give her was enough. The Scot had decided not to come with them and she supported that decision. It wasn't worth the risk. She did wish that she could talk to him though. Some of his guidance, however growly, would be welcome right now.

"You're going to make Alastair proud, don't worry," Lily said.

It was hard to know when she was listening in, but Hallie didn't mind. There wasn't a lot that she kept private about her life and she wouldn't hide anything from Lily.

"I don't know. It still felt like we were only really getting started."

"He would tell you that the best way to truly get better at this is to go out there into the field and learn on the job. If the fight goes ahead, then you'll learn very quickly what you are capable of doing," she said.

"I really hope it doesn't," Hallie said.

"I know, me too. If she and Ezra and the others can figure it all out, then it could mean exciting new things for all of us."

"But particularly you and Caleb," Hallie smiled.

"Yeah," Lily said, choosing not to be coy for once.

"You really like him, huh?"

"To be honest, I had begun to give up hope that anyone like Caleb would come into my life. I could never get serious with anyone because…" she tapped her head. "But then he walked into in my shop and bam! It was practically instantaneous. His mind was just so… beautiful."

"I sort of know what you mean, it was like that for me and Kiara too. Cupid hit me with one of those ridiculous little heart arrows of his and suddenly all I could think about was her. What she was doing, when I was going to see her next, the way that she smiled… I'd never felt like that before and I'm not sure I'm ever going to feel like that again."

Lily looked sad for her.

"I know that the day we lose her will be one of the hardest of our lives, but don't count your heart out, Hallie. Maybe someday you'll have a different love for another."

"Yeah, maybe."

There was a crashing sound from outside in the hallway, then a yelp, and she heard Caleb curse loudly.

"What the hell?" Hallie said, both her and Lily running over to the door.

Caleb was stumbling down the corridor trying to support a very tall man between him and a tiny, young woman. The guy was beaten and bloody, he looked like he was barely alive.

"Oh my God!"

Hallie met them halfway, taking over from the woman so that their new patient wasn't sagging so much on the one side.

"What happened?"

"The camp turned against Diana," the woman said between deep breaths. "Caleb had to come rescue us."

"Jeez. Where's your Mom?"

"She's fine, she said she was going to find somewhere to wash up," Caleb said.

The elevator pinged again, and another woman ran out of it, catching up with them quickly.

"How's he doing?" she asked.

"I can barely feel anything," Hallie said. "He's slipping away."

They picked up the pace, squeezing through the doorway so they could lift the man up and place him on the cot that Lily was standing by.

"You, whatever your name is, start on his chest, I'll take his head," the older woman ordered as she pushed everyone but Hallie back.

She had blood smears on her dress, but no wounds. They must have been from holding him.

"It's Hallie."

"Eshe. This is Aaren."

"And I'm Priya," the young woman added.

Hallie wasted no time ripping open Aaren's jacket and shirt, so she could get a better look at his wounds.

How many people had he been fighting off? There was so much bruising, she was surprised he hadn't died already.

Laying her hands on the center of his massive chest, Hallie closed her eyes and gave it everything she had. Usually she felt an improvement instantaneously, but she had never dealt with injuries that were so extensive.

"I'm not sure it's working."

"Just stay focused," Eshe told her. "If you give up now, he'll certainly die."

Hallie squeezed her eyelids even more tightly shut, chanting over and over in her head so that she was sure that she was giving it all she had.

Slowly, but surely, she started to feel the life breathe back into him. As he grew stronger, she started to feel Eshe's power merge with hers. It was like they were touching each other without any physical contact.

Hallie was so distracted by what was going on that she didn't even realise that her own energy was draining.

"Stop," Eshe told her, but Hallie didn't hear her properly.

Instead, a pair of hands gently pulled her backwards, breaking her connection with Aaren. She had to stop losing control like this, otherwise she was going to be no good to anyone during the real battle.

"You okay?" Caleb asked.

"Yeah, I think so," she said. "How's he?"

Eshe opened her mouth to speak, but Aaren replied instead by simply going:

"Ow."

"I'll take it," Hallie said, then let Caleb guide her over to the cot opposite so she could sit down.

Priya rushed forward in her place, holding one of Aaren's thumbs in her small hand.

"I'm so glad you're alive," she said, sounding like she was going to cry.

"Yeah, me too," he said. "Or, I will be, when I don't ache so much."

"That sounds fair to me," Eshe patted him softly on the shoulder.

"How did we get to the Citadel?" he asked, carefully tilting his head. "And where's Diana? We didn't leave her behind, did we?"

"One question at a time," Eshe told him.

Caleb stepped forward again, catching Aaren's attention.

"Well, that answers one of my questions," Aaren said.

"My Mom's around somewhere. She has a bump on the head, but she's all right," Caleb told him, covering the other too.

Aaren looked relieved.

"What happens now?" Lily asked.

"The others gave chase but fell back when they realised they weren't going to catch us," Eshe said.

"They'll attack first thing. It's the smart thing to do considering they've already lost five of their own, including their leader," Caleb said.

"Then it's probably a good idea if we all get some sleep," Lily suggested.

"I'll stay with Aaren, make sure he's okay," Eshe volunteered.

"You can come with me, Priya. My girlfriend and I will take care of you," Hallie said, thinking that was probably best considering what she had been through.

"Girlfriend?"

"Yeah, you're going to love her."

~

Diana hadn't known where to go after Caleb and the others ran Aaren up to the infirmary. She had injuries of her own, but she didn't want to join everyone quite yet. The events of the last day had been quite shocking, from Will's departure and Ezra's visit, to her change of heart and the rescue. She should have found somewhere to wind down and clean herself up, but instead she found herself wandering towards the south wing.

Everything looked much the same as the last time she was here, except for an update in the decor and an upgrade to the technology. People were shooting her looks as she walked down the hallway, but news had already begun to spread about what had happened. She could hear them whispering, wondering why she was truly there, but she didn't have the energy or the inclination to explain. It would be time wasted when she knew that she could prove her change of heart by fighting alongside them when the time came.

Diana looked up at the door in front of her and saw that Ezra's room hadn't moved. There was a fingerprint scanner outside the door which looked a lot fancier than the one from her memories. Surely, he had removed her from his permissions?

Much to her surprise, he hadn't. Was that out of forgetfulness or sentimentality?

Diana shrugged to herself as she pushed the door open wider and stepped inside, leaving it open behind her in case anyone thought that she was trying to sabotage his room.

Ezra's had always kept his room tidy, even in his twenties. It was something that his parents drilled into him that he had never let go. He didn't let go of a lot, it seemed, if he still refused to let go of her even after all these years. She supposed she had done the same through her anger and hatred.

Approaching the small bookcase by the bed, Diana ran her finger over the lid of the dusty, wooden box where she knew Ezra kept his most prized possessions. It didn't have any carvings on it, but she could feel that their initials were both still etched into the back. Sentimentality, then.

"I heard you were here, but I didn't quite believe it," Ezra said, making her jump.

She hadn't realised that she wasn't alone.

"I can't believe you still have this, I would have thought that Master Talbot would have found it and taken it away long ago."

"He doesn't know everything about this place," Ezra said, staying by the door. "Besides, I'm a Master too. If he did, it would be tantamount to petty theft among Elders."

Diana laughed, something that she thought she would never do in response to any of his jokes ever again.

How things had changed.

When he didn't move to stop her, Diana carefully opened the box and surveyed what was inside. His parents' wedding rings, his grandmother's copy of the Torah, a couple of old pictures and coins, then, at the bottom...

"This..."

Diana pulled out an old comic book and held it up, so he could see.

"This was Caleb's."

"I know."

Looking between him and the colourful cover, she wasn't sure what to say, what to feel. How did he have this?

"He gave it to me when I saw him and his aunt onto the plane back to America, said something about how I should track down the hero from the story and ask him to become a Guardian. He thought he would be a perfect fit." Ezra smiled and shook his head. "I was surprised when he didn't recognise me when he came back here as an adult, he didn't remember much of anything. Too much time had passed, I suppose. Or it was a side effect of the head injury."

Diana was clutching the comic now, staring at it rather than him.

"I meant what I said when I've tried to do my best by him, as much as the others would allow. If they had suspected that I was showing too much favouritism, they would have kicked both of us out, and I knew how much all of this meant to him."

When she continued to refuse to look him, Ezra took a step closer, touching the comic with a finger.

"Caleb was the only way I could make amends for what I did. I didn't understand just how painful it was for you to be separated from your child, it was only when I sent my own family away that I came to regret blindly following orders."

Diana didn't shift away from him, but her stance didn't change either. There was far too much to forgive for it to be solved in one conversation. However, she could see how Ezra's influence had affected her son. That level headedness that lay under his words and actions could never have come from her sister-in-law.

Before either of them could speak again, the sound of footsteps trampling quickly through the hallway outside reminded them that there were more important things to be tending to right now.

"If we survive this, you owe me a proper apology," she said, pushing the comic against his chest.

Ezra nodded in agreement as he wrapped his arms around it protectively.

Diana stepped to leave but stopped herself, looking up at him again. "If I die, you make sure my boy wants for nothing, Elders be damned."

"I swear."

"Cross your heart," she said.

"And hope to die," he finished.

That was how she knew he meant it. Even after all these years, that simple promise was everything to them.

Chapter Twenty-Nine

Caleb had been right. The sun had barely begun to rose when he woke to the sound of Ezra banging on his door. Scouts at the highway had seen a convoy of cars heading north. They were less than an hour away. Caleb needed to be ready.

All the Guardians who were fighting on the front line had congregated in the lobby to wait for their orders. Caleb searched for Kiara in the crowd and found her talking to his Mom and Ezra.

"Here he is," Kiara said, giving Caleb a quick hug when he appeared.

"Hey," Caleb said. "Are you all ready?"

"As we'll ever be," Diana replied.

Her attention suddenly shifted away from him and she called out, "Will!" as she raised her hand in the air to catch his attention.

The three of them watched as she made her way to him, the two of them sharing a look before they embraced.

Caleb hadn't thought about it before now, but Will must have been the closest thing that she had to family these last few years. It would be difficult for them not to fight side by side, but he had decided that he was going to help protect Hallie, Lily, Eshe and the others in the infirmary with Aaren and Priya. It made sense, so no one argued.

"May we see each other again," Caleb saw her say as she touched Will's cheek.

"In this life or the next," Will replied.

Caleb hoped it was this one.

"I'm not sure I can take the suspense," Kiara said when Diana joined them again, bobbing up and down on her heels.

"You won't be saying that in a minute," Ezra told her. "All of you, follow me."

The three of them kept close behind Ezra as he forced his way to the front of the crowd, stopping just in front of the double doors.

"Everyone, quiet!"

Silence fell within an instant.

"You all have your orders, but I wanted to take a moment to tell you myself how honoured I am to be fighting alongside you all today. Whatever happens, be strong and remember that you are only to harm another if it is absolutely necessary. We want to resolve this as bloodlessly as possible, so we stand a chance of negotiating our way to a better future for all Guardians. Understood?"

There was a great cry of 'yes!' from everyone there.

"On me," he told them, gesturing for the doors to be opened.

They all took a few steps back, the doors swinging wide to bathe them in the morning sun. Caleb remained close to Ezra as they made their way out into the courtyard, forming a defensive line between the main gate and the building which was three layers of people deep. He had Kiara to his left and his Mom to his right, who was standing between him and Ezra.

The people from the camp were already amassing on the other side of the gate, surrounding a truck with a metal battering ram on the front of it. They were going to break through within minutes.

"Caleb?"

He turned his head to look at his Mom, who had her fists up already, prepared to strike the moment they made it into the courtyard.

"Yeah?"

"I love you."

There a loud crash, but the gates held. Caleb almost got so distracted by it that he forgot to reply.

"I love you too," he said.

There was a lot that they had to talk about if they made it through this, but deep down, he knew that he would always love her, no matter what she had done.

The truck's engines revved again and this time they were successful in sending both iron gates flying.

"Steady!" Ezra yelled as the campers came piling through.

They didn't stop to form any sort of line, instead they came right for the Guardians and started to pull out their weapons. He was waiting for exactly the right moment to move, when their counterattack would be the most effective.

"Now!"

Their front line took off at a sprint, ducking the first wave of gunfire as the two groups collided, so they could come at them swinging.

Caleb skidded on his knees, sending a person soaring right over the top of his head. Kiara cleaned up behind him as he struck forward, disarming a woman by grabbing both her hands and pointing her gun in the air, so the shot fired over their heads, then twisted the weapon from her grasp. His Mom jabbed her across the face, knocking her unconscious.

No one tried to shoot him around his family and got away with it.

"Keep pushing forward," Ezra called out to them, hoping to keep the fight outside the Citadel if possible.

"Roger that," Kiara said from behind Caleb, slamming her knee into the private parts of a man who had tried to disable her.

With any luck, this all would be over before it had really begun.

~

Hallie slapped her brother upside the head.

"Stop looking at her like that," she hissed, obviously meaning Lily, as Will had been staring at the woman's side profile for a solid minute now without blinking.

"Why?" he asked quietly, rubbing the back of his head.

"Because she's all but taken."

"What's the guy waiting for?"

"Things around here to change."

Surely Will could have figured that one out. He had been instrumental in putting together the group of people gathering outside, the ones who wanted to tear down the Citadel and restart the Guardian order from the ashes.

Hallie had already made it known to several people how dumb she thought this stupid rule was and they were inclined to agree now so many of their order had rebelled. Hopefully, once this was over and the Elders came to their senses, there would be nothing in the way of Caleb and Lily having a proper relationship.

"I can hear both of you, remember?" Lily said, although when she looked over her shoulder at them, she was smiling.

"I know, which is why I was stopping his mind from wandering in the first place," she said, narrowing her eyes at her brother as one final sign to back off.

Will held up his hands. "Okay, okay, sheesh."

"What are you lot going on about?" Aaren asked from the doorway, looking at the three of them with a raised eyebrow.

"Nothing important," Eshe assured him.

"When do you think the assault will begin?" Priya asked them from where she was guarding the side door.

"Any minute now," Lily said. "I can hear a lot of angry voices coming from outside the walls."

"I still think it's weird that you can read our thoughts," Aaren said.

"It's helpful in this case," Hallie told him. "She's sort of our early warning system."

"Way to depersonalise me, Hallie," Lily snorted.

"You're welcome."

Their humorous looks died when they heard the first crash from outside.

"Here we go," Aaren said quietly.

"Be prepared, the first people needing our help will be making their way up to us shortly," Eshe said, shooing Will towards the side door.

There were several other healers waiting beside cots further inside the room. The plan was for Hallie and Eshe to check everyone who came in and send them further back if they needed more serious healing, so they could get people who weren't too badly injured back out into the fight.

They only had to wait a few minutes after the fighting started before they heard the elevator ping for the first time.

"Two gunshot wounds incoming," Aaren warned them as he walked to meet the couple part way.

When he appeared, he was carrying a middle-aged woman his arms and had a young man holding onto his elbow for support.

"Hop up on here," Hallie told the man, grabbing a medical kit so that she could remove the bullet if she needed to before she healed up the worst of the wound.

Aaren laid the woman down in front of Eshe, who immediately went to work as well, tending to his stomach wound.

"If they brought guns, what else did they bring?" Lily asked.

"Depends how much time they had to grab stuff before they left. We could be dealing with some pretty nasty stuff," Will said.

"Fannnntastic," Hallie grumbled.

"We can handle whatever they throw at us," Eshe said. "We just have to remember to only heal what's necessary."

"Right," Hallie said, knowing that was going to be the hardest part for her.

Hopefully the fight would be over before that became a problem.

Chapter Thirty

When the initial wave of campers ran in, it looked like the fight was going to go in their favour if they could keep them staggered. Unfortunately, as time pressed on, the campers started to gain a foothold throughout the courtyard by using grenades, with the Guardian's numbers dwindling fast. It was proving difficult to fight against their weapons as it gave them a solid advantage.

Kiara had got herself pinned back against the wall of the courtyard, blood dripping from a wound in her arm which had been slashed with a knife. She shifted to the side, making her assailant smash his fist into the wall rather than her face. He growled with pain and made a sloppy move towards her, which she was able to deflect. This unfortunately meant that she missed the woman to her left who seized her wounded arm and tightened her grip to the point where Kiara screamed.

This cry didn't go unnoticed as suddenly both Caleb and Ezra were there, dispatching the pair of campers before they had the chance to strike again.

"Kiara, you need to go to the infirmary," Caleb said.

"No, not yet, it's not that bad," she told him. "I'll only be distracting them from more important things."

"Okay," he didn't argue, knowing that he didn't have the time. He did, however, turn to Ezra. "We need to pull back into the corridors, give them less room to work with so that it's easier to fight them."

"Agreed," Ezra said.

"Retreat into the Citadel," Caleb shouted to those around them, protecting Kiara as they skirted along the wall and made their way inside, Ezra and Diana right behind.

"We need to divide their attention," Diana said once they were in the lobby.

"Caleb and I will go that way, towards the infirmary," Kiara said.

"Ezra, you follow me then."

As they parted ways, what remained of the campers began to enter the building, some through the main doors and others through the parking garage, so they could spread throughout the building.

"Over here!" Kiara called out, a bullet narrowly missing her as Caleb pulled her out the way.

"That was close."

"Too close," he agreed, pushing open the door to the stairwell. "Up we go. Keep your head low."

They barely made it up two flights before the four campers following them caught up. One of them tugged Caleb's foot out from under him, making him fall against the stairs with an 'oof!'

Kiara levelled her foot with their face in retaliation, sending them tumbling over the railing and back down the steps. Caleb was able to turn over and pull one to the floor, but another leapt over them both and collided with Kiara. As they bashed into the wall, the man lost his footing, which allowed Kiara to slam her palm into his chest, then boot him in the side when he fell to the ground.

"Give up already!"

"Never!" a blonde-haired woman cried out from below.

Tired of their dogged determination to ruin everything, Kiara pulled a gun out of the hands of the man she had just kicked and threw it directly at the woman's head. It bounced off the side of her face with a crack and she collapsed, dazed.

"Nice throwing arm," Caleb commented, looking impressed as he picked himself up off the stairs. He was leaning slightly to one side, compensating for an injury.

"I was always the bowler whenever we played rounders at primary school, my team rarely lost a match."

"No kidding."

"Shall we?" she said, nodding up the stairs.

"After you."

~

Diana and Ezra found themselves sprinting down the long corridor towards the south wing. If they kept going all the way round, eventually they would meet up with Caleb and Kiara at the infirmary, but they had to deal with those following them first.

And those ahead.

"Duck!" Diana cried when she spotted them.

They moved quickly in opposite directions, flattening their bodies against the walls of the corridor so each group ended up shooting at each other. That took care of three of them without either of them having to lift a finger. Diana ran towards one group and Ezra went for the other. She lost sight of him as she attacked the two that had been trying to ambush them by coming up from the parking garage.

They both looked apprehensive when they saw the sheer focus on her face, having never come to blows with her before. She dropped into a roll at the last moment, sweeping their feet out from under them. In a flash, she was standing again and delivering a boot to the side of one of their heads. The other dodged out of the way and spun around on their back, aiming at their gun at her. A bullet lodged itself in her shoulder, but she didn't stop. Ripping the piece from their hand, Diana leaned over and smashed the barrel of it into their face three times, leaving behind a broken nose and two missing teeth.

Diana whipped her head round to see where Ezra had got to and found that he had been shoved against the wall, a man's hands around his throat.

"HEY!" she boomed, her voice echoing through the corridor.

The distraction was enough to make the man loosen his grip. Ezra struck out so quickly with his knee that the man ended up stumbling backwards. Diana shot him in the kneecap before he could regain his balance and he screamed, falling back against the nearby window. He banged his head against the windowsill and knocked himself out. She knew what Ezra had said about not badly injuring people unless it was necessary, but they had gone far past that point.

"Still quick on the draw, I see," he said.

"And you haven't got complacent with age, I'm impressed."

"By most Elders' standards, I'm still a young man."

"Don't let them hear you saying that," Diana said with a wicked smirk.

For a moment, it felt just like old times, then a burst of gunfire from upstairs brought them crashing back to reality.

"Let's go take care of them," Ezra suggested.

"I'll be right behind you."

~

It hadn't taken long for things in the infirmary to get hectic. Hallie was already starting to feel overwhelmed as person after person piled in, some looking for a quick fix, others who were out for the count and needed patching up just enough so that they didn't slip away while they were busy taking care of everyone else.

They hadn't had anyone attack yet, the benefits of being on the top floor, but they could hear the fighting getting closer. Lily was doing everything she could to keep those in real distress quiet and calm while they waited for a healer to become available, but that was tiring work.

"How much longer is this going to go on for?" Hallie asked as another person hobbled in through the door with a gash in their leg.

"However long it takes for one side to win," Aaren said.

"Can you tell whether one side is making headway over the other?" Will directed his question to Lily, as she was the one who was able to sense those around them.

"No, it's a mess out there," she said, shushing a young woman who had tears streaming down her face, her arm was burned so badly.

He didn't really get a chance to look disappointed, as Aaren suddenly called out, "Incoming!"

"This way too!" Priya shouted back.

As the three of them stepped out into the corridor, Hallie returned her focus to the older man whose stab wound she was cleaning.

"You are Hallie, right?" he asked her.

His breathing was shallow as he had already lost a lot of blood.

"Yes, just try to stay quiet if you can. I need to be able to concentrate to heal this up," she said as softly as she could. She didn't want the stress to make her snappy.

"I fear my wounds might be too great."

"Not if I have anything to say about it."

He ignored her. "Will you do something for me?"

The man was only just able to get the end of the sentence out before he started coughing, blood seeping out from between his dry lips.

He beckoned her closer with a tilt of the head and she obliged, only because she believed he was going to continue to be stubborn if she didn't do as he asked.

"There's a letter in the top desk drawer in my office, give it to Ezra after the battle is done. He's the only one I trust to carry out my last wishes."

"You're not going to die," she tried again.

"Just don't forget," he whispered, his voice fading.

Hallie pulled away from him, laying her hands on his chest so she could start healing, but she couldn't feel anything. All she could see within him was cold and darkness. He was already gone.

"Damn it!" she cursed, kicking a nearby crate.

"We can mourn him later, pick another patient and start healing," Eshe said.

Hallie knew that Eshe was right, that she couldn't waste time because of the sheer amount of people who needed their help, but she still took a couple of seconds to carefully slide his eyelids closed. Whoever he was, she would make sure Ezra got his letter.

~

Caleb and Kiara managed to make it to the top of the staircase without any more mishaps, stopping to take a breather once they were in the corridor.

"The infirmary is around the corner and down the end of the next hallway," Caleb said, leaning against the wall. "Once we're there, we can check on everyone, see how many people they've had make their way up here so far."

"Okay," Kiara agreed.

When he could hear his breathing again over the sound of his pounding heart, he righted himself and started to make his way down the corridor, only for the end of it to be blocked by a massive man, covered in all sorts of weapons.

"Oh crap," he said.

The man thundered towards them, each step making the walls and floors shake. He and Kiara looked at each other and set off at a run, linking hands so that they formed a barricade with their arms. As their barrier collided with the man's stomach, they all bounced off each other, getting tossed every which way.

Caleb was the first to his feet, snatching up a blade that had fallen off the man's belt. He intended to disable him with it, but the large fella snatched a flash bomb off his shoulder strap and lobbed it at Caleb. Without even thinking, Caleb batted it back then turned away as it went off in the man's face, violently blinding him.

The noises that the man made in response to his loss of vision sounded like he was about to erupt like a volcano. This wasn't good.

Caleb prepared himself to take another run at the man, but he as was spinning around and flailing in pain, he was shaking other things loose from his small armory. He watched in horror as a grenade with no pin bounced its way down the hallway towards them, coming to a stop at his feet.

The elevator pinged behind them and Caleb turned on his heel, hurling his body against Kiara's. As the explosion went off, they were both thrown onto the floor of the cabin, which shook from the force of the blast. There was a moment of silence where he thought that his plan had worked, then, with an ear shattering screech, the elevator dropped, taking them both with it.

Chapter Thirty-One

Kiara let out a shriek when the lift came to a shuddering halt, having only fallen a couple of floors. The failsafe must have kicked in for now.

"Hey," Caleb said, touching her arm. "Are you hurt?"

"I'm fine. You managed to push us out of the way in time," she assured him.

"Good," he said. "Because it looks like we might be trapped."

Oh no. This was Kiara's worst nightmare, she hated small spaces.

"Just breathe, okay?" Caleb told her, punching the emergency help button as he got back onto his feet.

"What's that going to do?" she asked, knowing that no one was on the desk downstairs, they were all too busy fighting.

"If someone passes by, maybe they'll hear it and come get us."

"What do we do until then?"

"Try the doors, see whether or not we're between floors," he suggested.

Together, with a lot of brute force, they were able to pry the doors open far enough to see about a foot of the next floor's exit.

"If we can get those open, we can get you through," Caleb said.

"Surely you should go first? I'm the one who can't die if things go wrong."

"There's no way I'll fit. Better that you get out there and find some help, just in case this thing doesn't hold."

Kiara didn't look so keen.

"Just, trust me, okay?"

"Okay."

Caleb crouched down so Kiara could sit on his shoulders. Once she was up, the lift creaked a little, but didn't move.

"I think we're okay. Go ahead."

Kiara decided to focus on one of the doors first, forcing it as far as she could push without losing grip, before doing the same with the other.

"Great, now get down and I'll give you a proper boost."

Kiara slid down his back, landing as softly as she could so she didn't disturb anything, then used his linked hands as a springboard to catch onto the edge. She let out a groan as she pulled herself through the small gap, the weight of her entire body supported by her arms. If it weren't for all the training that Caleb had put her through these last couples of months, she wouldn't have been able to do it.

"You got it," Caleb said from below her, supportive as always.

It took some wiggling, but she got clear of the door and lay on the floor for a moment, panting.

"You okay?" Caleb called up.

"Yeah," she shouted back, pushing up onto her hands and knees.

Thankfully, there was no one around, so she was able to crawl back around to the opening without being disturbed.

"I can try to open the doors wider, then you can crawl through," she said, wanting to at least try and get him out.

As she looked around for something to use as leverage, the lift let out another almighty creak and shifted slightly, making them both stop dead.

"Caleb?"

"Get back," he told her.

"Caleb, no, we have to get you out of there!"

"If I move again, it might fall."

"All the more reason for you to make a break for it. Come on."

They locked eyes, Caleb slowly shaking his head.

"I think it's going to go."

"Caleb!" Kiara pleaded, desperately searching for some way to save him.

"It's been an honour being your teacher, Kiara," he told her sincerely. "Don't waste the time you have left."

"No! You're not dying! Just jump!"

Kiara stretched a hand out, willing him to take it. But it was too late. The sound of the cable snapping echoed through the hallway. Kiara only just managed to pull her hand back before the lift crashed down out of sight, taking Caleb with it.

~

"Fuck off!" Will heard Aaren grunt as he seized the collar of a woman trying to slip past him and tossed her on the floor.

It seemed that most of the campers were making their way up to the infirmary as they knew that was where the remaining Guardians were headed. They were having to fight off group after group as they tried to take the last remaining stronghold in the building. Will could feel himself growing tired, even with the adrenaline pumping through his veins. If this didn't end soon, then they might just break through.

"Seriously, why haven't they given up already?" Priya complained, flopping back against the wall so she could breathe for a second.

"Both sides must be on their last legs," Will said. "It could go either way."

A loud explosion from the other end of the floor startled them, as did the noises that followed.

"That can't have been a good thing," Aaren said.

Will was trying to figure out what might have happened when a group of several campers rounded the corner, led by Ricardo. They looked like they were out for blood.

"Watch out!" Will tried to say as they slid a smoke bomb down the corridor.

They had to duck out of the way, back into the infirmary as smoke obscured everything that they could previously see.

"What's going on?" Hallie demanded, but no one got a chance to respond.

A woman with a knife appeared through the smoke and tossed it, hoping to hit someone, anyone really. There were screams, but it embedded itself in the wall rather than slicing anybody.

Aaren grabbed her throwing arm and pulled her inside, slamming her into a pile of medical supplies, but got stabbed in the back of the shoulder while he was distracted. As he stumbled forwards onto one of the cots, Priya stepped up and kicked the sword from the person's hand. She was able to fend off two of them by using her size to her advantage, but they soon overwhelmed her too.

All their attention was pulled in that direction, so no one noticed the shooter entering through the side door until it was too late.

They pointed the barrel of the shotgun directly at Hallie's chest and pulled the trigger.

To Will, everything moved in slow motion. His eyes followed the line of the gun to Hallie and suddenly he was lunging, his body travelling inch by inch until it completely blocked hers.

Pain spread throughout his chest like someone had set it on fire.

Burning, *burning,* all he could feel was BURNING.

As his body hit the floor, his eyes rolled up and he saw the shooter in the doorway get ripped backwards by a pair of hands, a woman's hands.

"WILL?!"

The cry bounced around his eardrums, but he couldn't comprehend where it was coming from. Instead, his vision began to go white. Everything around him dissolved away into nothing and the last thing he remembered thinking before he lost consciousness entirely was:

'Is this it?'

~

"NOO!" Kiara cried, her eyes fixed on the space where Caleb's face had been only moments before.

Scrambling to her feet, Kiara kicked open the door to the stairwell and charged down the first flight, missing every step that she possibly could without falling face first onto the floor. She had never moved so fast in her life, it felt like she was flying.

At the bottom, she burst into the hall and looked at the doors where the lift would usually open. They had been blown outward slightly by the force of the fall, which had been several storeys.

Kiara ran forward and pulled on one of the doors, yelling loudly as she used all her strength to force it open. She had to do the same again with the inner door, using her feet so she could get even more power behind her push.

Eventually the inner door gave way and she fell inside, landing next to Caleb's limp body.

"Caleb?"

Kiara tugged at his top, hoisting his head up into her lap. There was blood oozing from a terrible gash on his forehead and one of his legs was bent completely out of shape. His eyes were closed. It didn't look good.

"Caleb? Caleb, please, wake up," she shook him gently, unsure whether he was dead or alive. It was tough to tell through the tears.

Pressing her ear to his chest, she prayed that she would hear a heartbeat or feel his chest moving. It took a moment with all the other noises going on around the building, but she heard it. He was alive, just.

"Stay with me," she told him, thanking whatever power in the universe had allowed him to survive such a terrible fall.

Lifting him by herself wasn't an option. He was dead weight and it was going to be impossible to maneuver him through the doors without hurting him even more.

"Somebody! Anybody! Help!" she screamed, holding onto Caleb tightly, like he might slip away if she let him go.

"PLEASE! HELP ME!"

It was agonising howling the words again and again, only for no one to respond. Kiara was about to give up hope when suddenly a voice called back.

"Where are you?"

"IN HERE!" she bellowed, waving a hand in the air in case they could see it.

There was some creaking and groaning as two people she didn't recognise, but had clearly been caught up in the fighting seconds ago, pushed the doors down to get to her and Caleb.

"Oh my gosh," the woman gasped, quickly crouching down beside Kiara to take Caleb's pulse.

"He's hanging on by a thread, we need to get him to the medical area now," Kiara begged, looking at them both, her face wet with tears.

"Please, help me. He can't die, I need him."

The pair could see how desperate she was feeling. Caleb wasn't just her teacher, he was becoming family. She couldn't lose her family, not again.

"Don't worry, sweetheart, he won't be going anywhere if we can help it," the woman said, squeezing her arm softly.

"Now, help me get him up," the guy said.

They positioned themselves by each of Caleb's shoulders, making sure that they had a secure grip on him.

"Okay, on three."

Kiara nodded.

"One, two…"

~

Hallie's world had come to a shuddering halt.

One moment she was staring down a shotgun, certain that she had already taken her last breath, and the next her brother was lying on the floor with blood spilling out of his chest.

Her voice didn't sound like her own as his name tore its way out of her throat. She dropped to her knees and clutched at his shirt, her hands quickly becoming slick with his blood.

"Hallie."

Someone was trying to talk to her, but she didn't want to listen.

All she could see was red.

A pair of hands held her shoulders as Eshe and Diana materialised on the other side of Will. Hallie hadn't even realised that Diana was here.

"Heal him," she choked.

"I'm on it," Eshe promised, running her hands across the top of Will's shrapnel wounds. As they glowed brightly, Hallie felt her heart fill with hope. But as time passed and nothing happened, despair started to creep in instead.

"Why isn't it working?"

"It must be his time," Diana said, her eyes filling with tears.

Hallie shook her head. That couldn't possibly be the reason. He had made promises he had to keep, he couldn't die now.

"He told me once that he knew he had four years, but the Oracle never told him exactly when he was going to die," Eshe said. "He's been living in limbo all this time, wondering when death was going to catch up with him."

They were all giving up. Why were they giving up?

"No, no, NO! This can't be it, we have to do something!"

"Hallie."

It was Lily's voice that came from behind her, she must have been the one trying to comfort her.

"They're right, once he's gone, he's gone."

"NO!" she screamed, slapping her hands against his chest. If they wouldn't do anything, then she would! She could bring him back.

"Heal," she pleaded, her sight of him going blurry. "Heal. Heeeeal."

Still nothing.

"HEAL GOD DAMN IT."

A second pair of arms wrapped themselves around her, joining Lily's.

"I'm so sorry, Hallie," Priya said.

"Noooo," Hallie wailed, screwing up her face because she couldn't bear to hear it.

"He loved you so much, Hallie, you were everything to him."

It was that love that had got him killed.

Killed.

Hallie felt her heart shatter into a million pieces as she yelled out with anguish. The only things keeping her tethered to reality were Lily and Priya's arms, cradling her, supporting her, giving her the room she needed to fall apart.

If it wasn't for them, she might never have come back.

~

"Help! Somebody help!"

Kiara and the other Guardian tripped over the bodies in the hallway trying to get Caleb into the crowded infirmary.

They brushed by everyone as they made straight for the nearest cot. Kiara was sort of half aware that a bunch of people were currently huddled around on the floor, but she didn't get a proper look on the way past.

"Why is nobody helping?!" she declared as she turned and looked at them.

That was when she saw him.

The reason so many people were on the floor was because Will was down there, flat on his back, soaked in blood, and Hallie was falling completely to pieces.

"Oh my God," she gasped.

Or, at least, she tried to, but was completely drowned out by Diana crying out at the sight of her son.

"Caleb!"

The previously still room sprang into action.

Diana and Eshe almost fell over each other trying to get to Caleb's cot. Hallie pushed Priya and Lily away to look to Kiara, her eyes bloodshot with grief.

Her expression said it all. She was hanging on by the slightest thread, if anything else happened then it was going to push her straight over the edge.

"Someone help me up," she croaked.

Ezra obliged, gently lifting her over to Caleb's bedside, which is where they all knew she wanted to be.

"What happened?" Diana asked Kiara as the two healers assessed the damage.

"Someone tried to blow us up. Caleb knocked us both into a lift, but it became unstable. I managed to get out but he…"

She couldn't relive that moment over again, not right now.

"He's barely holding on," Eshe said. "Hallie, give me your hand."

Hallie did exactly as she was told.

"We're going to channel each other, like we started to do last night with Aaren. Feel my power and use it, I'll do the same with you. Got it?"

Hallie simply nodded her head and closed her eyes.

They each placed their free hand on Caleb's arm and began to chant softly. It was something that Kiara knew Hallie did in her head when she was healing, but this time they were both doing it out loud. The longer they chanted, the brighter their linked hands glowed.

Eventually it got to a point where everyone had to look away, their power was shining so brightly.

Kiara wasn't sure what was happening. She wanted so desperately to look back, but she knew she wouldn't see anything if she did. For once, she was having to go on blind faith. Together, they could do it.

Together, they could do anything.

The sound of Caleb coughing was like music to her ears.

When she opened her eyes, the bright light was gone, and Diana was holding Caleb's head in her arms, pressing kisses to his cheeks.

"I thought I was going to lose you," she whispered, tears trickling from her eyes onto his face.

"I thought I was going to lose me too."

There was something about what he said that hit Kiara like a freight train. All of a sudden, she was crying, sobbing even.

"Hey, it's okay," he said. "I'm going to be okay."

"Yeah, but--"

Kiara couldn't finish. Her eyes met Hallie's and that only made things worse. How was she supposed to tell him that while she was so relieved that he had pulled through, she couldn't express it because of what had happened just minutes before.

In the end, Ezra spoke for her.

"We lost Will."

Caleb's face…

"Hallie--" he tried, but she cut him off.

"I can't. I'm happy you're alive, but I can't, Caleb."

That was the last straw. With a shake of the head, Hallie ran from the room, unable to take it anymore.

A mournful silence fell across the room.

"I need to go after her," Kiara said after a moment or two, looking round at all their sad faces.

"Of course," Ezra said. "We'll take care of everything else."

"Give her our love," Lily said.

"I will," she promised.

Hallie was going to need all the love in the world right now if she was going to get through this. Thankfully, that was something that Kiara could give.

Chapter Thirty-Two

It had been two weeks since the battle and Hallie still felt raw. She wasn't expecting that to change any time soon, neither was anyone around her. The respect they had for her grief was exactly the sort of level that she would expect from them. No one overwhelmed her, tried to give her advice when she didn't ask for it, they just supported her. They had all been through something like this before, so they understood that, in the end, what she needed was time.

Hallie hadn't known, but Kiara had managed to convince Will to phone their Dad the day before he died. As he had promised he would be on the first flight home after the fight, their Dad insisted that he be buried in Australia, for his and Will's Mom's comfort. Ezra moved heaven and earth to make sure that this happened for them, for which they were all appreciative.

There had only been two other casualties. A woman who was found in the courtyard after the battle was over, who had been caught by one of her own grenades, and Master Talbot, who had been the old man that had given the message to Hallie. It turned out that he was the Elder who was the casting vote when they had to make any big decisions. She wished she had known this at the time, but she didn't know what difference it would have made.

They had their funerals in a church near the Citadel. A lot of those from the camp were allowed to attend, although most of them hadn't accepted the opportunity to re-join the Guardian order. There was too much pain and shame there. The main instigators and those who killed Master Talbot and Will were arrested and were expected to be sentenced to life, which was less than they deserved in Hallie's eyes. Although, the man who killed Will had been ripped a new one by Diana in the moments after he fired, which helped to add to the justice served.

When it came time to fly out to Australia, Hallie wasn't alone. Kiara came with her, of course, as did Caleb and Lily for moral support. Diana decided that she wanted to come too, to pay her respects, and so Ezra joined them to be there for her. It was a long and quiet plane ride, none of them saying very much. Hallie drifted in and out of sleep, but every time she closed her eyes, she saw the image of Will lying there, covered in blood. She had woken up screaming several times since it happened, with Kiara right there to hold her and calm her down.

How was she ever supposed to let go of something like this?

The day of the funeral ended up being the worst. Hallie barely got any sleep and refused to talk to anyone at breakfast, not even her Dad. Once she was changed into the black dress and flats that Will's Mom had picked out for her, she retreated out to the gazebo in the back garden, looking out over the ocean.

This had been Will's favourite place to sit, he had told her, whenever he needed to be alone. The sound of the waves washing up on shore was so peaceful.

Hallie didn't realise that there were tears sliding down her cheeks until a soft hand carefully wiped one of them away.

"Hey," Kiara said, sitting down beside her. "I wondered where you got to."

"I couldn't face everyone, not today."

"They understand."

As Kiara's hand dropped back down into her lap, Hallie caught it, running a thumb over her babe's pale skin.

"I don't think I ever thanked you for what you did with Will, getting him to call home. It would have been so much harder to explain to my Dad if he hadn't heard from Will first," Hallie said.

"Of course. I knew how important it had been to have Lily back in my life, I wanted to give your Dad and Will that same sense of relief. I just didn't realise that… it would be the last time they would talk."

"I know, but I still see it as a blessing. They reconnected in a way that they never would have without that conversation. That was one less regret for them both."

Hallie didn't like the idea of Will being somewhere up there, worrying about all that he hadn't been able to do for his family. It was better to think about it this way, that he had got the chance to reconcile with his family and learn just how much they all still loved him.

"That's good," Kiara said with the smallest of smiles.

It showed that Hallie was already making progress. Very slow progress, but still.

"What's everyone else doing?" Hallie asked.

"I saw Diana in Will's room as I passed by to come downstairs, and I think Caleb and Lily are both getting ready. I'm not sure about Ezra. We're all just waiting for the cars to take us to the church."

Hallie was dreading the car ride, following Will's casket all the way. But at least she could draw on Kiara for strength.

"Do you think what happened will change anything?"

Hallie asked Kiara because she knew that she had been talking to the others while she had been shut away in her room, not saying very much to anyone.

"They're still talking about it, but things are looking hopeful. There is no way that they can risk anything like this happening again, the Elders have decided that much."

Any loss of life would have been too great for them. The fact that they lost three people had to be forcing them to reassess what truly mattered.

"I hope they do let Guardians have families again," Hallie said. "It's what Will was fighting for."

Kiara hesitated, which made Hallie frown.

"What?"

"I don't agree," she said. "That's not what he was fighting for in the end."

"Then what was he fighting for?"

"For you, Hallie."

Hallie's bottom lip wobbled so hard that she had to bite it to make it stop. She looked at Kiara with a fresh set of tears in her eyes.

"Please, don't, Kiara. I already feel so guilty."

"Why?"

"The bullet was meant for me. If he hadn't been fighting for me, then…"

"He would have done it anyway."

Hallie sniffed loudly in an effort to control her sorrow, but it was too strong.

"It took sheer force of will to put himself in front of that gun and take that hit. He would have done it over and over again if it meant saving your life. It was a combination of his choice, the shooter's choice, and fate that took him from you."

Kiara placed a hand on either side of Hallie's face and looked at her with her earnest, hazel eyes.

"I know it's not what you want to hear right now, but you're not guilty for any of it. I'm going keep reminding you of that until you believe it yourself. *That's* what Will would have wanted."

Hallie pushed Kiara's hands away from her, but only so she could lean into her chest and hug her tightly.

"I love you so much, Hallie," Kiara said quietly as she pressed a kiss to the top of her head.

"I love you too," Hallie murmured

Hallie had felt like the unluckiest person in the world for the last two weeks, but now she realised that she was the luckiest, and that no one could take that feeling from her so long as she had Kiara's love in her life.

~

"Caleb? Can you give me a hand?"

The Guardian had been sitting on the bed, staring at the tie that he was supposed to be putting on, unable to do so for the last fifteen minutes. This was the same story that Caleb had been living for the last fortnight; unsure of what to do, confused about how to feel. Of course, he was happy that he was alive. When that elevator dropped, he had thought for sure that was it for him. It was a miracle that he survived. He didn't believe in God, but if he did, he would say that he obviously had other plans for him, which meant that he had to be alive to see them through.

Whatever gratitude he felt, though, was always marred by the fact that Will died while he lived. They could easily have traded places if Will wasn't a Chosen. The timing of his death was so unbelievably unfair. If it had come a month, a week later, there was so much that Will could have done in that time which would have made it easier on his family. But it wasn't to be. He performed his act of heroism knowing that it could very well be his end and fate, ever the cruel mistress, decided that was it for him.

All that was left was to pick up the pieces, but they couldn't do that until they had said goodbye.

"Caleb?"

Lily poked her head around the door to their bathroom, looking at him expectantly. They had been given one of the guest bedrooms, which had a double bed that could be separated into two singles. Caleb wouldn't have minded the double, but he had no idea where they stood, whether he was allowed…

"Hey. Come back to me."

Caleb's thoughts had been drifting a lot lately, she had to be getting frustrated with him by this point.

"I'm sorry," he said, sliding off the bed.

"Don't be, I know you have a lot on your mind."

"That's no excuse to ignore you, whether I mean to or not."

"You don't mean to."

She was right, he didn't. He was never that rude, but he still felt like he was being an ass.

"It's just the zip," she told him, turning her back to him so that he could do it up for her. He did so gently, straightening out the shoulders of her dress when he was done.

"There you go."

"Thank you."

Lily spun back around slowly, looking up at him when he didn't move away. Being close to her was one of the only things that brought him comfort right now.

"I know that you're conflicted, Caleb," she told him, placing a hand on his chest. "We all are."

"I don't know, I wouldn't say Hallie was."

"Don't say that. You know that she's glad you're still with us."

"That wasn't..." he sighed. "I just meant the grief she is feeling outweighs everything else."

"I don't think you know what you meant. Your mind is so muddled that I can barely make sense of it."

"I'm sorry."

"Stop apologising."

Caleb went to apologise for apologising too much, but Lily placed a finger over his mouth before he could speak.

"Look, I know that this is hard, and I know that there are a lot of things that are unsure at the moment, but there are some things that you can be sure about. The first is that you have a family that loves you. Your Mum, Ezra, Kiara, even Hallie. If you were gone, they would be just as devastated, some even more so. I don't want you thinking that there is any sort of even trade that could have been made between you and Will. That's not something you get to carry anymore."

He had forgotten what it was like when she took charge like this, how she could command his attention and his feelings if she wanted.

"And the second?"

"That regardless of whatever the Elders decide, I want there to be an us," she said. "If there's one lesson that we should all take away from what happened it's that life for people like us can be short, regardless of prophecy. We have to seize the moment and I want to seize the moment with you."

"You do?"

"I do."

Pressing up on her toes, Lily touched her lips to his in short but sweet first kiss.

Caleb had imagined many ways that this moment could go, but he hadn't thought they would be able to find it here; a few seconds of calm certainty in the middle of a tumultuous storm of grief and pain.

"I want that too," he whispered.

"Good."

He leaned in to kiss her again, lingering longer this time. When he pulled back, his mind was clear for the first time in weeks. All that remained was the scent of her perfume and the taste of her lips.

"That's more like it," she said.

"The next one will be even better," he promised.

~

Diana had been apprehensive at first about attending the funeral. She felt a great deal of responsibility for Will not having more time with his family. If she had been less tied up in her own anger and grief and allowed him more freedom, maybe...

Maybe.

It was Caleb who convinced her that she should go. He knew how important it was for her to be able to say goodbye after what had happened to them all those years ago. If she didn't, then that decision was going to haunt her forever.

She hadn't asked Ezra to come with her. Like always, he simply volunteered with very little fuss. He was still attuned to what she needed, despite the vast amount of time that had passed.

Diana had meant to go downstairs to wait with Will's parents, but she had got distracted on the way by a sign on one of the doors. 'Will's Room'. As she pushed open the door, she wasn't surprised to find that it was exactly how Will would have left it. His parents hadn't touched it, probably to preserve a part of him while he had been gone.

The walls were painted blue, although you could barely see the colour for the number of posters that were plastered over every single wall. There were movies, bands, pictures and ticket stubs, a massive collage that made up his early years. His bed sheets were a tumbled mess and his dresser had half the drawers poking out slightly, revealing old shirts and underwear. There was a desk in front of the window which was the neatest thing in the entire room, only because it had so little on it. This must have been where most of the belongings he had carried with him to France had previously been. Handing his possessions over to his parents had been the first thing she had done when she arrived. By rights, they belonged to them now.

Diana made her way over to the desk and found a flight confirmation for his trip to New Jersey, the trip he had taken before he received his prophecy. There was a travel notebook with bits and pieces sticking out of the sides, leaflets about where he had wanted to go before his Dad shut him down. Flicking through the pages, she was glad that she had been able to take him to some of the places on his list: London, Moscow, Tokyo…

The only other thing was a crumpled picture of him, his Dad and Hallie's Mom, which he must have forgotten to take with him. He was only seven years old in the picture, holding newborn Hallie is in short arms.

She sighed quietly, touching the pendant around her neck. It was where she kept the pictures of her own family, John and Caleb. She would have to find one of Will to add to it. It was the best way she knew how to keep him close.

There was a gentle knock at the door, followed by a, "Hey."

It was Ezra.

"Hey," she replied, still holding onto the necklace.

"So, this is Will's old room."

"It almost mirrors what the inside of his tent looked like back at camp," she said. "He was such a mess, in so many ways."

"But he wasn't in the end."

"No, far from it."

Ezra joined her by the window, looking out at the sparkling water.

"It's my turn to be surprised by something I didn't realise you still had," he said.

Diana looked down at the pendant enveloped in her fingers.

"I wear it every day."

"I would have thought that you would have discarded it because it reminded you of me," he said.

"I would be lying if I said I didn't consider doing that once, back when I was first expelled from the order. But I realised that it had come to symbolise so much more than what we meant to each other all those years ago."

"What was that?"

"That was I was always carrying a little bit of love around with me, for those I care for and those who cared for me."

"That's beautiful," Ezra said.

It was funny to think that, in a way, Ezra had been the person who had kept a part of her grounded all this time because he had given her one of the most important things that she owned.

"I appreciate you being here," she said. "And I appreciate all that you've done for me these last couple of weeks, from the moment you risked your life to come to camp to talk some sense into me. If you hadn't have done it, then I probably wouldn't be here right now."

"You don't need to thank me," he said.

"Oh, but I do."

Diana grazed her the tips of fingers against his palm, letting him close his hand around hers.

"All this time, I've been so angry at you, thinking that you were the reason that Caleb was taken from me. But the truth is that I wouldn't have Caleb without you, and that's a debt that I can never repay."

"You don't owe me anything," he tried to insist.

"Would you just be quiet for once and accept my gratitude?" she asked, looking up into his familiar brown eyes.

"All right," he replied, bowing his head to her.

They stood there like that for a few minutes, letting the hatred and pain of the past slip away from them so they could start again.

"I have something I need to show you," Ezra said, breaking the silence.

"Oh?"

He let go of her hand so that he could pull a folded letter from his pocket. It was addressed to him in Master Talbot's handwriting.

"Hallie told me about it the day before we came out here. She was asked to pass on a message from Talbot in the moments before he died."

"What does it say?" she asked.

"Many things, mostly thoughts and regrets," he said. "But his last wish was that I take over his position as the deciding vote on the Elders' council."

"Really?"

"Apparently I was the best student he had ever taught, and he wanted me to lead the Guardians into the future."

"Ezra, that's--"

"I want you to know that the first thing we're doing as soon as we get back is changing the rules surrounding families. Everyone deserves to have that love in their life."

"I would have been supportive regardless, but thank you," she smiled.

"You're welcome," he said. "If we're going to move forwards, then we have to do it together."

"I agree."

"Which is why, if you agree to come back, I want to put you forth for my old spot on the council."

Diana opened and closed her mouth, a whole flurry of thoughts and doubts whirling through her head all at once.

"You don't have to decide right away. I know you've been through a lot and that convincing people to accept you will be difficult, but I would feel better knowing that there was another person on the council that I could trust."

Diana let out a shaky breath, looking back at the ocean rather than at his face. His generosity was almost too much to bear.

"I'll think about it."

Ezra smiled softly.

"That's all I ask."

~

The ceremony was perfect. There was very little pomp and circumstance. Will's cousins read a couple of poems and his Dad gave a short speech about how proud he was about what his son had achieved in life, short as it was. They buried Will in a plot closest to the cliff, so that his body would forever be by the ocean he loved so much. Kiara couldn't imagine a better send off, even though she barely knew him.

She wished she had got to talk to him more, but she had already learned the hard way that you had to take whatever you were given and cherish it. They would definitely cherish their memories of Will.

His parents held a wake at his Dad's house, where everybody milled about in the sunshine, eating from the barbeque and telling stories about their crazy family shenanigans. It was lovely.

As the sun began to set, Kiara found herself sitting on the beach, her eyes on the horizon. A definitive line that you could never reach. It felt symbolic in a way, but she couldn't put together why.

Slowly, members of their group started to join her. Hallie first. Then Lily and Caleb, walking together hand in hand. Finally, Diana and Ezra, who sat just to her right. No one wanted to speak. They all wanted to feel the one thing that had been impossible to find these last few weeks: peace.

"I can feel him," Hallie said without warning, making them turn their heads.

"Will?" Kiara asked.

"Yeah, it's like... I can feel him smiling at us, wherever he is. He's happy that we're all together."

"I can believe that," Kiara said.

"As can I," Ezra agreed.

"It's good," Hallie said, managing a smile for the first time since the battle had begun. "I hope that we can make him proud."

"We will," Diana said, looking at Ezra. "I've decided, I will let you sponsor me for your old slot on the council. Resolving our issues is the best way that we can honour him and the others who lost their lives or left us."

"From rebel leader to Elder," Caleb said, sounding amused.

"But always your mother."

"I wouldn't have it any other way."

"We'll also be doing away with the ban on Guardian's having families. I think we've all suffered enough," Ezra said. "Although, I see you two have had a head start."

Kiara noticed that Caleb and Lily were still holding hands, and not just as friends.

"That's exciting," Hallie said, and she meant it. "You two deserve each other."

"Thank you, Hallie," Lily smiled.

"If I say more nice things now, can I call dibs on being a bridesmaid?"

They all laughed.

"Let's not get ahead of ourselves, shall we?" Caleb suggested.

But Hallie whispered, "Dibs," in Lily's ear anyway.

"What's going to happen to the Citadel?" Kiara asked.

"We'll repair and rebuild. I'm not ready to give up on it just yet," Ezra said.

That made sense. Despite what had happened there, it was still home to so many. They wouldn't let fall to ruin if they could save it.

"What will we do next?" Hallie looked at Kiara.

"I hear New Zealand is very nice this time of year," she said. "If you're up for it?"

"I think a little travelling might do me some good," Hallie nodded.

"We can work out everything else once we're back," Kiara concluded.

"By the time you're done, we should have everything back up and running," Caleb said. "And then our real work will begin."

"Kicking ass and taking names the world over," Kiara smirked.

"Sounds like a plan."

Three Weeks Earlier
Epilogue

"Are you in the bathroom?"

"It's the only place that I can get a little privacy around here! They've got four of us in a room together, it gets a little crazy sometimes."

"You'd think with the amount of tuition we pay, they'd be able to get it down to two a room," Noah remarked.

"I don't think it would be any less silly. We'd all just pile in together anyway," Sophia said, giggling at a shriek that came from the other side of the door.

"Well, I know how you're finding the hotel. How about Vienna itself?"

"GREAT! So great, I can't even... The opera house was stunning. And La Traviata!"

Sophia jumped up and down, waving her phone around, which made him a little motion sick.

"Oh my God, their voices. I thought they were going to bring the whole building down."

"I'm glad you're having such a good time."

"How's London? How's Faizal?"

"Busy. He's got me trailing after him all over the city, going from meeting to meeting. I was hoping to see the sights, the closest I've got has been staring at them from the cab window while we're stuck in traffic..."

"Noah, sorry, I missed half of that because they've started fighting. Give me a minute."

Noah waited as his sister ducked past the quarrelling girls, out of the room, and made her way down to the pool. It was the middle of the night, so no one was around to bother them.

"That's better," she sighed. "I heard something about you wanting to see the sights, then you were drowned out by a screech of 'THE GUMMY BEARS ARE MIIIIINE!'"

Noah laughed. "What I had to say wasn't as interesting."

"Was the gala fun at least?"

"I got to do some schmoozing. Met a very cute redhead who would have been perfect for you, but she dashed off before I could start up a meaningful conversation."

"Are you sure you didn't scare her off? Those dimples are a lot to handle."

"They are, but I made sure she knew I was taken. I thought that would make things less tense, but it wasn't enough to stop her from darting away into the crowd before I could say goodbye."

"Ah well, it wouldn't have worked out anyway, I suck at long distance anything if it's not you or Mom," Sophia shrugged.

"And even then..." he teased, expecting a chuckle or a retort.

Instead, she was distracted.

"You okay?"

"What? Oh, yeah, I thought I saw someone. It was probably just a reflection in one of the windows."

"Yeah, probably. How's your head been?"

"Pretty good, actually. The blocking technique we figured out has been working. I've been able to go out in crowds without getting overwhelmed and I've been able to find my friends' voices through the crowd as well, so I haven't got split up from them."

"That's awesome, Soph," he smiled.

"Right? I treated myself to some Linzer biscuits as a reward, they're delicious."

"I've never had them before, but their chocolate is the best."

"I'll get you some before I--"

Sophia was cut off mid-sentence by a hand suddenly covering her mouth. Her eyes went wide, and she let out a muffled scream before the phone fell.

Noah watched in horror as the world tumbled across his screen, his words getting caught in his throat. He heard glass shatter, then the call disconnected.

"Soph?"

He didn't know why he was only saying this now, not ten seconds ago when someone was in the middle of kidnapping her.

"SOPH!"

Yelling at his phone wasn't going to help her either.

Noah rolled off the bed, barely stopping to grab his shoes as he bolted for the door. As he yanked it open, he almost ran headlong into his fiancée, who just about caught him.

"Noah, what's wrong?"

"I think someone just kidnapped my sister," he stammered, trying to wrestle himself from Faizal's grasp.

"How do you know?"

"We were having a video chat, someone grabbed her, and the call disconnected."

"Are you sure it's not just her classmates pulling some sort of prank?"

"I--" Noah cut himself off, stopping his struggle for a moment. "She sounded scared."

"Have you got the number for the hotel? Let's give them a call."

Steering Noah back into the suite, Faizal sat him down on the bed and pulled his own cell from his jacket pocket. It was a quick call.

"They've found her phone, but there's no one by the pool. None of the kids are hanging out in the lobby either. They're going to do a thorough search and get back to me. If they can't find her, they'll call the police right away."

Noah buried his head in his hands, his leg jiggling up and down furiously with nerves.

"I just sat there," he said, berating himself. "I didn't say anything, I just watched as they took her."

"There wasn't anything you could do, she's half a continent away."

"I could have shouted something, made them think twice."

"Noah, stop. If she's truly been taken, then we'll do everything without our power to get her back. You know we will. Between us and our contacts, we can have her safely back home tomorrow."

Noah was too stressed to truly believe what Faizal was saying. Between their family's money and her psychic powers, there was too much in her life that could put her in jeopardy. But he knew that if he didn't calm down, then they couldn't do what they needed to in order to get her back, and she was his number one priority right now.

"I hope you're right."

Acknowledgements

I'd like to take a moment to thank my family and friends for their support while I was writing this book. It's taken a long time to get here, including an entire rewrite with all new characters and an entirely different plot, but we got there!

Special thanks goes to my Mum, Anthony and Carmen for their feedback, which was invaluable.

And to all those on Twitter who cheered me on while I posted flail gifs to celebrate my progress, keep being wonderful!

I hope you all enjoyed this book as much as I enjoyed creating it.

Printed in Great
Britain
by Amazon